FINDING
ROOTS

A novel by

J.B. WEBB

Acknowledgments

Thank you, Johnny, for your love and support,
not only for this book but for our life together.

Table of Contents

Page Left Blank Intentionally

1

Rob knew the day would come when he would have to face his past and his family again. He hadn't meant to hurt them when he walked away, but he could not face a lifetime of the daily grind he'd seen his parents endure. His father, coming from the old school and being a generational farmer, couldn't understand why his only son would not continue in the life he was raised. And when he left home four years ago, his whole family was upset with him. And they haven't spoken since.

The shrill ring of the telephone interrupted Walter Cronkite's news broadcast just as Rob had settled on the sofa with a highball in hand. Walter was his idol, and he had recently been named the evening newscaster for the CBS network. While Rob had no aspiration to be a TV journalist, he was still captivated by Walter's journalistic history in the printed word. Those were the steps he planned to follow.

The phone rang again.

"Damn." He'd had it installed on the bedside table, so he stood up, took his drink with him, and walked over to the corner of his studio apartment. He sat down on the edge of his bed. Expecting it to be his girlfriend Eleanor, he answered playfully.

"Hello there, darling," he crooned as he picked up the

receiver from its cradle.

"Rob, it's Betty," here was a voice from the past. Betty was his older sister. His relaxed mood instantly vanished.

"Betty," he answered back, not sure what to say. He paused and then said, "I assume you are not calling for a friendly chat." His voice held more sarcasm than he intended, and he instantly regretted his tone. Must be the Jim Beam, he thought.

Betty sighed on the other end of the line. "Rob, we are going to have to be civil to each other to make it through this." Her voice was a little harsher, and she sniffled. "There's been an accident, and we have serious problems."

He closed his eyes and braced himself for the bad news he expected next. His past was here. Whatever she was about to say would not be welcome news. When he graduated summa cum laude from Georgia State last week, he'd not heard a word from his family. No call, not even a card. Then again, he hadn't expected to.

"I'm sorry," he said much softer as the knots tightened in his stomach. "I don't mean to be a prick. Please, tell me what happened."

"Connie was driving mom and dad into town," Betty continued. Connie was their younger sister, born three years after Rob.

"She wanted to take them out to dinner for Mom's birthday." Rob's ears started pounding, and he set his glass on the table by his bed. Finish the damn story, he thought.

She continued, and all he heard were the major points. "Accident. Connie died on impact. Dad in ICU. Mom is critical."

"Holy shit," Rob whispered. Connie was now; he racked his brain, trying to remember her age. 19 years old. Far too young to die. The last time he'd seen her was when he walked out the door of their family home. He turned around and saw her staring at him. Chewing a piece of Bazooka gum, she blew a bubble almost as big as her face. She didn't say a word when he gave her a farewell salute.

Until this moment, everything had fallen into place in his life, and he began to feel settled with hope for his future. He moved into his modest apartment over the weekend and loved it. No more sharing the john with his college buddies.

Even though it was small, he still had more room than he'd had in the college dorm. He now had his own little kitchen with a two-burner stove and a Frigidaire. No more sharing space for groceries. The place came furnished. He had a small dinette in the corner of the room. A sofa, chair, and small black and white TV took up most of the space in the living room area. A bed, dresser, and nightstand were tucked in the rear of the space. And the bonus was his own private bath, complete with a shower.

"Rob?" Betty's voice brought him back to the present. His head started pounding. He would begin his new job as an apprentice journalist with the Atlanta Constitution next week. He didn't want to jeopardize his new position, but he knew he had to go home.

"Let me make some arrangements, and I'll be there as quick as I can," he muttered to Betty. "I'll have to check the bus schedule. I don't have a car. I have to clear things with my new job, talk to Eleanor, and pack some clothes." He was rambling, but his thoughts were jumbling together in his brain.

"Just let me know what time to pick you up at the bus station." And the line went dead.

Rob sat on the bed and stared down at his feet for what seemed like an hour. In reality, it was only a few minutes. He downed the rest of his highball and stood up, not even sure where to start.

"Damn, and double damn," he screamed into the empty room. Why Connie, the youngest member of the family? He thought about the years when they were growing up. She was always a quiet child who seemed to observe more than she spoke. Now, they would never speak again.

He grabbed a notepad and pulled the Atlanta phonebook out of his nightstand. It was much thicker than any phonebook he'd seen back home. He found the number for the nearest Greyhound station and listened to the schedule. If he caught the first bus in the morning, he would arrive in north Florida in the late afternoon. Perfect.

He pulled his duffel bag out of his tiny closet and packed a few essentials. He had no idea how long he'd be gone. He didn't want to be away from his new job any longer than he had to.

Eleanor was out with friends for the evening, so he wrote her a note that she would find when she got home. Her apartment was in the same building, two floors up from his, and he had a key. He ran up both flights of stairs, let himself in, and left the note on her dinette table. He would be out the door early in the morning. They probably wouldn't have time to speak, but he promised to call once he arrived in Florida. The last item on his list was to swing by the paper in the morning. He would need to clear his schedule with his editor. Rob felt sure he would understand and give him a few days to be with his family.

Rob fixed another highball, turned off the television, and sat in silence. He always knew he would have to return home one day. He never guessed it would be under these circumstances. He sipped his drink slowly and wiped away the tears falling softly on his face. Tomorrow, he was going home.

2

The bus trip from Atlanta to north Florida took a little over six hours. Rob's mind didn't shut off the entire trip. He thought about the day Connie was born. At only three years old, he remembered the sound of his mom in the bedroom crying. Little Rob sat in the corner of his room, crying in fear for his mother.

Eventually, she grew quiet, and soon after, he heard the wailing of a baby. When he saw her for the first time, she looked like a wrinkled doll. She grew into a cute little sister, though, and he didn't mind her toddling around after him. She learned to work in the fields. He admired her work ethic even when she became a sullen teenager.

While his parents never talked about it, there were two other children who didn't make it past childbirth. Old enough to remember the births of each of them, he knew that each was tiny and blue. And each baby was a boy born a year apart. Two tiny coffins were buried in the family plot. Rob saw the heartbreak in his dad's eyes, knowing that he lost two sons. One of them might have been a more dedicated son to the farm than his oldest.

Betty was waiting at the bus stop when Rob stepped off. The beautiful and glowing young woman who greeted him was a pleasant surprise.

"My God, you're pregnant!" Rob exclaimed.

Betty offered a weary smile. "Due any day. Baby number two."

"Why didn't I know you had a child?" Rob asked, genuinely surprised. Betty shot him a look.

"Really?" she snarked. "How many times did you call to check on your family?"

Rob breathed out a heavy sigh. "Touche," he conceded. "Let's not get into this now," and his tone changed. "How's mom and dad?"

"Neither one has woken up yet, so we don't know how much they know or the full extent of their injuries." Betty paused, not sure how he would handle her plans for him.

"I'll drop you at Mom and Dad's place so you can settle in."

Those words stung Rob. His family had openly written him off when he left. His childhood home was no longer his home.

"The key is in Dad's old truck, so you can drive it wherever you need to go. They are both in Faith Memorial, so you'll have a 20-minute drive each way, depending on traffic."

Rob grinned at her, trying to lighten his mood. "You haven't seen traffic until you visit a city like Atlanta." He tried to make a joke, but Betty shot him a look, letting him know he wasn't funny.

"They only allow one visitor in each room per hour and then for only 15 minutes." Betty swallowed hard to keep from crying in front of her brother.

Both were silent for a few moments, lost in their own thoughts.

Betty sighed. "I was at the hospital most of the night, and I'm exhausted. Ned is stretched thin, trying to keep both farms going. He's also lining up crews for gathering tobacco at both places. Cropping starts next week," she glanced sideways at her brother.

"If you'll keep vigilance at the hospital and keep me updated, that would be a huge help."

"Of course," Rob said with a little too much enthusiasm. "Happy to help any way I can," he looked towards his sister. "That's why I'm here."

Betty turned into the driveway. The home Rob grew up in had changed very little. The family lived within their means in a modest farmhouse that belonged to Rob's grandparents. His parents had installed several window air conditioners to help provide relief from the incessant summer heat. Otherwise, it was an old house made into a home. A picket fence lined the front yard where Charlotte's rose bushes stood. They looked a little sad to Rob today. Probably needed extra water from the soaring Florida heat. Betty watched Rob for a moment and then spoke again, "The key is still under the mat."

Rob gave her a slight smile and slid out of the vehicle. He grabbed his one duffel bag and turned towards the house. Without another word, Betty backed the car out of the driveway and headed south towards her home.

When Rob unlocked the front door and stepped inside, he was greeted with familiar sights and smells. Family photos lined the fireplace mantle. Some he'd seen before, and some were new. Connie's face, wearing a cap with a dangling tassel, was center. She graduated high school a year before, and he doubted she had plans to leave their little town. There were photos of a baby and then a toddler. Rob recognized them as Betty's child. He looked just like her. Rob scanned the other photos. Betty and Ned were smiling on their wedding day. His parents holding a pearl handled knife to cut a cake on their 25th anniversary. He felt a pang of guilt that he missed the celebration. And tucked in the back, he found a 5x7 photo of him at his high school graduation. He was surprised to see any of himself.

As he walked through the living room, the furniture was all

familiar. Nothing much had changed. The couch and chairs were old and worn but clean. He peeked in the kitchen. Nothing new. The old farmhouse dining table was the same with the same buttercup yellow China cabinet his mom loved.

He went down the hall and opened his old bedroom door. It was exactly as he left it, which surprised him. He expected it to be turned into a guest room or sewing room. His bed had the same crisp spread and pillows. The books he'd left behind were still on the shelves. And tucked into the corner of his dresser, he found the letter he'd written to his mom after he arrived in Atlanta. She probably read it and tucked it there so her husband wouldn't notice it. She had never answered Rob, but he didn't expect an answer anyway. He just wanted her to know that he was okay. The few clothes he left behind were still hung in his closet. The dresser drawers were empty. He almost felt like his mother expected him to come home one day. And here he was.

After a quick shower and change of clothes, Rob was ready to ride over to the hospital. He wanted to give Betty a call first and thank her for picking him up earlier. The phone still rested on its stand in the hallway between the bedrooms. He picked up the receiver to dial his sister's number.

"Myrtle, I'm telling you. I don't think that boy will come home even for his sister's funeral," Rob heard someone on the line speaking. The joys of a party line, he thought.

As a young boy, he would sit and listen to the old biddies gossip on their party line for hours. Then, he would write stories using their adventures. Betty used to become so mad when she wanted to call her friends, and the ladies wouldn't give up the line. She'd cry to Charlotte to make the ladies quit talking. But they always said if it wasn't an emergency, then she didn't need to make a call. Rob smirked as he knew they were talking about him.

"Well, Louise, if he don't, he didn't grow up to be much of a man, now did he? Such a shame what this family has gone through. Him leaving his daddy in the lurch like he did to go to some high falutin school up north. Broke his mama's heart, that one. And now they've lost their baby girl."

Those words hit him hard, and Rob couldn't listen anymore. With a soft touch, so the other party couldn't hear, he put the phone back in its cradle. Coming home would be tougher than he thought. Not only did he have to face his parents, if they pulled through. He also had to face the damn nosey small-town gossiping biddies.

3

Rob had forgotten how beautiful the north Florida countryside was, especially in the twilight hours before sunset. As he drove his dad's old rusty Ford towards town, he admired the surrounding landscape. He could almost smell the scent of the tall, stately pines and freshly plowed fields, clean and ready for their new crops. The soft glow of lights from the occasional home he passed gave him a warm feeling. He saw children playing outside, not allowed back in until Mama called them in to wash up for supper.

Family gatherings were important in this time and place. After working in the fields helping with the crops, the moms would toil in the kitchen to put a hearty dinner on the table for the family. Menus often consisted of farm-fresh fried chicken, mashed potatoes, and fresh vegetables, all from the garden. And no country meal was ever complete without homemade biscuits and gravy and freshly made sweet tea.

Rob's stomach started to rumble with hunger just thinking about the meals his mom made. Since moving to Atlanta, he started eating healthier without the lard and starches he was used to. But all of a sudden, he had a hankering for fried chicken. Without thinking, he pulled into the local diner located at the main intersection in town. He decided to grab a bite to eat before facing what lay ahead in the hospital beds.

The little bell clanked over the door as Rob walked in. Atlanta restaurants were full this time of evening, but only one table was occupied at Gram's tonight. Rob slid into a booth by the window. Lost in thought, he barely noticed when the waitress brought him a menu and a glass of water.

"What can I get ya, cowboy?" He heard a sweet southern drawl from the past.

"Patti?" he looked up into the eyes of his high school crush. She had not changed a bit, including waiting tables at the local diner.

"Rob!" the waitress exclaimed. "I didn't realize that was you. Give me a hug."

Rob stood up and embraced Patti. They had dated off and on in high school. He had been a shy teenager and often found himself tongue-tied around the young beauty. Besides, his dad demanded he be home early to help on the farm, and Patti worked all the hours after school she managed to fit in. She'd been waiting tables for as long as he remembered.

Patti sat down across from him in the booth. Her voice was sincere. "I am so sorry about Connie and your parents. I'm glad you came home. Is there anything I can do for you?"

He remembered those sweet blue eyes all too well. Patti was always the one he felt most comfortable with, other than his favorite teachers. She was the one hesitation to leave their little town. But his feelings for her were not strong enough to hold him there. The little bell rang over the door, and Patti glanced away for a second.

"Ya'll have a seat anywhere you like, and Peggy will be right with you," she said to a young family as they entered.

"It's nice to see you, Patti," he said and looked down at his hands. He had left town without even telling her goodbye, and he always felt like a coward for doing so. He had been afraid that if she tried to talk him out of leaving, he might have stayed.

He saw concern on her face. All of a sudden, his stomach rumbled so loud it could have woken up the dead.

Patti snickered. "Sounds like you need a good meal."

Rob nodded. "I only ate junk out of those vending machines at the bus stops coming down, so yeah, a good meal would be great. You still serve that amazing fried chicken?" he smiled.

"The best in town!" she answered. "I'll get ya fixed up," she said, rising from the booth. She turned and walked towards the kitchen.

Rob glanced around the little diner and noted that it appeared much cleaner and fresher than when he was last here. Gram and her husband opened the restaurant around the time Rob was born. It soon became a staple in their little town. Gram's husband passed away suddenly, and the elderly lady was left to run the place by herself. She did an honorable job keeping it open. But in the last few years before Rob left, the strain on Gram became clear both in her demeanor and the ambiance of the diner. Both were starting to look worn. Rob noticed that everything was now fresh and sparkling clean with new décor and even an updated cash register.

Patti brought out a plate piled with fried chicken, homemade mashed potatoes, collard greens, and cornbread. Peggy brought over a tall glass of iced tea so sweet it could make your blood sugar rise. Both ladies smiled sweetly at him, and Peggy turned to check on the other customers.

"Enjoy," Patti said. "Some good old southern nourishment will perk you up, and we'll chat later." She smiled and then turned and walked away.

Rob had not enjoyed a meal that delicious since leaving home. Everything was freshly cooked, and he was sure the potatoes and greens had come from local farmers. Probably the chicken, too. Just the smell of the fried chicken brought back memories of long days in the tobacco fields. After working from sun up to noon, everyone would pile into the dining room or back porch of the farmer's home where they were working. The neighboring ladies would put out a spread equal to a Sunday dinner on the grounds at church. There would always be fried chicken plus a ham and another meat or two. The vegetables would line the table – collard greens, mustard greens, turnip greens, butter beans, string beans, squash casserole, baked beans. And there was always a heaping plate of fresh hot biscuits, fluffy mashed potatoes, and gravy to cover it all.

The men would eat first. Then the ladies would feed the children before preparing their own plate. Once the men finished all they wanted, they would find a seat on the porch and lay their heads back in their chairs and snooze. In about 30 minutes, the foreman of the day would stand and announce, "back to work." The men would head out to the field, and the women would clean up the massive number of dishes while they chatted about their children or gossiped about local troublemakers.

"Did you save room for apple pie?" Patti's voice guided Rob back to the present. She stood next to him, holding a delicious-looking piece of homemade pie. He remembered apple was Gram's specialty.

"I'm afraid I can't swallow another bite," Rob smiled at her. "I'm sure I'll be back soon, and I'll save room that day."

"Sounds good, hon. I'll have a piece warmed up and ready for ya," Patti smiled. Looking into her eyes brought forth a feeling Rob couldn't quite put his finger on. His stomach tightened up a bit, and he didn't think it was from the food.

"It's great to see you, Patti," he stammered as he laid down enough cash on the table to cover the bill and a generous tip. He winked at her and headed out the door. He felt a tug in his gut that made him want to sit and chat with her for hours. But he needed to get to the hospital and check on his parents.

4

The parking lot of the small hospital was nearly empty, so Rob maneuvered the old pick-up close to the main entrance. There was nothing stately about the structure. It was a modest red brick, one-story building that had been built around the time Rob came into the world.

When he walked through the front door, he noticed a small reception area in the center of the foyer. A small waiting room was on the right. If you made it past the receptionist, the main nurses' station sat behind it. Beyond that, two wings flanking each side led to the patients' rooms. There was an emergency room at the back of the hospital with a separate entrance. If you were inclined, you could walk the building from end to end in less than five minutes. This was a far cry from the large Atlanta hospital structures he'd seen.

As soon as he entered the building, a pleasant-looking middle-aged woman approached him.

"Mr. Mathis, we've been expecting you," a warm voice greeted him. "Thank you for making the trip so quickly." The woman flashed him a down-to-earth smile that combined business with a genuine welcome. "I'm Margaret, head nurse in charge. I'm here to answer any questions and assist with both of your parents."

"Thank you," Rob responded as he returned the smile.

"Please, call me Rob."

"Of course, Rob," she said. "Let's step into my office, and I'll bring you up to speed. Would you like some coffee?"

"That would be great," Rob replied. They stepped into a small room behind the nurses' station. The room was painted pastel blue with a small desk and two side chairs in front of it. Rob noticed a tall metal file cabinet with a vase of pink flowers on top and two small, framed photos. There were framed certificates on the wall. He assumed they were the charge nurses' college diplomas and other various certifications she held. She seemed to be a smart woman and definitely carried the air of authority of a charge nurse.

As soon as he sat down, a young woman stepped in carrying two steaming mugs of coffee. She set one down in front of each of them. Her starched white nurse dress was covered in a red and white pinafore. She flashed Rob a bright smile as she set the mug in front of him.

"Thank you," Margaret said and nodded to the young girl. As the door closed behind her, Margaret said, "She's one of our newest candy stripers, and I think she'll make a good nurse one day. But now, let's discuss your parents."

Rob took in every word while he sipped on the hot coffee and Margaret explained the condition of his parents.

"Your mother suffered severe head injuries and has not yet gained consciousness," she paused to let him absorb her words.

"She was sitting in the back seat and, unfortunately, was tossed around quite a bit upon impact. We've not found any internal bleeding, which is good." She studied Rob's face.

"What's next?" He managed to choke out.

"Well, we stitched her superficial wounds and reset and cast her broken arm. However, until she wakes up, we can't fully gauge the extent of her head injuries." She paused.

"I'm sorry. I know this is a lot for you to take in."

"No, please continue. I need to know what we are about to face. How is my father?"

"He has been drifting in and out of consciousness and responding somewhat to lights and sounds. That's a positive sign. He had some internal injuries which have been repaired with surgery." Again, nurse Margaret paused.

"His left leg was crushed under the dashboard of the car." Rob bit his lower lip and closed his eyes, not sure how much more he wanted to hear.

"Only time will tell if he will be able to use that leg again."

He opened his eyes and looked at the nurse. She had finally finished the updates and was patient while Rob absorbed the news. She had given him a lot of information in a short amount of time.

Rob blew out a long sigh.

"Wow," he said. "You live your life from day to day with a plan in mind, and in the blink of an eye, your entire world can change beyond your control." In his mind, he thought, 'Not only had his parents' world been blown apart, but every plan he had for his future melted a little more with each word the nurse had spoken.'

"May I see them?" he managed to choke out in a whisper.

"Of course," Margaret said warmly. "Dad, first?"

Rob nodded, and they both rose from their seats. He felt like a child again as Nurse Margaret opened the door for him and ushered him into the middle hallway.

The intensive care unit was placed between the main hallway and the emergency room. Two swinging doors with a sign that read "Authorized Personnel Only" offered the only way in or out.

When they entered, Rob noticed how quiet the entire unit was. The only sounds were the soft beeping of machines attached to the few patients in the beds. Rob scanned the area.

He saw five small rooms along the back with glass walls and an open door to each room. The nurses' station, where two ladies sat, was in the center of the larger room. They stood behind a counter positioned so they were able to view each of the patient's rooms at any given moment. Soft lights glowed in three of the tiny patient rooms. The other two rooms were in complete darkness.

"We currently have three ICU patients," nurse Margaret explained. "Two are your parents."

Rob swallowed hard. He had never been inside an ICU ward, and this felt foreign to him. And he had no idea how his father would react to his presence. He looked nervously at nurse Margaret.

"My dad and I parted ways on not-so-good terms. I'm not sure how he will react when he sees me here," he whispered to her.

"Your sister gave me a heads-up. If he seems too agitated, we'll cut your visit short," she smiled at him. "I think it's worth a shot to show you care."

He took a deep breath and followed the nurse's lead into the tiny room with soft lights and beeping machines. Nurse Margaret busied herself, checking the various tubes and wires connected to his dad. Rob expected the worst, but what he saw in the bed was even more than he imagined. His father looked frail, and his breathing sounded uneven. There were bandages around his head, a cast on his right arm, and various tubes and wires came out from all parts of his body.

"It's ok to talk to him," Margaret advised. "I'm going to be outside if you need me. Just remember, less said is better right now."

Rob nodded and tried to fight back tears as the nurse stepped out and partly closed the curtain. She gave them enough privacy to talk but left them the opportunity to enter back if the need arose.

"Hey, Dad," Rob whispered.

His words seemed shallow after the way they had last parted. Rob found himself at a loss for words. When there was no response, Rob sat down in the chair next to the bed. Why did he come alone, he thought. He had to find out the medical facts. But trying to talk to his father, especially in his current state lying in the hospital bed, was difficult. He sat for a few minutes and, not knowing what else to do, decided to leave. He stood up, patted his dad's hand, and turned to leave the room.

As he reached the door, he heard a mumble or a grunting sound and turned back. His father's eyes were open and focused on him. Rob walked back to the bed and studied his father's face for a moment. "Hey," was all he managed to say.

"I must be in a hell of a condition," Robert muttered, "for you to be here." There was no hardness in his father's eyes like the last time they spoke. His face had a look of tired resignation.

"I'd say you're not in your best form," Rob spoke in soft tones. "I hear you had a bit of an accident, so I wanted to be here for you." He struggled to find the right words without giving away too much.

"Where's your mother? And your sisters?" his father asked.

"I haven't seen mom yet. She's in the next room," Rob replied. Then trying to keep it light said, "you know, we should try to move you both into the same room. Maybe they'd give you a discount." He chuckled, but dad didn't respond.

"I'm tired, Rob. I'm going back to sleep." Robert closed his eyes as if to dismiss his son. Rob was thankful that he did not have to go into any details about Connie. He knew his father was not ready to face that reality.

When he walked out of the partitioned door, nurse Margaret met him.

"His body is tired," she said, with a note of apology in her voice. "He doesn't say much to anyone."

"That's probably best at this point," Rob stated. "He adored his baby girl, so it's going to be tough on him when he finds out."

Margaret nodded and led Rob to the next room. "Your mom has not woken up yet, so don't expect much. It might be nice if you talk to her, hold her hand, rub her arms, whatever you feel comfortable with. Human touch is best right now."

Again, she led him into the room and checked the tubes, wires, and bandages before smiling at Rob and walking out. When Rob saw his mother, he was saddened. Her beautiful face was bruised and swollen. She had cuts all over her face and body and more bandages than he could count. Dried blood matted her hair. She looked nothing like the beautiful woman he remembered from a few short years ago.

He sat down next to her bed and gently took her hand. He wanted to rub her arm, but she had so many cuts and bruises he feared he would hurt her.

"Hey, mom. It's me, Rob." That was a stupid thing to say, he thought. But he couldn't think of any other words. *I'm the prodigal son, coming home because your life has been turned upside down* didn't seem like the appropriate comment at this time. Nurse Margaret warned him that she probably would not hear anything he had to say. It was worth a try to show her he was there and that he cared.

"Look, I'm sorry I haven't called or written since I left," he began speaking from his heart. "I have missed you, and I wanted to pick up the phone so many times. There's no excuse. I just didn't." He swallowed back tears and continued. "Mom, I love you. The past four years have been hard, but I accomplished so many of my goals. My dreams are coming to reality. I've landed a great job with a major newspaper. I've met a girl I really love. I think you would be proud of how I put myself through college." He paused to see if there was any reaction from her. There was none. She continued to sleep peacefully.

"I wish things would have been different between us. Maybe it took something like this to bring us back together, even though no one deserves to go through what you and Dad are facing now. Just know that I'm here for you. Even though I can't make up for what I put you all through, I want to help the family. Please believe that." For a second, Rob thought he saw the slightest twitch in his mother's face. "I love you, Mom." Rob squeezed her hand slightly before reaching up and wiping the tears from his eyes.

The nurses were in the middle of their shift change, but the night nurses who were on duty assured Rob they would call if there were any changes. He didn't see Margaret, but the new nurses encouraged him to get a restful night's sleep and be ready to face the days ahead. The doctor would make his rounds mid-morning, they explained, so he needed to be back by then.

5

The old Ford rumbled out of the parking lot, and Rob headed east toward his family home. The two-lane highway was dark and deserted, far different from the streets of Atlanta. An occasional headlight passed him heading west, but those were few and far between. With such little traffic on these roads, Rob wondered how such an awful accident had happened to his family. He made a mental note to meet with the sheriff tomorrow to hear his report.

Rob cranked the window down to let a little breeze blow through the truck. The night air was still humid, but he was used to that after living in the south all of his life.

He let his thoughts wander. He remembered his favorite teachers in school who encouraged his love of books. He smiled at the memory of kissing Patti behind the tobacco barn when he was only 12. And he could almost feel the mud on his feet as he remembered running barefoot through puddles after a sultry summer rain. He did have some sweet memories from childhood. Unfortunately, other memories were not so good.

Probably his worst memory was the day after his high school graduation. Rob broke the news to his parents that he was leaving the family farm to attend college. Mrs. Cherry, his high school guidance counselor, had recognized his talents. She helped him apply, and he was accepted into the Journalism program at Georgia State University.

"I've saved money from working part-time at the newspaper," he announced when Robert bellowed that he would not financially contribute to such nonsense. "I've also been awarded a full scholarship for four years."

Needless to say, Robert Mathis hit the roof.

"You are my only son!" he shouted. "This farm has been passed down in our family for several generations. You are betraying the Mathis legacy!"

His father continued to rant for most of the night. Charlotte cried and tried to soothe her husband. Betty was newly married and living with her husband half a mile away. Robert called her to come home and try to talk some sense into the boy. Connie, 15 at the time, stayed in her room with the door locked. The night was hell for Rob with his family turning against him. Even Betty told him what a scum he was.

Rob ended up staying home through July that summer to help with the annual tobacco gathering. But on the first day of August in the year 1960, the young man boarded a Greyhound bus bound for Atlanta. He never looked back. His father didn't say goodbye. His mother cried and packed him a brown bag lunch. Betty's husband Ned drove him to the station. When he graduated Summa Cum Laude four years later, not one family member was at the ceremony to cheer him on. And now, only a week after his graduation, he had come home.

"Shit," he said aloud when he realized that he forgot to call Eleanor and let her know he'd made it home. She would be worried, sick, and mad as hell at the same time.

He decided to call as soon as he stepped in the door at home. It should be bedtime for the biddies, so maybe he would have access to the phone with no interruptions or listening ears.

Most people in Atlanta were fortunate to have private telephone lines, which were foreign to Rob at first. It didn't take long, however, to enjoy the opportunity to pick up the phone and dial whenever you wanted and not have to worry about the ladies down the street listening in.

Rob turned left on Main Street and noticed the diner was still open. Patti was inside wiping tables and getting ready to close up for the night. It was just after 8 pm, and the sidewalks of the tiny town had rolled up.

"Why in the world is that girl still waiting tables?" he said to no one. She had been a smart girl in high school with a good business head and had shown a drive to succeed. He figured she would have been long gone from this two-light town just as he had. He made a mental note to speak with her before he left town. Seems his list of meetings was growing.

As soon as Rob turned into the driveway of the old home, he noticed a light glowing in the back of the house. He was almost certain he turned all the lights off when he left. Great, he thought, after the day he'd had, now he was going to have to face an intruder.

His dad's rifle was in the gun rack in the back glass of the old pick-up, but he had never liked to shoot. He jumped out and found a tire iron in the truck bed, and hoped for the best. The front door was locked as he had left it, so he figured the intruder had gone in around the back. He crept around the house looking for foot tracks but didn't see anything. The back door was locked. The windows were open, but the screens were intact, so he saw no sign of forced entry.

Maybe he forgot to turn off a light. If that was the case, he would be severely reprimanded if his dad found out. Electricity was a luxury not to be wasted, Robert had always preached.

He got the key from under the mat, held on tight to the tire iron, and entered the house. The light came from a small lamp in the dining room, and he found a note propped on it. Rob let out a breath, thankful that he wasn't going to have to hit someone over the head with the tire iron. He propped it by the wall and picked up the note.

Dear, Rob. First, let me say thank you for coming home. I know we had our differences growing up, but we are first and always family. I honestly don't know what the immediate future holds, but I do know I could not face this without my little brother. I've never been good at putting my thoughts in words like you are, so I decided to write you this note. Please stay and help us. You are now the glue that will hold this family together. Ned and I will help as much as we can, but with a toddler and a new baby (any day), we have our hands full. You can do this, Rob. I believe in you. And I love you. Betty. PS – I hope you didn't eat because your supper is in the oven.

Rob read the note several times as tears welled in his eyes for the third time today. When he walked out of the family home four years ago, he did not look back. Not that he was cold or unfeeling for his parents and sisters. He just believed he was a major disappointment to all of them and thought it best to stay out of their way.

Reading Betty's note brought back the sense of family bond that he had long ago buried. He vowed that he would step up and be the leader his family needed him to be.

Before he ate, he knew he should call Eleanor. He pictured her settled into her cozy sofa, reading the latest Harlequin novel. She would be worried about him. He sat down at the small phone table in the hallway and quietly picked up the receiver. If the biddies were on the line, he didn't want to get into a discussion with them. He smiled when he found the line clear and dialed 0 for the operator. He listened to the clicks as she patched him into the number he provided. After one short ring, Eleanor picked up.

"Rob, this had better be you!" was her greeting.

"Hello to you, too. Sweetheart," he answered warmly. "I'm sorry I worried you. It's been a hectic day, and phones are not as accessible here as they are in Atlanta."

"I thought your parents had a phone," she said.

"They do, but we are on a multi-party line, and there are others who like to keep the line tied up. In fact, we need to keep the steamy talk out of our conversation when we're on this line. Never know who's listening," he chuckled.

"Baby, I've got to get you out of the sticks and back home to me," her voice changed. "How are you, darling? How is your family?"

"I'm fine. A little travel weary and emotionally tired, but a good night's sleep will help." He went on to tell her about his bus trip down, which was uneventful, the visit to his parents, and his plans for tomorrow. Then, a thought occurred to him.

"Sweetheart, I could talk to you all night, but my dad will hit the roof when he sees the phone bill," he said apologetically. "Unfortunately, we need to keep these calls brief since every minute adds up. I love you and will call again as soon as I can."

"I love you, too, and miss you. Please be safe."

The dinner Betty left him tasted amazing. If he keeps eating like this, he'll gain 10 pounds in the first week, he mused to himself.

6

Rob woke up early the next morning feeling refreshed and ready to face the day's challenges. There had been no phone calls during the night from the hospital, so maybe that was a good sign that his parents had rested peacefully.

He made a mental list of things to do. When he added a funeral home to that list, tears welled up again. Connie was such a young, bright star, and it wasn't fair that she was taken so soon. He wanted to call Betty and thank her for dinner and the note and meet with Ned about next week's tobacco harvest.

His stomach rumbled, so breakfast needed to be on his list as well. Maybe he'd stop in Gram's and see if Patti was working. Surely, bagels were on their menu these days.

Not thinking, he snatched up the phone's receiver and started to dial the operator.

"I don't know who picked up on this line, but I'm talking right now," a scratchy voice yelled in his ear.

Rob rolled his eyes. Here we go, he thought.

"Miss Myrtle, is that you?" he used his most charming voice with a gentlemanly southern drawl.

"It is," the scratchy voice came back, not phased one bit by the attempted charm. "Who the hell is this on my line?"

"Well, Miss Myrtle, it's my line, too, I believe. This is Rob Mathis. How ya doin?"

Myrtle was not one to be silenced, but for a brief moment, she was at a loss for words. Then she found her voice again.

"Well, look who came home," she said. "I can't believe it. I was telling my sister just yesterday that you were far away and wouldn't come home even when your family needed ya." Rob didn't take offense because, in all of his 22 years, he had never heard Myrtle say anything positive on this line.

Another voice chimed in. "Leave the boy be, Myrtle," the voice chastised. "He has come home, and that is wonderful for his family. They have enough grief right now, and you need to play nice."

Rob grinned. He wasn't sure who the other voice belonged to, but he enjoyed listening while Myrtle was being put in her place.

"Donna Sue, don't you go telling me how to act!" Myrtle slammed back. "This boy left his family and never even wrote them a letter, let alone call. I also heard tell he's laid up with some woman in the big city of Atlanta."

"OK, ladies," Rob chimed in. "Donna Sue, it's nice to hear your voice." He and Donna had been friends in high school, even though they didn't have much in common. Donna was one of those sweet souls who saw the best in everyone.

"And it's not nice to hear mine?" Myrtle asked with a note of hurt in her voice.

"Of course, it's very nice to hear your voice, Miss Myrtle," Rob soothed. "And I can't wait to catch up with all of you lovely neighbors. But I have a lot to do today, and I need to make a quick phone call. May I have the line for just a minute, please."

Both ladies said a quick goodbye to each other and promised to visit. Even Myrtle hung up, however, grudgingly.

Rob dialed the operator and asked her to patch him through to Betty's phone. She answered on the second ring, and a toddler crying in the background.

"Hey, sis," he said, and then he heard a slight click on the line.

"Hey, little brother," she answered. "Did you sleep ok?

"Well, I would have, but these two blond bombshells came over, and I didn't get a wink of sleep. I hope the noise didn't wake you down the street." He heard a gasp and a receiver slam loudly in his ear. That would teach Myrtle to try and listen in.

The duo laughed and made plans to meet after Rob returned from the hospital. Before they hung up, Rob checked on the baby's status, and Betty told him nothing had changed with her. He told his sister that he loved her, and she told him back. He could feel the new bond forming between them.

Rob checked his watch and figured he had time to grab a bite at the diner before heading over to the hospital. As the old truck rattled into the parking space, he saw they were much busier for breakfast than the previous evening. He also watched Patti bouncing from table to table, taking orders, smiling, and chatting with the customers.

"That girl must live here or must really need the money," he thought to himself.

The little bell clattered over the door when he walked in.

"Have a seat, hon. I'll be right with you," Patti called out before turning around to face him.

"Oh, it's you!" she exclaimed, and a big grin broke out on her face. "How ya doin this morning?" She set down a pile of dishes on an empty table and ran over to give him a quick hug.

"I'm good," Rob replied. "Just thought I'd grab a quick bite before I head back to the hospital."

"Have a seat, and I'll bring you a menu. We're a little swamped this morning, and my other server called in sick, but I'll take great care of you." And she swooped up the dirty dishes and was back in less than a minute.

"I'll just have coffee and oatmeal," he smiled sheepishly. He figured they still specialized in everything fried, but it took him almost four years to get a lifetime of grease out of his system. He didn't want to overwhelm his internal organs with greasy food so soon.

"That's not the country boy I remember," Patti laughed, and Rob caught himself thinking how much he enjoyed that laugh. He smiled up at her and managed to avoid her eyes without seeming rude.

She came back with the coffee and patted his shoulder.

"Maybe we can catch up when you have some time," she said with sincerity. "I'd love to hear about your Atlanta life, and I'm here to help with anything you need while you are home. Your sister was such a special young lady."

"Thanks," he said and this time he stared straight into her eyes. He had forgotten what a deep blue they were, and he got lost in them for a second.

He thought he saw her cheeks flush slightly. "Well, I'm pretty busy right now," she said. "But please, stop by when you can. I'm almost always here, and I'd really love to chat."

"I'll do that," he assured her, and she turned to go back to work.

He ate quickly and drank one cup of coffee. Patti had not brought his check, but she was busy. As soon as a table cleared, another patron was waiting for the seat. He left more than enough cash on the table to cover what he assumed the bill would be, plus a tip and headed out the door.

The drive back to the hospital was uneventful except for the occasional tractor on the road. When he began driving as a teenager, the tractors on the highway always annoyed him. As a novice driver, he was afraid to try and pass them, but they went so slow that his dad's old pickup would almost choke out. Today, he enjoyed the snail's pace and didn't even attempt to pass, which annoyed the drivers behind him.

All of the farmers in the surrounding area knew each other

and, for the most part, were happy to oblige when their neighbors needed help. He didn't realize he was smiling as he allowed himself to remember the days in the field that he hated. Now, they didn't seem so bad after all.

Sometimes, Connie would chase him down a tobacco row with a hornworm in her hands and threaten to throw it on him. He thought about the days they sat on the back of the planting wagon. They would sing silly songs at the top of their lungs as they dropped the tiny plants in their prepared holes. While he was the serious one, Connie could be the comedy relief. How had he forgotten that? They had shared a bond, and he broke that bond when he walked away from her four years ago. Now, she was gone to him forever. Damn it, he thought. He pounded the steering wheel one good time. And he fought back the tears trying to surface.

Nurse Margaret greeted him when he stopped at the nurses' station.

"Right on time!" she said and led him into a small office close by. "Dr. Barnes will be in soon and give you an update," and she closed the door softly as she stepped out.

In less than a minute, there was a knock on the door, and the doctor stepped in. A stately gentleman with graying hair, stylish horn-rimmed glasses, and a starched white coat, he gave an air of authority.

"Rob, it's good to see you again. I am very sorry for these unfortunate circumstances in which we have to meet," he shook the younger man's hand, and Rob noticed he had a strong, assuring grip.

"Thank you, sir, even though I'm not sure when we have seen each other previously," Rob replied.

The elder man chuckled. "Son, I delivered you, so I was the first to see your naked butt," he laughed. "I set your broken arm when you were," he paused to think a second, "ten, I believe, and treated you for the measles and various other childhood illnesses."

"Wow," Rob laughed. "You're Dr. Bee," he mused. "Man, you know more about me than I know." Everyone in the community called him Dr. Bee rather than his true name. One of the kids had started that when they couldn't say "Barnes," and it stuck. The doctor never minded and played along with his new name.

"Well, I've been your family's doctor since your parents married," he said. "I came here fresh out of med school and never left." He hesitated a second and then said, "Your family is very special to me, and my heart breaks for what you are going through. I'm glad you came home."

Rob wasn't sure what to say. The doctor made it sound like he came home for good. That was not at all his intention.

Dr. Barnes changed his tone. "So, let's talk about your parents, the loss of your sister, and where we go from here."

The younger man nodded. "How are they this morning?"

"They are stable and have come through the first 48 hours, which is the most critical time following such a trauma. While they are not out of the woods yet, their vitals are getting stronger. There are no signs of further internal injuries that we haven't already treated. Your father woke up a few times last night," he hesitated and looked at Rob. "He asked for you a couple of times."

Rob's eyes widened.

Dr. Barnes continued, "Your mom is stirring more, and I expect her to wake soon. If they continue to improve, we should be able to move them from ICU into a room together. I believe that will help them heal even more by being together."

The doctor stopped speaking to let Rob take in everything before they had to approach the next difficult question.

Rob knew what was coming next. "When do we tell them about Connie?" his voice choked.

The older man sighed. "Once they are fully awake, we won't be able to keep it from them. They will want to know where she is. I'm just not sure how that will affect their medical conditions." He paused to choose his next words with care. "They will need the full support of their family, so having you here is most beneficial. However, Betty is due to have a baby any day, so she may not be in a condition to offer full support." He paused again and peered straight into the younger man's eyes. "I'm afraid the full burden of this is on your shoulders, son."

Full burden, Rob thought. This was the furthest thing from his mind when he threw a few clothes in a duffel bag and boarded the bus headed south. He had left home on the worst of terms and vowed not to look back. But here he was, back on his home soil with the "full burden" of his family on his shoulders. His head was reeling, and he needed to think. Dr. Barnes watched him closely but didn't speak.

"I need a little time to get my thoughts together," Rob finally said. "This all happened so fast I," Rob stammered and for once in his life, could find no words.

"I understand," the doctor said softly. "You've got some time. If you'd like, stop in and visit with your parents. Talk to them and let them know you're here. They may not respond, but they may feel your presence. I know you have a lot of planning to do with the funeral and the farm to take care of."

Rob thought for a moment. "I'd like to hold off on the funeral until they are awake and can possibly attend," he said.

"Absolutely," the doctor responded. "Talk to the funeral director. He can help with that, and I'll help with your parents when they are strong enough to deal with it."

Both men stood up and shook hands, and then Dr. Barnes reached over and hugged Rob. "You can handle whatever is thrown at you, son. You and your dad may have had your differences, but you are still blood. I know your dad was hard on you kids, but he is a farmer from many generations, and that's the only way they know to be. Let go of the past and focus on family right now. You have a community to support you." He patted Rob on the back and held the door open for him. "I'll check on you later," and he turned and walked away.

Rob spent his allotted 15 minutes with each parent. Neither of them seemed to wake up, but he talked non-stop to each of them. He visited his dad first, and while he patted his arm, he told him about his life in Atlanta. He met Eleanor during his first year of college, and they had been inseparable ever since. They shared goals and both planned to pursue careers in journalism.

"She's a looker, dad," Rob chuckled. "And she has a brain to match. She's smart, funny, and down to earth. I think you'll like her. We're starting to talk about marriage now that our careers are taking off."

And then, as an afterthought in case Robert could hear him, he added, "But I'm not leaving here until I know you're ok and the farm is taken care of. They'll hold my job for me." At least I hope they will, he thought to himself.

His conversation with his mother was pretty much the same. He shared more about his college life and how living in a dorm wasn't so very different from home.

"I had a roommate, and we shared a bathroom with two other guys in the adjoining room," he shared with her, not knowing what else to say. "Since I'd shared a bathroom with two sisters and my parents, it didn't bother me."

"I've met people from all around the country and made some great friends," he continued. "They called me farmer boy because I came from north Florida."

He hesitated, looking for any sign that she was hearing his words. He put his hand on hers.

"I love you, mom," he hesitated. "I hope I can make you proud."

There was little traffic and no slow-moving tractors on the drive back to the farm. It was high noon, and most farmers stopped for lunch and a short rest before finishing the long day in the fields. As he passed Gram's, he noticed the full parking lot and the waiting crowd spilled outside. He was glad to see Grams so busy, at least for breakfast and lunch.

His sister's house was about a half mile past his parents' home. She and Ned built a very modest frame home on the far edge of Robert's land. He portioned off an acre for them when they married and built their modest home. They designed it with two bedrooms and one bath, and Ned planned the home so it would be easy to add on as their family grew.

Rob turned the old pickup into the driveway and right away noticed that the house had a warm and nostalgic feeling. The yard had been recently mowed, and a small white picket fence bordered a part of the front. Rose bushes in shades of red and pink lined the fence, and even in this Florida heat, they looked perky and happy.

A small front porch held a swing at one end. Rob imagined his sister and brother-in-law sitting at the end of the day, holding hands and watching the sunset. Ned's pickup was in the yard, as it was lunchtime. Rob knocked on the screen door and called out, "It's me, big sis."

"Come on in," Ned called, and he heard the squeal of a toddler. "Come in," the baby mimicked his dad.

Rob opened the door and stepped in. He immediately noticed how neat and tidy the house looked and was impressed by his sister's housekeeping skills. Farm life was not easy on a woman, and his sister had the added burden of pregnancy, along with a husband and toddler to tend to.

"Hey, little brother," Betty said as she tried to rise from her chair. He was so tired after the bus ride yesterday that he hadn't noticed how pregnant she looked. When she said she was due any day, he believed it. She was glowing, however.

"Don't get up, sis," he said and gave her a kiss on the cheek. "You look wonderful, by the way."

He shook Ned's hand before turning to his nephew. He marveled at the cute toddler sitting in his high chair and waving a spoon towards his uncle. The child looked a lot like Ned and had the cutest chubby cheeks he'd ever seen.

"Meet Dennis," Betty said with the smile of a proud mama. "Dennis, this is your uncle Rob."

"Unky Wob," the child smiled wide and waved his spoon towards Rob again. This time, applesauce splattered on Rob's shirt, but he laughed.

Betty offered him a napkin to wipe his shirt and invited him to sit and have lunch.

"I'm sorry to intrude on your meal," Rob said, but he really knew around here you never intruded on a meal. When food was served, everyone was welcome to sit and eat.

"Nonsense," Ned said. "We were expecting you, and Betty had already set a plate for you."

Rob noticed the extra plate and pulled out a chair. True to form, Betty laid out a spread for lunch just like their mom used to. All of a sudden, he was hungry, so he loaded up his plate with beef tips and gravy over rice, fresh garden peas, and homemade cornbread. Betty poured him a glass of sweet iced tea, and while it was delicious, it almost reminded him of syrup.

While they ate, Rob shared what Dr. Barnes had said and about the time he spent with each parent. They all agreed they would take it day by day, and with Betty's current condition, Rob said he would travel to the hospital twice each day.

"I'm afraid I'll be traveling to the hospital before long," Betty laughed. "Then you can visit all four of us."

"Four?" Rob seemed puzzled.

Betty pointed to her bulging belly, and everyone laughed.

When they finished eating, Betty stood up and started

gathering the dirty dishes.

"I'll take care of this," Rob stood. When Betty started to protest, he insisted.

"I've learned my way around a kitchen living on my own. I'll take good care of the dishes and leftovers. You sit and rest with Ned, and then we'll talk about how to handle funeral arrangements."

Rob had the dishes washed, leftovers put up, and the kitchen cleaned in no time. Betty was a neat cook, and her kitchen looked like it had barely been used when she finished cooking. He remembered his mom always saying, "If you wash as you go, your load will be much lighter after the meal." He now understood what she meant.

Betty and Ned were sitting on the front porch swing, and he joined them, sitting in one of the rocking chairs. Betty had already put Dennis down for a nap, and she and Ned were in the swing and fanning themselves in the Florida heat. Rob noticed Betty's ankles were swollen slightly which he assumed was part of the pregnancy.

"People are asking about arrangements," Betty said. "They want to bring food and send flowers, and I don't know what to tell them."

Rob remembered how the community came together when there was a death of a loved one. When his grandmother died, the house was filled with so much food, they didn't have room for it all.

"We can't do anything until Mom and Dad are strong enough to help make decisions," Rob said, and they all agreed. "I can go talk to the funeral director today and get his recommendations if that works for you."

Betty and Ned not only agreed. They would be grateful if he would take care of that. Ned was finalizing the schedule for tobacco gathering which had to start next week, and Betty was too big and uncomfortable to be dragging a toddler around.

They sat in comfortable silence for a spell. Each was lost in thoughts of a younger sister they would never have the chance to see again. Rob noticed Betty wipe away tears and Ned hugged her close. He was happy that his older sister had a loving husband and a beautiful family of her own.

Ned stood up. "It's back to the fields for me."

Rob stood to meet his gaze, and Ned slapped him on his back. "It's good to have you back," he said. "I'm sorry it has to be under these circumstances."

Rob nodded at this brother-in-law, and Ned strode towards his truck. After giving his sister a peck on the cheek, Rob turned the old truck back towards the parents' house. He thought it might be best to call and see if the funeral director had time to see him before he went into town and just showed up. He learned in Atlanta that you had to have an appointment for anything.

He should have known making a phone call in the middle of the day would be next to impossible. When he picked up the phone, Myrtle was in a conversation with someone complaining about her leg cramps. That was all he needed to hear, so he set the phone back in its cradle, not very gently.

He waited two minutes and hoped she'd get the hint and tried again. She was still talking. This time he set the receiver down a little harder. After another two minutes, he picked it up again. This time the old voice chastised, "I don't know who keeps interrupting my conversation, but I am using the phone. Everybody on this line knows this is my busiest time of day to talk."

"Why hello, Miss Myrtle," Rob said using his most charming voice again. "I didn't realize that was you. I mean, all I heard was you talking about your leg cramps, and I thought you are far too young to have those." He smiled to himself.

"Don't you try and sweet talk me, Rob Mathis!" Myrtle retorted. "You know good and well, I'm an old biddy. Not only do I have leg cramps, but the gout wakes me up at night, and most nights, I don't get no sleep at all. Of course, you don't know anything about your neighbors now that you've been gone for four years." Another voice grunted in agreement. "You ought to be ashamed of yourself, running off like you did. Your mama cried for days, and your daddy wouldn't hardly take to no one. And poor Patti was ..."

Before she could finish her sentence, the operator cut her off.

"Myrtle, I'm afraid you are going to have to give up the line. I have an emergency call for Mr. Mathis."

"I ain't through with you, Rob. Why don't you come over for a visit, and we can finish this conversation."

"I'll try to do that, Miss Myrtle. Thank you for hanging up now." And the line went click.

"The nurse wants to talk to you, but she said it's not an emergency. I wanted to save you from any more of Myrtle's foolishness," he heard the laughter in the operator's voice. "I'll patch Margaret through."

"Rob, this is Nurse Margaret," the voice was efficient and pleasant. "I wanted to let you know that your mom has opened her eyes, and Dr. Barnes thinks she is beginning to wake up. You might want to come earlier for your visit this evening, and maybe she will be fully awake."

"That sounds great," Rob replied. "Thank you for letting me know. I have a couple of errands to run, and then I'll head that way."

7

Not wanting to risk another chastising from Myrtle, Rob decided to ride over to the funeral home rather than call first. That is how people do in North Florida anyway. Just show up, and more times than not, you are welcomed with open arms. If they were having a service or were too busy to see him, he'd make an appointment for tomorrow.

The old truck rumbled into the parking lot of the funeral home. There were only two cars in the lot, so Rob figured his chances of talking to the funeral director were good.

Actually, he was greeted at the door by the director himself.

"Rob!" the director exclaimed. Mr. Stewart was an older gentleman with a kind face, balding hairline with a slight combover on top, and a belly that proved he enjoyed his daily fried chicken. And his smile was always genuine.

"It's good to see you, son. I heard you were back in town. I am truly sorry for what your family is enduring. We are here to help with whatever you and your precious family need."

"Thank you," Rob answered back, feeling comforted by the man's words.

Just then, a younger man stepped into the foyer. Rob recognized him as Ralph Wheeler, one of his few friends in high school. Ralph laughed at Rob's look of surprise.

"Hey, stud," Ralph chuckled and slapped Rob on the back.

"Guess you're wondering what I'm doing here. I just started working for Mr. Stewart. Let's catch up later, once you have some time."

Mr. Stewart ushered both men into a small, tastefully-decorated room next to his office. Rob could tell at one glance that this was the room where grieving families made final plans for their loved ones. As if he read his mind, Mr. Stewart said,

"I know you're not ready to talk about arrangements yet, and that is fine. We'll take care of your sister until your parents are able to help with the planning." He paused. He'd seen many family members break down in this room. He could already see the effect that being here was having on Rob. "As I said, we're here to help in any way we can. Is there anything we can do for you today?"

Mr. Stewart was right. At that moment, Rob's grief hit him hard. He put his head in his hands, and the floodgate of tears opened. Embarrassed that he couldn't stop himself, he also realized that releasing the tears felt good. The other two men sat quietly in their chairs as Rob worked through his range of emotions.

After several minutes, he spoke, "I'm sorry. I don't know what came over me." And then he hiccupped.

"Rob it's perfectly normal," Ralph spoke with a softness in his voice.

"We'd be worried if you didn't let your emotions go. My gut tells me you haven't had a cleansing cry since you got that first phone call from Betty."

Those last words surprised Rob. How would he know about that phone call? But he was right. With the travel plans and worries about his parents, Rob had yet to acknowledge the deep grief he felt at the loss of his baby sister.

"And besides," Mr. Stewart winked at him, "why do you think there is a box of tissues next to every chair?"

The three men rose and rather than shake hands, they

hugged each other. Mr. Stewart promised to stay in touch and again assured Rob not to worry about a thing.

"Let me walk you out," Ralph said.

The two young men walked outside into the bright Florida sun. Even though the day was still young, the temperatures were rising quickly. Without thinking, they sauntered under a big oak tree in the corner of the parking lot, where a park bench was placed for family members and friends to sit and chat.

"It's good to see you, Rob," Ralph said quietly, not sure if he should continue the conversation as he wanted. He didn't want to add to Rob's grief or obvious feelings of guilt.

"Good to see you, too, my friend," Rob answered quickly. The two men sat in silence for a few minutes.

"I was sweet on her," Ralph finally said.

Surprised, Rob looked over towards his old friend. He tried to absorb the meaning of what Ralph had just said.

"You and Connie?" he finally asked.

"Yeah. We went to the picture show a couple of times. I had just gotten the nerve to hold her hand." Ralph let his words drift away. He didn't want to burden Connie's brother with his own grief.

"Aw, man, I'm so sorry," Rob looked away and swallowed hard.

"You two would have made a great couple," he squeezed his eyes shut.

"She sure was a sweet gal," Ralph said.

Both men sat in silence, letting their own thoughts and grief wash over them. Another life outside the immediate family was changed. How many other lives had been touched by his sister that he didn't know about, Rob thought to himself.

Wanting to change the mood, Ralph nudged his friend with his elbow.

"Hey, remember the time you helped me chase the goat

down the highway?"

Rob chuckled at the memory.

"Oh my God, that was a riot."

"I had just stopped at the main red light in town. My brother wanted that goat, and I was delivering him to his farm. I felt the truck shake and looked up to see that dang goat jump out of the back bed! He had wriggled himself out of the container I had him in and in seconds was gone. Good thing you were close by!"

"Yep, I had just come out of the diner, and all I saw at first was you jumping out of your truck and sprinting off down the middle of the highway! You just left your truck running at the stop light. Someone came up behind you and was honking their horn. It was a sight."

"Hey, man. Thanks for moving my truck and then helping me in the chase."

Both men were laughing now at the memory. If Ralph could have only seen how he looked in his cutoff blue jeans as his cowboy hat went flying off his head while he was running. The goat made it almost a quarter of a mile down the road.

Luckily, the traffic had been light that afternoon, or there could have been an unhappy ending. Some kids had seen the chase and joined in and were able to stop the goat from getting any further away. The two men had secured him back into the truck bed, and he was finally delivered safely to his destination.

The men got quiet for a moment, thinking of other memories. Finally, Ralph stood and said he needed to get back to work. They shook hands awkwardly and then gave each other a quick hug.

"Thanks for everything," Rob said, "I'll always consider you my brother."

8

Rob decided to make a quick stop at the newspaper office. Since it was just a couple of blocks away, he decided to walk despite the rising temperature.

Few people were on the sidewalk, but each one nodded and spoke with the same greeting, "Hey, how ya doing?" He smiled to himself, thinking how no one speaks when they pass you on the streets of Atlanta. So, to each person who spoke, he responded with a smile, "Good, and you?"

A friendly young receptionist greeted him as soon as he entered the newspaper office.

"Rob!" she exclaimed. "A little birdie told me you were home. Give me a hug!"

It took a minute for Rob to recognize the young woman.

"Mary Ann!" Rob remembered his former high school classmate. They dated once or twice, and he thought she continued to have a crush on him even when he started dating Patti.

"It's so good to see you," she hugged him a little tighter than he was comfortable with. "Let me look at you!"

She stepped back and looked him over from top to bottom. "Handsome as ever," she smiled.

"It's nice to see you, too, Mary Ann. How's your family?"

"Fit and fiddle as ever," she answered. Then, her tone

changed.

"Oh, Rob, I am so sorry ..." her words trailed off as a booming voice interrupted.

"Rob! I was wondering when you'd make it by here," Freddy Black, also known as the old publisher in town, slapped Rob on the back. "Boy, I have missed you."

The newspaper office had been Rob's place of solace in high school. He visited as often as he could, and Mr. Black appreciated the young boy's love of the printed word. He also recognized the writer's talent in Rob and encouraged him to pursue his love of writing. He even let the young boy pen a few articles for the weekly paper.

The two men chatted for over an hour. Mr. Black pulled out the article he had written about the accident and asked Rob to read it. As a fellow journalist, Rob knew the accident would be big news in this small town and would be the main headline on the front page.

The old publisher was sensitive to the family's needs, however. In the spirit of small-town living, he cautioned his readers that Mr. and Mrs. Mathis must hear the news of the loss of their daughter from family members only. He asked the community not to try and intervene. He also mentioned that the funeral arrangements would be made once the parents were well enough to come home, and he would inform the community at that time.

When he received Rob's approval of the article, the older gentleman changed his tone.

"How are you doing, Rob?" he asked with genuine concern.

"I'm ok. Just trying to help the best I can. Looks like Betty may have that baby any time, so we certainly have a lot going on. Ned is working to line up plenty of help when tobacco gathering starts next week," he sighed. "You know that's not my favorite place to be, but I'll help however I can."

Mr. Black nodded. Not every country boy was meant to be a

farmer.

"Well, I have it on good authority that you don't need to worry about your new job in Atlanta," Mr. Black smiled. "They will keep it open for you."

Rob gave him a confused look, and the older man winked. "I have friends in high places," he laughed. "But on a serious note, son, remember that family comes first. Sometimes, life deals us a hand that we aren't expecting and certainly don't want. Our plans may work out, and sometimes they won't. You have to decide what's best. You've grown up since you walked away four years ago. You're a smart man with a big heart and a good head on your shoulders. You'll do the right thing."

Rob thanked him, and the men stood and shook hands. "You're welcome here anytime," Mr. Black said.

Mary Ann was still sitting at the receptionist's desk when Rob stepped into the lobby.

"Hey, handsome. I'd love to grab a cup of coffee while you're in town and catch up with ya," she said.

Rob noticed that she had matured into a fine young woman, far from the girl he left behind. Her slim figure was accented by a pale pink suit that hugged her curves just right. He noticed the cut of her jacket was a little low and thought it was too low for the workplace. Her auburn hair was now redder, perhaps from a dye job, and her lips shined a bright ruby red. She definitely was a looker, he thought, and not Rob's type at all. Being polite, he answered, "Sure, that would be great."

"See ya soon," she smiled as Rob opened the door.

He strolled back to the truck. It was time to drive back to the hospital. Even though he had plenty of time until visiting hours, nurse Margaret told him to come early. They were hoping to coax his mom awake. As he passed the edge of town, he glanced towards the diner. He wanted to stop and say hello to Patti, but he had spent enough time in town already. So, he continued on.

Nurse Margaret met him in the ICU ward and was happy to report that both parents were out of the danger zone and showing signs of improvement, however slight.

"We'll take our improvements one step at a time," she smiled.

Her smile was genuine, and he marveled how her starched white uniform never showed a wrinkle and her white cap sat perfectly on her head. All of the nurses looked neatly manicured, yet he saw they worked hard to ensure their patients received the best care.

"Want to see Mom first today." Even though it was a question, he could tell in her tone that it was a strong recommendation. He nodded, and they headed to her room together.

Margaret spoke first. "Mrs. Mathis. Look who came to see you."

Rob was surprised to see his mother's eyes flutter for a moment, and then she opened them and focused on her son's face.

"Rob," she whispered hoarsely.

"I'm here, Mom," and Rob took her hand. Nurse Margaret discreetly disappeared behind the curtain.

Charlotte's eyes were full of questions, but she only whispered, "Thank you."

"I love you, Mom," Rob said, trying to hold back tears. "You had quite an accident, so I wanted to be here with you."

"I'm glad," and she struggled to keep her eyes open.

Nurse Margaret stepped from behind the curtain. "You need to rest, Mrs. Mathis. Rob's going to stick around until you're all recovered, so he'll come back and see you soon."

Charlotte nodded and Rob thought he saw a slight smile on her face before she fell back asleep.

"Great progress," Margaret said. "Now, let's see how your

dad is doing."

Rob noticed there weren't as many wires hooked to his dad, and the older man was awake staring at the ceiling when his son walked in.

"Hey, Dad," Rob whispered.

The older man's eyes showed a hint of surprise when he saw his son.

"So you are here," he said weakly. "I thought that was a dream."

Again, Margaret stepped behind the curtain. She didn't want to pry, but she needed to stay close in case her patient became agitated.

"Not a dream, Dad. I'm here." Rob hesitated. He didn't want to say too much that would trigger his dad to ask questions about Connie.

"We have to gather next week," Robert stated. His voice was flat.

"Yes, sir," Rob answered. He should have known his first thoughts would be about the tobacco crop. Not his wife. Not his daughter. "Ned is working on getting a crew together. We'll get it done for you."

"Ned is a good man," Rob nodded and tried not to show the sting in his dad's words as he agreed. What did Robert think of his own son?

Robert closed his eyes, and Rob could feel some of the old fury coming back. He knew he had to keep his emotions in check, but he felt like the berated kid again.

"Get some rest, Dad. I'll be around for a while," Rob said, grateful when Margaret stepped back into the room.

"You're in good hands, Mr. Mathis," Margaret said as she adjusted her patient's covers and began checking his vital signs. Rob thought he heard his father grunt as he stepped into the main larger room.

Margaret caught up with him as he was about to exit the ICU ward.

"You're doing great, Rob," she said as she put her hand on his arm. "Your dad may not show it, but he's glad you're here. Just remember, farming has been his entire life. It's what he knows best. I sense he was never an emotional father?"

"That's putting it mildly," he said blandly. "He had emotions. Just not the right ones."

"You're not the little boy or the teenager anymore," she said. "You're a mature, responsible man, from what I can see." She paused for a brief moment. "Maybe it's time you showed him the way it should be," she smiled.

"I'll try," he said. And he walked out of the hospital.

9

Rob pulled up at the farmhouse just before 8 pm. He realized he wanted to talk to Eleanor just to hear her sweet voice. There was a note on the front door from Betty inviting him to supper, but he knew it was too late. By now, they were getting ready for bed, as Ned needed to wake up early and start on his farm work. He decided to just call and fill her in on their parents' progress.

He figured it was too late for Myrtle to be on the party line. As much as she talked during the day, she would probably be hoarse in the evening. When he picked up the receiver, he immediately dialed 0, not thinking anyone would be on the line.

"Hey, I'm talking here," a young girl's voice reprimanded. Great, he thought. Now, he had to contend with teenagers on the line.

"Sorry," he said. "How much longer will you be?"

The girl sighed quite loudly as if to make a point.

"I can't talk during the day because Myrtle won't give up the line. Now I'm interrupted at night. Who is this? Did they put another party on the line?" he smiled at the frustration in her voice. She reminded him of the days he, too, waited impatiently for a chance to have a turn on the party line.

"This is not a new party. This is Rob Mathis," he said. "And who do I have the pleasure of speaking to?"

"Oh my God! Rob?" the voice squealed. "This is Helen from down the road."

Rob chuckled. He remembered Helen. She was about 12 years old when he left. She had a head full of flaming red hair and a face full of cute freckles. She followed him around the farm, swooning over him. She'd had a little girl's crush on him.

"Well, Helen," Rob smiled. "It's good to hear your voice. You sound like you've grown into a nice young lady," he said in his most charming voice.

He could almost see her blush through the phone. "I'm sixteen now," she said. "I'm a grown woman."

"Well, I look forward to seeing you again. In the meantime, may I have the phone for just a few minutes? Then I'll be finished, and you can have it the rest of the evening."

"Of course," she answered. "See ya soon," and he heard two clicks on the other end as both parties hung up.

He dialed Betty first, as he knew they would be headed to bed soon. Eleanor was a night owl and was hours away from slumber. He filled his sister in on his brief conversations with his parents. She was relieved to hear they had not asked about Connie yet. They made plans for Betty to ride to the hospital with Rob tomorrow during his morning visit.

Eleanor answered on the first ring. "Rob?" she sounded hopeful.

"Hey, sweetheart," he said. "Yep, it's me."

They chatted for a few minutes, mindful of the long-distance charges Rob was running up on his father's phone bill. She told him about the new story assignment she had gotten and gossiped about the new reporters at work.

"So, how are you holding up, darling?"

He informed her that he was okay and his parents were out of danger. He heard the phone click a couple of times and smiled. Helen was checking to see if she could have the line back.

"I'll call again in a couple of days," he said, knowing that he needed to end the call. "It was great to hear your voice. Keep up the amazing work on your stories," and he ended with, "I love you, darling."

"Me, too," was all she said as they clicked off the line.

10

When Rob arrived at Betty's house to pick her up the next morning, she handed him the keys to her new Oldsmobile.

"We'll be more comfortable riding in this," she chided. "And it has air conditioning, which I need right now."

Rob laughed and opened the door for Betty. It took her a minute to get her very pregnant frame inside and settle into the seat.

"We had a better-than-average crop last year, so Ned felt it was time we bought a family car," Betty explained. "Isn't she a beauty?"

Rob admitted that the car was sweet. It was a four-door, perfect for a growing family, and painted powder blue with chrome trim. The hubcaps were even rimmed in blue to match the paint on the car. The cloth seats were cushiony, and he had ample room for his long legs. And the air conditioner was definitely a plus in the sweltering heat.

The little downtown area bustled with Saturday morning activity as Rob and Betty passed through on their way to the hospital. Farmers went to town on Saturday to buy supplies for the week. Often, the kids were given pocket change to spend in the general store. Rob remembered the thrill of looking for the newest book or magazine and then filling up his little bag with penny candy. He'd stretch his candy to make it last all week while Connie gobbled hers up in the first couple of days.

Nothing much had changed. Lines of pick-up trucks were parallel parked in front of the stores on Main Street. Men were loading up their feed and fertilizer for the week while the ladies shopped in the stores looking for household supplies and an occasional treat for themselves.

His mother had rarely bought anything for herself, but he did remember one Saturday before Easter when she splurged on a new pair of white dress shoes for herself. She was so proud of the patent leather shoes with a buckle strap and chunky heels. She didn't buy them until all three of her offspring had new Easter clothes and shoes, and Robert had a new tie for church. Rob smiled sadly at the thought. Mom always put herself last.

As they passed the little diner, Rob saw Patti inside, taking orders from her customers. Her blonde ponytail bobbed as she chatted and laughed with the patrons.

When Rob turned onto the highway leading to the hospital, the brother and sister maintained a relaxed atmosphere. Neither spoke for a while, each lost in their own thoughts and each a little unsure as to what to say to the other.

"Look, Rob," Betty broke the silence. "I'm sorry for how I acted right before you left. I got caught up in Dad's drama, and with you leaving, I didn't know what would happen to the farm."

"Think no more of it, big sister," Rob smiled at her. "Think about it this way. What would have happened to the farm had I stayed? I don't know much about farming, no matter how much Dad tried to teach me. I only did what he told me to do, and I had no ambition to learn anything more. My head was in my studies and my books. I wouldn't have been much help had I stayed. And I would have ended up resenting everyone."

"You're right. I hadn't thought about it that way. And Dad has done fine running the farm. I married a farmer, and he helps Dad when he can. Connie has no interest," she caught herself using Connie in the current tense and choked back tears.

Rob sighed. "What do you think she would have done with her life," he asked quietly.

"She worked at the general store and took night classes at the secretarial school. I think her goal was to be an amazing secretary, maybe for a law firm or banker."

Rob nodded his head. "I'm sure she would have been amazing." And then he muttered "Damn" under his breath. A wave of grief passed over him as he thought about his sister's life taken so soon.

"Damn is right," Betty said, and he saw tears fall on her cheeks.

They were silent the rest of the way to the hospital, both lost in their own thoughts. Rob parked the car in the nearly empty parking lot and sprinted around to open the door for his sister. He helped her out of the car and held her elbow as they entered the hospital. Nobody stopped them as they headed for the intensive care unit, and the nurse greeted them with friendly smiles. They stopped at the center desk at the unit.

"Look, I know the policy is one visitor at a time, but could you make an exception …" Rob began.

The head nurse on duty cut him short. "For you two, we will make an exception this one time. Just don't tell on me," she smiled.

"Thanks," Rob said and escorted his sister into their mother's room first.

Charlotte appeared to be sleeping so peacefully that neither wanted to disturb her. She didn't have as many wires hooked to her, and for that, they were grateful. She had bruises on her forehead and on her arms and neck. They stood in silence for a couple of minutes before Charlotte's eyes slowly opened. It was as if her mother's instinct kicked in, and she knew her children were nearby.

"Well, I must be a sight," she tried to smile. Charlotte was always meticulous about her appearance. Even when she worked in the fields, she had bandanas around her hair, and her clothes always appeared neat, even when they had Florida soil on them.

"You look beautiful, Mom," Rob smiled at her.

"Thank you for coming," she smiled back at her only son. Even though her voice was weak, she turned to Betty, "and you, missy, need to stay off your feet." She coughed lightly and tried to keep her eyes open.

"I'm fine, Mom," Betty said and took her hand. "I'm strong, just like you."

"I don't feel strong," Charlotte said. And then she asked the question they dreaded, "Where's Connie?"

Before they opened their mouths to speak, the nurse appeared. It was as if she stood outside the door waiting for the question they weren't ready to answer.

"Sorry, ya'll. Your time is up. Ms. Charlotte needs her rest," she said as she quickly pushed a shot into Charlotte's IV line. "This will help her rest better," the nurse said as she escorted Betty and Rob out of the little room.

"Dr. Barnes will speak with you after you see your father. For now, he wants us to keep them sedated until you are ready to talk with them about your sister."

They thanked the nurse and stepped into Robert's room. They found him awake and staring at the ceiling. His expression was blank when he saw Rob.

"You didn't need to come home," he said flatly.

His words stung. "I want to be here, Dad," Rob said, trying not to let the hurt in his heart show on his face.

"We've done just fine without you for the last four years," his father said with no bitterness in his voice.

"Dad, let's talk about this later," Betty intervened. "Right now, our focus is to get you all well. Rob is here to help. That's all."

Robert was silent for what seemed like an eternity. The siblings couldn't tell what he was thinking until he said, "Have you told your mother about Connie?"

"What do you mean?" Betty asked.

"Don't play games with me," Robert spat, and they saw tears slipping down the older man's face. His grief was raw and obvious.

They let him cry for several minutes, both lost in their own grief. None of them spoke. The nurse discreetly came into the room.

Finally, Robert spoke first. "I was awake at the scene. I saw a lot of what was going on. Connie took the brunt of the impact. She could not have survived any of that," his voice was broken.

He continued, "I've heard the whispers around here when people thought I was asleep. I know your mother is in the room next to me." He paused. "Does she know?" he spit out.

"No, sir, not yet," Rob kept his voice calm. "The plan was to tell you both together when you were strong enough."

Robert stared straight into Rob's eyes and started to speak. He changed his mind and grew silent. The fight had gone out of him.

"I want to tell her." And then added, "But not just yet. I don't think she's ready to handle it."

The nurse stepped forward with a shot for Robert. She pushed it through his IV and told him it was time to rest.

Betty stepped up and took Robert's hand. "I love you, dad. We are family, and we'll make it through this together." Then she saw Robert's breathing go steady as he fell into a calming sleep.

Rob stepped up and patted his father's shoulder. "I love you, dad. I'm here to help." But he knew Robert didn't hear him.

A petite young nurse met the brother and sister outside their dad's room and led them to a small waiting room down the hall. She explained that Dr. Barnes wanted to meet them and discuss a plan for the immediate future. She smiled politely and left the room in the most efficient manner.

Neither one spoke, lost in their own thoughts, and Dr. Barnes didn't keep them waiting long. As soon as he entered the room, he shook Rob's hand firmly and then touched Betty's shoulder.

"How are you holding up, my dear?" he asked gently.

"I'm fine," Betty smiled, "I'm in good hands with two caring men by my side."

"Glad to hear that," Dr. Barnes said in his authoritative voice. "This is a lot to go through for a woman in her late stages of pregnancy. You need to take care of you and our soon to be new resident first. No working in the fields this week, right?"

Betty smiled sheepishly. "I promise I won't be in the fields, Dr. Bee" she said. What she didn't say is there would be plenty of work in the barn and in the kitchen once the men started their field work on Monday.

"Good. Rob, you make sure she minds," the doctor ordered. He looked at Betty with concern on his face.

"Your hands are a little swollen, which is not uncommon in this heat. I want you to stay off your feet as much as possible and come see me in my office on Monday. I think we need to check you out just to make sure eclampsia is not setting in."

Betty sighed. She didn't like all this fuss over her. They had bigger issues to worry about, and her mother's instincts told her the baby was fine. He or she was kicking up a storm, especially around 2 am. Betty figured he was getting her ready for those around-the-clock feedings that would be coming soon enough.

"Yes, sir," was all she said.

"Our dad knows that we've lost Connie," Rob said.

"The nurse filled me in," Dr. Barnes said. "I'm sorry he found out that way. We tried to be discreet so he would have family around him when the time came. He's a sharp man, however. He's very astute, especially when it comes to his family." Dr. Barnes looked at Rob.

"So, what's next?" Betty asked.

Dr. Barnes explained that both parents were well enough physically to move into a regular room. He wanted to keep them close to the ICU ward but put them in a double room together. Since Robert was the stronger one at this point, his presence might help Charlotte heal quicker. And they would need each other to help with their grief.

"Since your father knows that you've lost Connie, I think it best to let him decide if he will tell your mother alone or if he wants his family with him." The siblings nodded that they understood even though they didn't necessarily agree. "We'll move them in the morning," Dr. Barnes continued. "We'll let them rest peacefully tonight with sedation so they'll be strong enough for the move. You can call in the morning to see how they are doing before making the trip back over."

Before he left the room, Dr. Barne's voice changed from authority to sympathy. "My deepest condolences to your family. I'm not just your family physician. I'm your friend, and I love each of you."

They rode home in comfortable silence, both lost in their own thoughts. The baby kicked and moved almost continually, and Betty smiled, thinking what a rambunctious child she was about to bring into the world. She loved feeling this new life move inside of her and was thankful the child was so active. She wasn't the least bit worried that she and this baby would be fine.

Rob pondered his immediate future. He had no doubt that he would eventually return to Atlanta, but at this point, the question was when. How long would they hold his new job for him? Did Eleanor love him enough to wait patiently for weeks? Would his father even want him around once he came home? His head started to pound. It was time to find a quiet place where he could put his thoughts on paper.

Ned had taken Dennis to the field with him, so the house was quiet when Rob pulled into Betty's driveway. He helped her out of the car and into the house and handed the keys over to her.

"Why don't you take a little nap while you have the house to yourself," Rob suggested. "I'll check on you a little later."

"I think that's a great idea," Betty agreed, and she headed towards her bedroom.

11

Rob was emotionally done. He wasn't surprised at his dad's comments to him once he became completely aware of his family's tragedy. He had not expected the truth that his dad knew they had lost Connie.

He needed to write. Putting his thoughts on paper made him feel better and sometimes turned into a story. He grabbed his notebook from his satchel, found a pen, and headed for his favorite oak tree in the backyard. The old tire swing his dad hung many years ago didn't look stable enough for even a child to sit on. Instead, he eased himself onto the ground and leaned his back against the tree.

The air was hot and sticky, but he closed his eyes and soaked in the warmth and the smell of the north Florida fields. Tobacco gathering started in a couple of days. He could almost smell the pungent odor of the leaves as they were cropped from their tall stalks by lanky men. A good cropper was worth his weight in gold and would help a farmer get his entire field cropped and loaded into the barn in a single day.

Rob put pen to paper. Words flowed easily for him on paper, and he wrote non-stop for at least 30 minutes. He recounted an argument he'd had with Connie when she was about 13. She dreaded tobacco season as much as he did, and they took their frustrations out on each other one hot afternoon. He couldn't even remember what started the argument, but he did remember some of the heated words they threw at each other. Their mother had chastised them and sent them their separate ways. He apologized to his baby sister the next morning, but the words hung in the air between them. They couldn't be taken back once spoken. Rob wrote until his printed words began to smudge from tears that fell silently from his eyes.

He stood up, closed his notebook, and wiped the dirt and leaves off his bottom. Sweat mingled with the tears, and he wiped his face with his shirt tail before deciding to take a walk around the yard. His mom's rose bushes were wilting from the heat, and the begonias and geraniums had dropped off all their blooms, leaving brown spots where bright colors had once been.

Rob put his notebook on the front porch swing and went in search of a water hose. He found the faucet and tested the first spray of water. Just as he remembered, the water was hot from the sun when it first emerged from the hose. He let the spray of water run for a full minute before turning it to the plants. He could almost see the greenery perking up from the coolness of the liquid.

Satisfied that the flowers were hydrated, Rob strolled around the perimeter of the yard and stared out into the fields. Tall tobacco stalks stood in the north field, ready for their leaves to be taken and prepped for market. On the back side of that field, the tobacco barn rose two stories high, and Rob was sure his dad had already prepared everything inside for the first gathering.

Behind the home, two large chicken coops held an assortment of hens who laid enough fresh eggs for the family and a few extras for the neighbors if they needed them. Rob made a mental note to gather the eggs in the morning.

The "back field" held the cows that Robert took to market twice yearly. They had plenty of grass to graze on, so they required little maintenance. To the south of the home was the corn field, and there had been plenty of rain this year, so the corn stalks were tall, green, and perky.

The rumble in Rob's stomach reminded him that he had not eaten, so he decided to freshen up and ride into town in search of food. He knew he was welcome at Betty's house, but he liked the idea of seeing Patti at the little diner.

He went inside and changed clothes, swiped on a little deodorant, and decided to try to reach Eleanor before he headed out. He picked up the phone, and as usual, another party had the line tied up. At least it wasn't Myrtle, but he didn't recognize the voice. He laid the phone back in its cradle and sighed. Maybe he'd find a pay phone in town and call her collect. At least that line would be private.

The old Ford rumbled into the parking lot of Gram's Diner, and Rob noticed a pay phone booth near the front of the building. A new addition to the old diner, he mused, and he pushed the door open to the little box and walked in. The sun had warmed the box through the glass walls. He left the door open, hoping that the cooler evening air would keep the little space from getting too stifled.

When the operator answered, he said, "Collect call from Rob to Atlanta, please, 55-1249."

He listened as the operator plugged the cord into the circuit board, and then Eleanor's sweet voice came on the line.

"Collect call from Rob," the operator's southern drawl stated flatly. "Do you accept the charges, ma'am?"

"Yes, operator, I'll accept," and the two were connected.

"Hi, sweetheart," Rob said as soon as the operator clicked off the line. "I sure do miss you."

"I miss you, too, darling," Eleanor answered back. "I just got home from wedding dress shopping, and my sisters and mother and I had the best time! I tried on so many beautiful gowns, and then we had lunch downtown. It was a wonderful day!"

Rob smiled, listening to her excitement. She was a breath of fresh air as she continued.

"I'm meeting the gals from work for cocktails in an hour. Then we're going to the picture show and out for a late-night supper," she went on.

As an afterthought, she said, "How are you? How's your family holding up?"

"They are as good as they can be at this point," he said. He told her about the conversation with his father and the doctor.

"Does that mean you can come home now?" Eleanor asked with hope in her voice.

"I don't think I need to leave yet," Rob responded. "Once they are well enough to leave the hospital, we will plan Connie's service. I need to stay through that, at least."

"Well, you need to come back to the city where you really belong," she pouted. "You must be bored to tears down there in the sticks."

Rob laughed. "I really haven't had time to be bored. There is a lot to be done at the moment. Enjoy your night out with the girls. I'm going to grab a bite to eat."

They hung up after words of affection and a promise that Rob would call again in a couple of days.

Rob wasn't surprised to see Patti working when he walked into the diner. There were two tables occupied, and she was talking and laughing with her customers.

"I wondered when I'd see you again, Mr. City Slicker," she said as she saw him slide into a booth. Without asking, she brought him a glass of sweet tea and slid into the booth opposite him.

"Do you live here?" Rob asked jokingly as he sipped the best iced tea he had ever tasted. This was far better than any tea he'd had in Atlanta. The glass was tall, full of ice, and had enough sugar to put him in a diabetic coma. But, damn, it was good.

Patti laughed. "I live close by, but I just love what I do, so I'm here most of the time."

Rob smiled back. "Well, I hope Gram pays you well."

Patti responded with a sweet smile, but she didn't answer. Rob ordered the Saturday night blue plate special of meatloaf, mashed potatoes and gravy, fried cabbage, and cornbread, and he ate every bite. When he finished, he was so full that he felt like the button on his pants would pop off any second. He didn't eat like that in Atlanta. Eleanor had turned him onto salads and finger sandwiches, and he hardly ate fried foods anymore.

Patti brought two pieces of pie and sat in front of him. "We have fresh baked lemon meringue and apple," she winked at him. "I seem to remember that your favorite is apple."

Even though he was stuffed, he couldn't resist Gram's homemade apple pie with a scoop of ice cream on top. He savored every bite, along with a cup of fresh brewed coffee, and watched as Patti effortlessly waited on customers.

The diner was filling up, and she was the only girl working on the floor, but she handled everything efficiently. She knew what the locals wanted as soon as they walked in, so she had their drinks on the table almost before they sat down. He could see why this place was so popular. It was much busier than he remembered when he was a local.

With a full belly, tiredness suddenly set in, and Rob figured he'd better get a full night's rest before dealing with his parents again tomorrow. He stood and dropped money on the table to cover his bill. Patti was busy with new customers, but she managed to speak as he left.

"Hope to see you again soon, Atlanta."

He waved and smiled and walked out the door.

12

The brother and sister sat in comfortable silence on the drive back to the hospital. They were in the Oldsmobile again and both were lost in their own thoughts, not sure what to expect in the hours ahead. The road was clear on this bright Sunday morning as most of the folks in the area had already arrived for Sunday School and church services. Betty would have been at the little country Baptist church, but Ned took their son and went without her so she could meet with her parents. He wanted to go with her, but little Dennis would have been a handful at the hospital, and Betty wanted to focus on her parents. She was grateful for a husband willing to take their toddler to church alone. She smiled thinking how lucky she was to have landed such a caring man. Most of her friends had husbands who didn't lift a finger in the care of the children. Not only did Ned help her with their son, he managed to take care of their farm and now her parents' farm. A flush came over her face and tears welled in her eyes as she also felt guilty. Her baby sister would never know such joy. A sob caught in her throat, and she hiccupped loudly.

Rob was jolted from his thoughts and looked over with concern.

"You ok?" She nodded but couldn't speak.

"Please tell me you are not about to have that baby in this

car!" Panic began to set in.

"I'm fine!" Betty wailed, and the tears started flowing. "Just keep going. I'm not in labor."

Not knowing what else to do, Rob mashed the gas and sped up. If she was about to have the baby, at least they were headed to the right place, and he wanted to arrive as soon as possible.

It wasn't visiting hours, so Rob parked very close to the front door. He pulled into the space and pushed the gear lever into park. He didn't switch off the ignition. He looked at his sister with concern. Her tears had stopped.

"I'm sorry," she said and hiccupped again. "I think my hormones kicked in, and I just needed a good cleansing cry."

Seeing the look of almost fear on his face, Betty started laughing uncontrollably, which scared Rob even more. He had never seen a female so out of control with her emotions. He was gripping the steering wheel so hard that his knuckles were almost white.

After a few minutes, Betty was able to breathe normally. She was no longer laughing and crying, and the hiccups stopped as well. She saw the mixture of confusion and concern on her brother's face and grinned at him.

"I guess you've never been around a super pregnant woman before, huh?"

"Only our mother and that was a very long time ago," he said. "I don't remember any outbursts like this."

She smiled. "I think she kept them hidden from us," she said. "I just had a lot of emotions going on in this tiny brain, and my hormones took over. Thanks for your concern," and she reached over and squeezed his hand,

Dr. Barnes was waiting for them in the lobby when they walked in. He smiled at Betty, at once recognizing from her face the emotions she had just experienced. He explained that they moved their parents early this morning after they both had rested well through the night. They eased off the sedatives, and

Robert was fully awake and had been very quiet this morning. Charlotte was waking up, and Dr. Barnes felt like she would be ready for the difficult discussion when Robert was ready to tell her.

Betty excused herself to the ladies' room to wash her face and freshen up. She didn't want to cause any undue worry for her parents about her condition. When she came out of the bathroom, Betty looked refreshed and was almost relieved that there would be no more secrets and whispers in hospital corridors. Robert had already figured out that Connie did not survive the accident. Was it possible that Charlotte had as well? They had purposely kept her sedated so her body could heal. Now, it was time to allow for grief and let the process of healing her heart begin.

Robert was sitting up and had been moved into a chair next to Charlotte's bed. He was holding her hand and sitting quietly. His right arm was in a cast, there were bandages on his forehead, his lip was swollen, and he had multiple bruises on his face. From where they stood, they couldn't see his lower body, so Rob couldn't assess the extent of his injuries.

Charlotte had casts on her left arm and left leg. She, too, had bandages and multiple bruises. Rob was glad to see that all tubes and wires had been removed, and the room was free from the beeping machines. An IV pole stood next to her bed with a single tube running into her arm. Her eyes fluttered open when Rob, Betty, and Dr. Barnes entered the room. Charlotte studied their faces for several seconds before she spoke in a hoarse whisper.

"There's a reason Connie's not with you, isn't there?" She spoke so low they weren't sure they heard her correctly. She searched the faces of her two oldest children, searching for the answer she didn't want to hear. Robert squeezed her hand, and she turned her gaze towards him.

"She didn't make it, sweetheart," he said softly, trying to be brave for his wife. But he couldn't be brave any longer. He'd known the truth since the night of the accident, but he'd held his grief inside. Between sobs, he said, "We lost our baby girl."

Tears came easy for Charlotte. Her mother's instinct had already let her know, but she had not been awake enough to fully comprehend that her youngest child had died. The older siblings gathered closer to their parents, and they all held hands, forming a family circle. They couldn't hug Charlotte yet, as they didn't want to cause her any physical pain, but they were there for her and for each other.

Dr. Barnes slipped out the door. He alerted the nurses to listen for signs of distress but to not enter the room unless necessary. The family needed their grieving time.

Several hours later Rob helped Betty into the Oldsmobile. Her face was worn, her feet were swollen, and he could tell she was bone tired. But she never complained and had kept up a good front for her parents.

They had all held hands and cried together and shared memories of the youngest family member. Even Robert had softened towards his son.

"Thank you for coming home, Rob. It means the world to us." Robert reached out for his son's hand.

Charlotte cried and looked at her son. "I have missed you so much over the past four years, but I understand your passion for becoming your own man."

"Thank you, Mom." Rob leaned down and kissed her on the cheek.

"I'll support you in whichever path you choose. I'll even travel to Atlanta if you want me to." That was a huge step for a woman who had never been more than 60 miles from her home.

Dr. Barnes stepped back into the room and ordered everyone to go home and get some much-needed rest. He was concerned about Betty's swelling feet, and he wanted to give the parents a mild sedation to help them rest. The day went much better than he'd anticipated, and for that, he was grateful. The next step would be to get the parents to a place where they could go home and be surrounded by family and friends.

Several cars were parked in Betty's driveway when they pulled in. Rob recognized Louise, the church secretary when she came out to greet them. She hugged Rob and helped Betty from the car.

"Everything is fine," she said, seeing the worried look on their faces. "We knew you were going to have a rough day and would be exhausted when you got home. Several of us came over to help." Rob remembered that he nicknamed Louise Mother Hen when he was a child. Whenever a need in the community came up, she organized the ladies at church so that every detail was taken care of. Short in stature but big in heart, she organized the most disorganized situation.

The house smelled heavenly when they walked in. There was a spread of food on the table that Rob had not seen in four years. There was fried chicken, fried pork chops, meatloaf, mashed potatoes, gravy, macaroni and cheese, squash casserole, butter beans, green beans, cornbread and biscuits. Rob took in the sight, and all of a sudden, he felt famished.

He looked around the room and took in the caring faces of his mother's friends and neighbors. When a neighbor was in need, the surrounding families rallied together and took care of them. Of course, the care usually started with food, but they would pitch in and do whatever was needed and stay until the work was done.

Several men were gathered in the corner of the living room talking with Ned, and Rob heard them discussing the week's fieldwork. Ned had already told him that tobacco gathering started tomorrow and that was a huge affair for these farm families. With Robert not able to be here, Ned had the burden of two farms on his shoulders, but these men would help them through it. He started towards the men when he felt a hand on his shoulder.

"Can I fix you a plate, Rob?"

He turned around and found himself face to face with a pair of swimming green eyes. It took him a minute to recognize the beautiful woman standing beside him.

"Karen?"

"In the flesh," she said with a true southern drawl so that flesh had two syllables.

Rob and Karen had played together since they were old enough to toddle around in diapers. They chased one another through the corn fields and played cowboys and Indians in the backyard. And they always picked each other to be on their team when they played softball in fields with the other kids. She had been his first crush when he was six years old, and they shared a first kiss at the age of 12.

His hormones kicked in during junior high school, and he learned what jealousy felt like when other boys flirted with Karen through high school. Somehow, they never dated, but they had been close friends. She was always a cute girl, but now she had blossomed into a beautiful woman. She wore a green dress that accented her tall and slim figure. Her blond hair fell gracefully around her shoulders, and she had it pulled back at the crown with a green scarf, which made her green eyes sparkle like emeralds. This was not the tomboy he remembered. All he could do was stare.

"Well, aren't you going to speak?" she asked. "I have really missed you and sure was hurt when you left without a word," she pouted her lips for just a second before she broke into a smile.

"You're all grown up," he muttered and thought how stupid that sounded. "I mean, you're," he hesitated, then said, "you're beautiful."

"Aw now, flattery will get you everywhere," she winked at him. "Come on and have a bite to eat. You must be starving."

He suddenly realized how hungry he was. He turned around and saw the rest of the men headed his way. They were ready to eat as well.

The men sat at the table while the women gathered in the kitchen. Karen checked on Rob often and made sure his plate and glass of sweet tea were kept full. The discussion at the table centered around the gathering schedule for the upcoming week. They would take care of Robert's crop tomorrow and Ned's on Tuesday. That way, if Betty happened to go into labor, Ned would be free of worry for this week.

"What can I do?" Rob asked, and the men all got quiet for a moment.

"You haven't worked in the fields in four years," Ned said hesitantly. "I don't think it would be a good idea to throw you out in the hot sun like that."

Rob was stunned by his words, but he did hate the cropping part of the work. Ned was right. You worked in the hot sun for hours, and he wasn't conditioned for it.

"Do you think you can coordinate the barn work?" George asked, breaking the silence. George was Louise's husband, and he always had a level head and a quick solution to any problem.

"I can do that," Rob said.

George smiled at the younger man. "Sounds good. You report at the barn at 5:15 in the morning. The croppers will start at 5 and should have the first load to you by 5:30."

The men nodded in agreement and pushed back from the table, stuffed from the massive meal they had just eaten.

Just then, the ladies brought in slices of Louise's homemade 12-layer chocolate cake. The men groaned in protest, but they ate every morsel on their plates. It didn't get much better than that for dessert.

The men gathered on the porch to finish plans while the women cleaned up the dishes and made plans for tomorrow's meals. They would cook lunch in Charlotte's kitchen since the first gathering was at their farm.

Rob noticed how tired Betty looked. He wished she would get off her feet and rest until the baby came, but he knew his sister would work as close as she could to the birth. He kissed her on the cheek and walked out to the old Ford. He was pretty tired himself and ready to hit the sack.

13

Monday morning came quickly, but Rob was refreshed and at the barn right at 5 am. He didn't want to be late and appear like the city boy he had become. As he looked around at the women and children approaching the barn, the sense of dread he'd had over the work ahead began to vanish.

Memories of when he was a young boy flashed through his mind. He would stand by his mother's side and hand her just the right amount of tobacco leaves. She would expertly tie them onto a stick that was held up by two homemade tobacco horses, a wooden frame that held the stick in place. She taught him how to grab three leaves from the table as fast as his little hands would let him. He made sure they were lined up straight and then handed them to her from the top. She would grab them and wrap the string tightly around the bundle. The first bundle was looped over the back side of the stick, and the next bundle was looped on the front side. Over and under. Over and under. Betty would also be a hander, and his mom could keep up with both of them so that the stick would be strung in less than 10 minutes. Then, one of the older stringers, if available and able, would take the loaded stick into the barn and lay it on a table for the croppers to hang later. If there was enough help, one of the teenage boys, lucky enough to escape the fieldwork, would pick up the loaded sticks. He would also unload the tobacco sleds when the full ones were brought to the barn. This routine was repeated all day until the field was completely gathered and about 500 sticks hung in the barn, ready to cure. Rob's job today was to unload the sleds and keep the sticks moving to the barn for the ladies.

Betty and a neighbor would be the stringers today. There were four children about 12 years old that Rob didn't recognize. The ladies were explaining how to hand the tobacco to them, just as his mother taught him. A table was set up in between the stringers, and Rob would pile them high with the fresh tobacco leaves when they got to the barn.

Rob could hear the young men in the field laughing and calling to each other. The sound of the tractor echoed through the leaves as it chugged down the row, pulling the sled for the boys to fill. Rob's last two years at home were spent in the fields as a cropper. He was never as fast as the other young men, but he tried to hold his own. It was back-breaking work. You had to bend over, grab the yellowing leaves from the bottom of the tall stalk, and put each large leaf under your arm until you could carry no more. Then the tractor, most often driven by his dad, would pull up, and you had to carefully lay your bundle of leaves in the right position inside the specially-made tobacco sled. Once the sled was full, Robert would pull it to the barn, unhook it from the tractor, hook up an empty one, and take it back to the field.

The day went by fast and without a hitch. Four acres of tobacco had their first cropping, and the green leaves were all strung neatly on their sticks. When the men finished cropping in the fields, they gathered at the barn and formed a human ladder to hang the leaves. Three of the men worked in sync as the one on the ground handed the heavy sticks up to the next man. He, in turn, handed it to the man balanced at the top of the barn. It was a job well done, and it had run like a well-oiled machine.

Everyone took a mid-morning break for water and a snack.

The ladies had prepared a huge country dinner for lunch, and by 3:30, they were all finished. They were hot, sweaty, and smelly, but all were proud of the first gathering of the season. Ned patted Rob on the back and congratulated him on doing a fine job.

"Now, go see about your mom and dad," Ned told him. "If you'll gather the eggs and put them up, I'll take care of the rest of the farm chores."

Ned explained that they were working at his farm tomorrow and asked Rob to take on the same role there. Then, he would have the rest of the week free to start working on funeral arrangements.

Rob showered and decided to head on over to the hospital before supper. He knew his dad would be anxious to hear how the gathering went, and Rob was excited to tell him of the day's success.

14

Eleanor was getting more irritated with Rob with each passing day. He'd been gone almost a week, and he had only called her twice. Both times, the calls were very brief. She understood his family "needed" him, but she had listened to countless stories from him about walking out of that hick town and never looking back.

They started to talk about marriage, and she knew Rob was a prize catch. It would be hard to find a man who would support a woman who wanted a career rather than a lifetime raising babies and keeping a spotless house. Eleanor saw their future as a power couple, especially in the growing competitive field of journalism. Rob was talented with a pen, no doubt about that. And her goal was to be one of the first female TV journalists. Together, they would take on the world.

She sat primly across the table from her best friend, Leslie. They met for drinks after work in a small bistro in midtown, and both had delicious, extra-dirty martinis in front of them. She smiled slyly at her friend.

"Let's make a plan to get my man out of that hick town," she said. The two ladies clinked their glasses together and discussed ideas.

15

The tobacco gathering the next day at Ned and Betty's farm went as planned. The day wrapped up just after 4 pm, and Ned gave Rob a friendly pat on the back.

"You haven't forgotten what you learned growing up, my brother," Ned said playfully.

"I guess you can take the boy off the farm, but you can't take the farm out of the boy," Rob replied with a smirk.

As a boy growing up and forced to work in the fields, Rob resented every minute of it. What he saw yesterday and today was the true camaraderie of family, neighbors, and friends as they came together to help each other tackle one of the toughest crops on their farm. The window was short to get things done, and they knew how to work together as a team. It was much easier when you helped each other. Such was the small-town life that Rob had walked away from.

After he tended to his dad's animals and watered his mom's roses, Rob showered and got ready to head into town. He was still stuffed from the massive lunch that Betty and her friends had prepared, but he had promised Patti he would come back for some apple pie. At least, that's what he told himself.

Dr. Barnes sent Rob a note earlier asking for an appointment tomorrow morning to discuss his parents' discharge plan. He didn't need to go to the hospital tonight, so he had some free time. Just as he cranked the old pick-up and got ready to back out of the driveway, a sleek red convertible pulled in behind him. He pushed the gear shift back into park and got out, thinking this was a weary traveler lost in the country. As he approached the car, the driver cranked the handle on the door to lower her window.

"Well, aren't you looking mighty fine this evenin'?" He heard a high-pitched southern drawl and noticed that evenin' had three syllables.

"Karen! It's nice to see you again," he almost stammered the words.

"You all dressed up with no place to go?" she winked at him.

"Well, actually, I thought I'd head into town and have a bite to eat at the diner."

As soon as the words came out, Rob regretted telling her his plans.

"I was thinking the same thing," she said with a big smile. "Hop in, and I'll give you a ride."

When he hesitated, she pouted her lips, "Come on, I promise to get you there safely. I took driver's ed in high school and passed my drivin' test on the second try." She laughed and continued, "And besides, it is no fun eatin' alone."

Rob was torn. He hoped to spend time chatting with Patti. If he went with Karen, she would monopolize his conversation. If he turned her down, she would probably go anyway, and she would still take over the conversation. He had no choice.

The car was nice, no doubt about it. This girl was driving a 1962 Ford Thunderbird, candy apple red, with a soft black top. She put the top down and navigated the vehicle onto the highway towards town. Rob closed his eyes and felt the wind surround him. Even though it was a hot and humid evening, the wind felt good and had a slight chill to it. He looked at Karen, and she was laughing at him.

"It's good to have you home, Rob. This little town hasn't

been the same without you."

The words stung him. He had never thought of himself as being important in the community. He did feel like a heel for running out and not telling anyone, but he was young and just wanted to escape.

"I'm sure the town has continued to run just fine without me," he laughed. He appreciated how the wind blew her hair around her face. She had it pulled back in a ponytail and a scarf tied sweetly around the top, but wisps of her hair were falling loose around her face. She laughed as she swiped at the strands and pushed them back into place.

They entered the diner laughing. Rob felt carefree for a change, and when the little bell tinkled over the door, Patti called out,

"Ya'll have a seat, and I'll be right with you."

She entered from the back with several plates of food that she expertly carried to a table across the room. Rob wondered again why she was always here working away. When she set the plates down, Patti turned their way. When she saw the two of them, Rob thought he saw her hesitate for a short moment and then she put a big smile on her face. Rob wasn't sure it was genuine.

"Hey, you two!" she exclaimed, looking from one to the other cautiously.

"Hey back," Rob said, "I see you're working again."

"Always," Patti sighed and slid into the booth next to Karen.

"So," Patti opened the conversation. "Is Gram's the best place you can find to go on a date?"

She laughed, but there was no joy in her smile.

"This isn't a date," Rob said, perhaps a little too quickly. "Karen drove up just as I was getting in Dad's truck and offered to give me a ride," he added. "You know, since we were both going to the same place."

"And I just love drivin' my new car," Karen beamed as she winked at the other girl.

Patti watched the two of them for a second, and then the bell tinkled over the door again. "Ya'll have a seat," she said as she pulled her eyes away from Rob's.

"What can I get you?" Patti asked as she stood.

"I'd love a cherry coke to start," Karen flashed a big smile.

"Same for me," Rob said and wondered how he could escape this awkward situation.

Patti dropped their drinks off and greeted the other customers who entered.

"Plan on stickin' around your hometown for a while?" Karen asked fishing for his plans for the future.

He hesitated before he answered. Whatever he said could potentially spread like wildfire through the community. Not that Karen was a gossip, but you only had to tell one person before the story began to spread and each person put his or her own spin on it.

"Honestly, I'm taking it day by day," he chose his words carefully. "Right now, my main priority is my parents and helping them with Connie's final arrangements." He glanced down at his hands. They were already feeling rough from the work on the farm the last two days.

Karen reached over and put her hand over his, and the feel of her soft hand on his shocked him. He looked up and saw genuine concern in her eyes.

"I'm so sorry, Rob. I know you must be dealing with a lot in that smart head of yours," her smile was as warm as her hand. "What can I do to help?"

"All of a sudden, I am beat," he said. "I'd just really like to go back to my parents' house and be alone to think. I need to sort things through."

"I understand," she said as they both rose from the booth.

Rob laid enough money on the table to cover the drinks, which they barely touched, and a nice tip. Patti was busy taking care of the other customers, so he didn't want to bother her. He held the door for Karen as they stepped into the thick night air.

Even though she was busy taking orders and running her tickets to the kitchen, the little exchange between Rob and Karen didn't go unnoticed. She couldn't hear their conversation, but she saw when Karen reached over and took his hand, and their demeanor changed. All of a sudden, they were ready to go and be alone somewhere.

"Just like a man," Patti muttered to herself. Karen chased Rob all through high school, and he'd been too naïve to see it. He'd been a sprawling boy more interested in his books than girls. Well, it looks like that boy had grown into a man, Patti thought. He jumped at the first pass made at him. He looked as though he couldn't wait to be alone with the other woman. Patti didn't know why, but she had to fight to keep back the tears that were stinging in the corner of her eyes.

16

After Karen drove away, Rob sat alone on the front porch swing. He'd always loved this, and memories of family gatherings on the porch flooded back to him. When he was a kid, his parents would sit on the swing at the end of a long day on the farm, and his dad would drape his arm over his mother's shoulder. He and his sisters would sit in the straight back chairs, and they'd talk about the day's work or the days ahead. He'd forgotten how nice those evenings on the porch had been. When he was older, he would often sit on the swing late at night and dream about his future and what he envisioned his life to be.

Rob sighed. He thought he had it all together in Atlanta, but now he wasn't so sure. When he headed north on that bus four years ago, he hadn't looked back. His childhood memories had been tucked away, and he never let himself reflect on what he left behind. He excelled in school, and his career was off to a running start. He had a sweet girl by his side to share his future with. But that life now seemed so far away, almost as if it didn't really exist.

He watched fireflies dance around his mother's begonia hanging on the far end of the porch and checked his watch. It was only 8:00, even though it seemed much later. He thought about Eleanor and realized he hadn't called her in three days.

She would probably be furious, so he decided to give her a call. When he picked up the phone, he heard the giggling of two teenagers. Their laughter made him smile, so he quietly put the phone back in its cradle. He'd try again later. They had to get tired of giggling sooner or later, he thought.

Rob wandered around the house, not really sure what he was looking for or if he was looking for anything at all. He noticed how spotless the house was. Even though his mother worked on the farm and cooked for all the farmhands, she managed to keep a clean house as well.

He studied the kitchen and noticed dishes stacked in the dish drainer. A fancy little tea towel embroidered with daisies and the wording "Family Makes a Happy Home" was hanging on the stove handle. The few glasses and utensils he used were lying in the sink, so he decided to wash them and add them to the drainer.

He walked into the hallway and picked up the phone again. Two young voices were still chatting away excitedly. He put the phone down and sighed again. It would be useless to try and talk his dad into springing a little extra each month to have a private line if they even offered them in this area. After using a phone for business purposes, he couldn't imagine having to wait patiently while your neighbors finished their conversations, especially when those neighbors were nosy old women and young, hormonal teenagers.

Without thinking, Rob opened the door to Connie's bedroom. He stood in shock for a moment, feeling as if he'd entered a sacred area. Her bed was neatly made and covered with a baby blue chenille spread. There were posters of Elvis and the Beatles on her wall and several 'Teen Magazines' scattered on her nightstand. Rob noticed one showing a smiling Annette Funicello on the cover and a tease into an article about her early fame as a Mouseketeer.

The top of her bureau held normal teenage girl items with a

jewelry box, a mirrored tray with a jar of Noxzema cold cream, and assorted cosmetics. On the end of the dresser, he found a thick notebook with PRIVATE scrawled in bold letters across the front.

Rob picked up the notebook and sat on the edge of his sister's bed. He stared at it for several minutes, struggling whether he should open it or not. He couldn't tell if this was a diary, but it appeared well-used, and the edges were worn. He hugged it to his chest and breathed in deep, hoping to catch a scent of his sister's smell. Would opening the notebook help him understand her better?

He felt torn, but in the end, he decided to take a peek inside. If there were things in there she truthfully had not wanted others to know; he could destroy the contents before they became public to others. Her secrets would be his secrets, and he vowed to forever protect her privacy.

When he opened the book, what he saw amazed and shocked him. The contents were not at all what he expected, and he knew by instinct that these secrets must not be kept. His sister was a gifted artist.

He slowly turned the pages and studied pen and ink drawings as well as pastel art and colored pencils. She had captured in minute detail his mother sitting on the wooden rocker on the front porch, shelling the day's pick of acre peas. There was a pencil drawing of her father on the old John Deere, and the likeness of his hard facial features was spot on. And when he turned the page to the next one, he broke down. She had drawn a stunning likeness of him sitting under the old oak in the backyard. No detail was spared as she captured the notebook in his lap, the pencil in his hand, and the studious look on his face as he was lost in thought with his writing. It was a much younger version of him, but it was him and was so realistic it could have almost been a photograph. He found a drawing of Betty in her wedding gown, another when she was pregnant, and several of the sweetest drawings of baby Dennis from his birth until recently. No details of his chubby cheeks and dimples and sparkling eyes had been missed.

Looking through her absolutely amazing artwork, Rob realized he'd never truly known his baby sister. She captured the souls of her subjects, and her work was flawless. Rob closed the book, hugged it again to his chest, and without realizing his actions, he slid off the bed onto the floor. He curled into a fetal position with the book tight against his chest and cried himself to sleep.

17

Eleanor slammed the phone receiver into its cradle for what felt like the hundredth time. She hadn't heard from Rob for three days, and she tried calling him multiple times tonight. Every time she dialed, she got a busy signal, and she remembered him telling her about the multi-party line his parents' line was on. What in the world could those old biddies have to say to each other for hours on the phone?

She missed him terribly, and she was beginning to fear that he might be settling back into his old hick life too easily. As she paced the floor in her apartment, she realized she would have to put her plan into motion faster than she hoped. She and Leslie came up with some creative ideas to get his butt back to Atlanta, and it was beginning to look like she would have to choose the most drastic one. It would be risky, but if she was careful, she could pull it off. After all, he was a family man at heart. First, she needed to hear his voice. She would call him early in the morning, hopefully before anyone else was awake enough to start gossip hour.

18

Rob felt like he'd been run over by a truck when the distant ringing woke him up. He was stiff all over from sleeping on the hard floor. He managed to scramble up, and after putting Connie's book on the bed, he hobbled to the hall and grabbed the phone receiver.

"Hello?" his voice croaked.

"Hey, buddy!" Ned's voice was on the other end of the line. "Sorry to call so early, but I wanted to share the great news with you."

Rob turned his neck and heard it pop. "Ow," he muttered under his breath.

"You're an uncle again!" Ned said excitedly. "Betty went into labor around midnight, and we got to the hospital just in time."

The news jolted Rob awake. "Aw, man, that is great news!" Rob said, "Congratulations!" And then he asked, "Boy or girl?"

"It's another boy," Ned laughed. "Perfectly healthy. He weighed a little over eight pounds and came out screaming. Betty was a champ," he continued. "Man, I sure do love that gal."

Rob smiled, thankful that his older sister was so loved.

"I know you have an appointment with Dr. Barnes later this morning, but I couldn't wait to tell you about your new nephew. Stop by Betty's room and see us while you're here," Ned told him.

"I sure will," Rob told his brother-in-law. "Tell my sister I'm proud of her."

"Will do, buddy," and the two men hung up.

The phone startled Rob when it rang again, almost immediately,

He picked up the receiver, "Hello?"

"Finally!" Eleanor's voice was on the other end. "I tried calling you for hours last night and kept getting a busy signal. And the first time I tried this morning, I got a busy signal. How many people are on that stupid party line?"

"Hello to you, too, sweetheart," Rob said with a laugh.

"I'm sorry, darling," Eleanor's voice purred. "I just miss you so much."

"I miss you, too, and believe me, I tried calling you for hours last night," he explained. "I guess we have a lot of teenage girls on this line," he tried to joke.

"Well, next time, you need to tell those kiddos to hang up long enough for you to call me," she pouted.

"I'll try that," he said, knowing he wouldn't. "How are you? How's the job going?'

Eleanor told him about a new story assignment she'd gotten and how excited she was about it.

"I'll be interviewing some of the highest government officials in Atlanta, so this is a big break for me!" she gushed.

She also mentioned that the paper had recently hired two new reporters. "I think competition for the big stories might be getting tougher, so we need to be on our game at all times."

What she didn't tell him was that these were student interns who would be moving on once school was back in session. She hoped to plant a seed that he might be replaced if he didn't come back to work sooner rather than later.

Rob listened to her with rapt interest even though his head was pounding, and his body felt like he had been hit by a truck. He needed coffee, but the phone cord wouldn't reach into the kitchen. He sat down in the little seat attached to the phone table and took in every word.

When she took a breath, she asked the dreaded question, "When are you coming home?"

Rob realized he didn't have an answer for that. With so much happening right now, he didn't know when he could, or would want to, leave.

"I'm meeting with the doctor today and should know more after that. I promise to let you know when I have more information."

"I'm beginning to lose my patience, Rob," her exasperation came through loud and clear. "You keep telling me you'll have an answer soon, and then soon never comes."

Her sudden outburst took Rob completely by surprise. Her voice grew cold. Before he could collect his thoughts to respond, she ended the conversation.

"Call me when you have something good to tell me." And the line when dead.

After she abruptly ended the call, Rob realized that not once had she asked how he was doing or, even worse, how his parents were.

19

The next few days brought a whirlwind of activity. Dr. Barnes cleared Robert and Charlotte to be released from the hospital, but there was much work to be done at their home in order for them to make the transition.

First of all, a wheelchair ramp needed to be added as both parents would be in wheelchairs for an undetermined amount of time. As soon as word spread in the community, volunteers showed up and skillfully built a perfect ramp leading up to the front porch. They were careful not to disturb Charlotte's beautiful begonias and prized roses and made the ramp fit perfectly within her landscaping.

Since the farmers were still busy gathering tobacco, they were unable to physically help, but they donated many of the supplies. Local businessmen and carpenters did the work. Even Sheriff Pete rolled up his sleeves and worked beside the men.

The ladies of the community had been waiting for their opportunity to shower the family with food. This was a tradition when a death occurred in the family that was generations old. Surrounded by women who came in and organized the kitchen, Rob watched the events unfold. They filled the Frigidaire and an extra freezer with mounds of casseroles and vegetables cooked fresh from the gardens. The counters were covered with more cakes and pies than Rob had ever seen.

He had no idea what he was supposed to do with all that food, but he didn't need to worry. The ladies came in and out, constantly fussing over him and making sure the food was stored properly and organized into hearty meals.

Rob cringed inside when he saw the red Thunderbird turn into the driveway, but he put on his best smile and greeted Karen cordially. She flashed him a big smile and made sure she brushed his arm when she went past him into the kitchen.

"You know we ladies are going to take great care of you," she purred as she moved in a little too close for his comfort.

"I don't need taking care of," he reminded her gently. "My parents are the ones who need and appreciate this wonderful help."

Karen's smile didn't fade as she answered sweetly, "Just know that I'm here for you whenever you need me."

The big day was drawing near and not only were Robert and Charlotte coming home, but Ned would be bringing Betty and the new baby home as well. The ladies had the house sparkling for his parents, and Ned's mother had been at their home taking care of Dennis and the house.

Rob relished what would be the last few hours of peace he would see in the house for a while. He walked back into Connie's room, picked up the book of artwork, and took it out onto the front porch. He sat on the swing and gently traced his fingers around her lettering on the cover. He smiled at the word "PRIVATE" she had scrawled, but his heart screamed that this book could not be kept private.

He slowly turned each page and marveled again at the artistic style his sister showed and how she captured the soul of her subjects. His breath caught when he turned to the page of Betty in her wedding gown. The sparkle in her eyes and every lacy fold of her gown was captured flawlessly in the intricate details.

He hadn't realized how long he sat admiring each of the pages. The dimming light made it hard to see, and the sound of mosquitoes began buzzing around him. Even worse, the little buggers had started nibbling on his neck.

He let out a deep breath and took the book into his bedroom. He felt a fierce need to protect his sister's wish for "private" at the current time. But he knew one day he would have to release her amazing art to those who would appreciate it.

Too early for bed, he thought, and he wouldn't be able to sleep anyway as his mind was racing in all directions. He wasn't hungry at all, but he suddenly had a desire to see Patti at the diner. It was almost closing time, so maybe they could sit and talk when her shift ended. He just needed a friend and someone who understood the range of emotions running through his head and his heart.

The old truck sputtered to a stop as he parked by the front door of the little diner. He noticed a couple still inside and saw Patti tidying up around them. The little bell clanged over the front door as he entered. Patti glanced up and showed surprise to see him.

"Hey, Rob," she said. "I can't believe you're here for a meal, as much food has been taken to your house."

Rob was surprised that she knew about all of the food that had been delivered. But then again, this place was probably the hub of the town, and not much went on that wasn't talked about here. He also noticed that she didn't call him Cowboy this time, and her eyes had not lit up as much as they had when she'd seen him the last few times. What else had she heard, he thought to himself.

He flashed his biggest smile. "You're right. I am not hungry," he told her. "But," he added, "I was hoping to catch up with an old friend."

Her face softened some, and she smiled back.

"I think I can help you out with that," she said with a little pep in her voice. "Have a seat, and I'll get you a glass of sweet tea. As soon as I'm done with these folks, I'll join you."

Rob began to relax as he sipped on the tea. He watched Patti skillfully take care of her last customer, and when they left, she locked the door and dimmed the lights. When she slid into the booth across from him, he noticed she looked a little tired, but she gave him her biggest smile anyway.

"Well, friend," she said as she sipped her tea, "what brings you here tonight?"

Before he knew it, an hour passed. Patti listened patiently to every word he'd said. She offered encouraging words of wisdom in between his pauses. He hadn't meant to tell her so much, but once he started talking, he spilled his heart.

He told her about his regrets of not keeping in touch with his family and he even shared a little about Eleanor. Patti showed a moment of dismay when he told her they dated all through college, but she quickly recovered and congratulated him. He never used the word engaged, and when the next words came out, he surprised even himself.

"Honestly," he glanced down and picked at a thread on his shirt and then looked Patti straight in the face. "I'm not sure I want to go back to Atlanta."

His words surprised not only Patti but Rob himself. The thought had fleetingly crossed his mind, and yet he had just said it aloud to a woman he cared about. They both sat quietly for a moment, lost in their own thoughts.

"Rob, you have a lot going on right now. My best advice is for you to take it one day at a time. Help your parents get well and work through their grief over losing their youngest child. Rebuild your relationship with them and then think about the future. If the paper doesn't hold your job, then it wasn't meant to be. And if Eleanor really loves you," she hesitated for a second, "then she'll wait for you to sort it all out. You're not the scared boy who left home with stars in his eyes anymore. You're an educated man who can conquer anywhere he chooses to be." She smiled and put her hand over his on the table.

Rob felt a slight jolt in his belly from her touch, and it was a pleasant feeling. He turned his palm over and took her hand in his, and they sat for a few moments longer. A wisp of hair fell across her forehead, and Rob had to fight the urge to reach up and tuck it behind her ear, but he didn't. Instead, he broke the silence.

"I know you have to be back here early in the morning, and I've got a big day tomorrow, so I guess we'd better call it a night."

She withdrew her hand from his, and he felt a pang of disappointment.

"Thanks for listening and for the great advice," he managed to say. "I could always count on you when I needed to spill my guts," he tried to joke and gave her his best smile.

"I'm here for you any time," she smiled back. "Just take your time, and don't run away this time. You'll figure it out."

She walked him to the door and as the hot air hit his face, he heard the click of the lock behind him. As he backed the old truck out of the parking space, he remembered that he hadn't asked her anything about her life. Why in the world was she still waiting on tables?

20

The first day home left Robert and Charlotte exhausted. They were brought home by ambulance, and the ramp worked out perfectly to help get them into the house. However, the long trip home, combined with getting them inside, left them in pain. Their energy was zapped. Other than thanking the ladies who were there ready to help, they had little to say to anyone. For the first time in their lives, they looked lost, confused, and old.

Ladies in the community were like a well-organized machine. They had met and come up with plans to keep vigilance in groups of three so as to not overwhelm the patients. They organized the food deliveries, laid out a laundry and housekeeping schedule, and prepared a notebook so whoever met with the nurse each morning could keep detailed notes. They all agreed the first day home would be rough for Robert and Charlotte, so they worked quietly in the background.

After a fairly restful first night in his own bed, Robert was ready to take charge of his family. After breakfast, he announced he wanted to talk to a preacher and to the funeral director. He also wanted to see Sheriff Pete and get a full accident report. And he wanted to see his baby girl one last time.

Rob was prepared to drive into town and make

arrangements for the preacher and the others to come to the house. He was surprised when the preacher knocked on the front door a short while later. It was almost as if he'd sensed Robert's wish to see him. One of the ladies brushed by Rob as she went to open the door and winked at him,

"I had a feeling they would need some extra comfort today," she whispered to Rob, "so I asked him to come on over early. I hope you don't mind."

"Not at all," Rob said, relieved that he didn't have to face the preacher alone. He was afraid he might hear a lecture about running out on his family the way he did.

Rob needn't have worried. Rev. Monroe was as cordial as always, and after gently hugging Charlotte and Robert, he shook Rob's hand and welcomed him home. The four of them sat together for over an hour, sharing memories of Connie, and the reverend offered words of comfort when Charlotte broke down in tears.

They discussed the service and chose to have it on the upcoming Sunday afternoon. Robert asked to have a private viewing prior to the service, and Rev Monroe promised to take care of all arrangements. Because of the wheelchairs and Robert's mobility issues, they needed to keep travel to a minimum. All visitations would be on the same day.

Throughout their discussions, the ladies helping had discreetly stayed in the background. But when the preacher called for a prayer, everyone gathered around Robert and Charlotte, held hands, and bowed their heads together. Rob was slightly surprised when he felt a peace wash over him that he had not had in a very long time. He squeezed his mother's hand, and she held on to his a little bit tighter.

As if on cue, Sheriff Pete arrived shortly after the preacher left, and he brought the accident report with him. Rob had just assumed the accident was Connie's fault, and to hear that a drunk driver ran a stop sign shocked him. The man was in custody and had been charged accordingly.

"Furthermore," Sheriff Pete said in a bit of a whisper, as he didn't want the whole community to know, "the driver had excellent insurance. You folks should get quite a settlement."

"I don't want any of that bastard's money," Robert spit out. "My baby girl is gone, and no amount of money will bring her back."

Charlotte began to cry again, faintly this time.

As the sheriff's words sunk in with the family, Sheriff Pete continued, "I know that money can never replace your daughter. But perhaps it will assist with some of the mounting medical bills you are facing. And Robert," he continued thoughtfully, "with the extent of your injuries, you may not be able to keep up the farm as you used to,"

Rob studied the faces of both his parents. A new wave of grief set in, knowing their youngest daughter had been killed senselessly by a careless driver. Rob knew that no amount of money would soften their grief, and it would take time for them to absorb everything Sheriff Pete told them. They all sat in silence for a while until Robert announced that he was tired and needed to rest. The sheriff excused himself, and Rob walked him outside.

"I figured your dad would react that way about a monetary settlement," Sheriff Pete said. "We'll let your parents work through all of this. Once the insurance company comes through, and believe me, they will with the information my office provided them, your parents won't have to worry for the rest of their lives."

"My dad is a proud man," Rob answered, "and stubborn as a mule. He's worked hard for everything he's gotten. He'll see this as a handout."

The sheriff sighed. "I know, and you're right. All we can do is take it one day at a time." He shook Rob's hand. "Call me if you need me. I'll be right over."

"Thank you, sir," Rob said as he shook the older man's hand one last time.

Rob sat on the back porch, lost in thought. His parents were resting and Geroma, his former high school guidance counselor, was keeping vigilance inside. Her hands were expertly working knitting needles as she sat close to his parent's bedroom door in case they needed anything.

The air was thick and humid, but he hardly noticed as he took in the familiar surroundings of the home he grew up in. In the very distance, he could hear the faint rumble of a tractor and the laughter of men and boys as they wrapped up another day in the tobacco fields.

The rotation would start again on Monday, and the Mathis farm was on the schedule. After the first two days of gathering, the men worked without Rob's assistance, and now he realized he missed the opportunity. As a kid, he hated the hot, sticky work. But as an adult, he realized that days in the tobacco field and under the barn brought everyone together in a certain camaraderie that only those in the thick understood.

His thoughts turned to Geroma inside. Although everyone around here called her by her first name, she would always be Mrs. Cherry to him. Even though he was a college graduate now, he could not bring himself to think of her as an equal.

He wondered what his parents thought about her helping in their house. After all, she was the one who encouraged and assisted Rob in leaving their little town and pursuing a higher degree and career. He sighed and wished they had listened and tried to understand his reasons for wanting to move beyond this town. But the realization that this town wasn't so bad after all sent a jolt of electricity through him. In just a few short days, his whole plan and whole world had begun to spin out of control.

Which brought him back to Connie. She was taking classes at the secretarial school, and Rob couldn't understand why.

Sure, secretaries were lucrative careers for young women; in fact, he planned to have one himself someday. A good secretary was the right hand and backbone of any successful man.

But Connie had the talent to be successful in the art world all on her own. Hadn't she known that? A wave of guilt washed over Rob for not taking the time and effort to really know his little sister and appreciate her talents. He wondered if his parents, or even Betty, were aware of the extent of Connie's artistic soul.

21

Once news of the service date and time spread around the county, activity at the house picked up. Flowers were delivered, and food kept coming.

Ned and Betty came over with the baby, so Robert and Charlotte could meet their new grandchild. A steady stream of visitors came in and out, but most of them kept their visits short, understanding that the elderly couple needed their rest.

Rob saw his parents getting physically stronger every day and was pleased with their progress. Either Dr. Barnes or Nurse Margaret stopped by every day to check on them. Both were happy to report that the parents were doing as well as expected.

His last phone call to Eleanor disappointed him.

"Honey, can't you come down for the funeral and to meet my family?" He had no doubt she would come, but he was wrong.

"Rob, I am still working on this big assignment. It may be a turning point for my career." Her voice sounded a little strange as she added, "And I just haven't been feeling well lately."

And then, she used her best flirty voice and pleaded for him to come home as soon as possible.

"I can't make any promises at the moment."

Eleanor was infuriated. "Do you realize that you have gotten completely immersed in the very situation you walked away from? Stay in that hick town. Give up everything you've worked for in the last four years. You'll never be a successful man."

Her words took Rob by surprise, but he kept his temper in check.

He sighed before he spoke. "I love you, Eleanor. We'll talk again soon." And he laid the phone quietly in its cradle.

Saturday evening was quiet around the Mathis household. Rob knew his parents were getting mentally prepared for Connie's service the next day. They sat close together in their wheelchairs and held hands a lot. He even saw them bow their heads in silent prayer. While their conversations were still a little strained, Rob felt like they were beginning to understand each other. While his dad may never forgive him for leaving home like he did, he came to respect him as a grown man and his only son. After supper, the ladies left, and Robert and Charlotte retreated to their bedroom.

Lost in thought, Rob wandered out to the front porch swing. Memories of days gone by washed over him again. This time, they were not happy memories.

Rob always believed he was a disappointment to his father. Even as a child, he sensed it. Born on the family farm in rural north Florida in 1942, all of the kids were expected to work the fields even at a young age. Rob was different from the other kids, and he knew it. Small for his age, he was a scrawny kid with fair skin and freckles. He hated being in the fields and preferred to hide in his room or sit under the big oak tree in the backyard and daydream.

As he grew older and learned to read and write, he loved to spend time soaking up books, writing silly stories, and just watching the people around him. Some days, when they needed extra help on the farm, his mom would keep him home from school to help plant or weed the crops. Those were days he hated most. He loved being in school surrounded by books. History and current events intrigued him. When summer came, and the massive doors were locked for three months, he dreamed of the day he could go back and begin the next grade.

Now, he had come full circle. He left the farm he hated so much, earned his degree in journalism, landed a great job, and had now come back home. The farm he hated didn't seem so bad after all.

He sat in silence and watched the fireflies dance around his mother's garden and admired the stars in the clear night sky. Suddenly, a wave of peace washed over him. The direction of his life was about to change. He didn't know how or where, but he could feel the change coming.

22

The service on Sunday afternoon was moving and beautiful. Rob had not been to many funerals, so he didn't have much on which to compare. But he thought, as funerals go, this one was sweet.

The neighbors and community members packed the church, and the choir sang "Nearer My God to Thee" and "In the Garden." When Rob glanced around, he couldn't find a person not crying, including himself. His parents were able to sit in the front pew with their wheelchairs close by. Betty and Ned sat next to them, and Rob sat on the far side, furthest from his parents.

He ignored the stares he'd gotten from some of the older ladies and made sure to nod at Myrtle when he made eye contact with her. The preacher talked about love and God's purpose, and the importance of family. He wasn't sure if that part was directed specifically to him, but he listened intently and felt the message hit a little too close to home.

Near the end of the service, the choir director asked everyone to join him in singing "Amazing Grace," and Charlotte broke down completely. Everyone continued to sing while the preacher went over and knelt down to console his parents. By the end of the fourth verse, his mother's shoulders stopped shaking, and both parents dried their faces with the linen handkerchiefs they had brought with them. Ned was consoling Betty, and Rob bowed his head. And he realized how alone he felt just then.

When the service moved to the graveside, the family was seated under a big blue tent while friends and family gathered around. Rob sat in the front row with the rest of his family. Ned held Dennis while Betty held the baby in her arms. Once the family was comfortably seated, the elderly were escorted to the remaining seats. Rob caught a glimpse of Myrtle being helped into a seat in the back row. She was more frail than he remembered, and he made a mental note to not lose his temper with her on the party line. Looking at her alone and bent over, he realized that her phone time was probably the highlight of her day.

Rob looked around at the familiar faces gathered outside the little tent and recognized most of them. He saw former teachers of his and Connie's, all of the neighbors, and young adults who were still adolescents when he left. Most of them were crying, and he realized that they would have been Connie's close friends. He closed his eyes. He had never been the biggest believer in prayer or God or whatever he had heard most of his life. However, he asked for guidance on how to move forward and provide the greatest amount of help for his family.

23

Later that evening, Rob asked Ned to take a walk with him. Several ladies had come over after the service and put out another spread of food, and Dr. Barnes had come by to check on his parents. Once everyone was settled down and Charlotte was holding the new baby, Rob wanted to run an idea by his brother-in-law.

"A walk would be nice right about now," Ned said. "All this extra food these past few days is catching up with me," he laughed and patted his belly.

"I know the feeling," Rob laughed. "I haven't eaten like this since I left these parts. My girlfriend keeps me on a tight diet, and I have to admit, I feel better when I eat healthier."

Ned's look of surprise was obvious as he glanced at Rob. "I didn't know you had a girlfriend," he said. "She couldn't come down for the service?"

"Nah," Rob answered, kicking himself for even mentioning Eleanor. "She is a career girl and is working on a big assignment right now. This could really boost her career in the journalism world."

"Ah, another writer, huh?"

"She is a good writer," Rob said. "But she has her sights set on television. She thinks broadcast journalism is the future. She wants to be in the forefront for women."

"Sounds like quite a gal," Ned was impressed. "Is it serious between you?"

"I guess you could say that," Rob sounded sheepish. "We're engaged."

At Ned's surprised look, Rob added quickly, "But keep it to yourself right now, ok? There's enough going on in this family at the moment. I don't need to rock the boat anymore."

"I've got your back, don't worry," Ned grinned. "I hope it all works out for you."

"Thanks." They were silent for a few minutes as they enjoyed the walk down the country dirt road. The twilight hour was setting in, and Rob appreciated the quiet as the two men walked in step.

He gathered the courage to begin the conversation that he planned to have with Ned.

"Ned, I want to take over some of the farm duties. Dad will never be at full strength again, physically or mentally, and you have your own farm to oversee," he took a deep breath. "It's time I became part of this family again and do my part."

Ned was quiet for a moment before he spoke.

"Rob, think about what you're saying. You left here and got a fine education all on your own. You are to be commended for that. Don't give up the last four years to go back to a life that you hated. You are smart and talented, and your parents see that even if they don't tell you. I know Betty is proud of you, and in their own way, your parents are as well."

Rob let Ned's words sink in as they continued to walk.

Finally, he spoke. "I'm beginning to feel more lost than ever," Rob said, not even sure what he meant by those words.

"What about your fiancé, the career girl?" Ned asked. "We are in the boonies out here. There is not a TV station in these parts. Do you really think she wants to move to a farm and be a farmer's wife?"

Rob didn't answer for a few minutes. "There is no way she would move here," Rob said quietly. "But right now, I'm confused on so many levels. I've got to figure myself out before I can bring a girl into my life."

"Wise words, my brother," Ned said. "If she truly loves you, she'll help you find your way."

Rob didn't respond to that. He knew Eleanor loved him. But there was something more with her that he couldn't quite put his finger on. He decided to change the subject.

"Tomorrow is gathering day for our farm," he said. "I want to be the man in charge."

Ned swallowed and tried not to show his concern when he answered.

"It's been several years since you've worked a tobacco gathering," Ned said with concern. "Are you sure you want to take on that responsibility? You did a great job leading the barn last time."

Rob thought for a minute. "Any of the older kids can lead the barn," he said. "I want to be the man in charge, as my dad would if he was able."

He peered over at Ned and then down at his feet. "I need to do this, Ned."

Ned nodded in understanding, even if he wasn't sure it was the best idea. He could discreetly keep a check on the day's progress, and he understood Rob's need to prove his true value to his father.

"I know you'll do a great job," he said, and he gently slapped Rob on the back.

24

Rob woke at 4 am, anxious to get the day going. He tried to stay as quiet as possible so he wouldn't wake his parents. He made a cup of instant coffee and took it out on the front porch along with his notebook. He outlined his plans for the day. He didn't know the names of all the men and boys who would be working. But they would know their jobs, so he would run the tractor and make sure everybody stayed on task. His goal was to be done by 3:30, and he looked forward to paying the workers and thanking them for a job well done at day's end.

He took a sip of his coffee and made a face at the bitter taste. He didn't know how old the jar of Folgers was that he found in the cupboard, but it sure didn't taste like the coffee from his mom's percolator. He didn't want to make a pot this morning, even though he loved the sounds of the coffee percolating in the pot on the stove and the aroma that seeped into the air. But he was concerned that the sounds and smell might wake his parents, so he decided to go with instant. This instant stuff was bitter and strong. He sighed and put the cup down. Too bad Gram's Diner wasn't open this early. He could sure use a cup of Patti's good coffee.

Rob arrived at the barn just before the men started gathering. He climbed on the old Ford tractor, and the engine came to life when he pushed the clutch and turned the key. Smoke sputtered from the stack for a few seconds, and he was ready to go. The tobacco sled was still attached from the last gathering, so he put the tractor in gear and headed to the first row.

He noticed the sun peeking over the horizon, casting a golden glow over the morning. Tall pine trees and rows of corn from the neighbor's farm framed the background for the rows of tobacco on the Mathis farm. The Florida heat and humidity were already rising, but Rob knew in his gut that it was going to be a good day.

He nodded to the young men who were already breaking leaves from the big green stalks and slapping them under their arms. Once they could hold no more, they would place them in the sled behind the tractor. This was the third gathering, so the work was a little easier than the previous one. The men worked swiftly. Grab a leaf, snap it off close to the stalk, slap it under their arm, and go to the next plant.

The work was hard, the pay was decent, and the boys just wanted to get the job done and move on to the next. For most of them, this was their chance to earn money during the summer when school was out. Sometimes, they earned spending money to take their favorite girl out on the town Saturday night. A couple of the boys were saving up to buy their first vehicle. And if their families were hard up, they were earning money to buy their school clothes for the upcoming year.

Ned worked at the barn, wanting to be close by in case Rob might need him. Just as the sun made its way fully into the sky, Rob pulled up with the first full sled to unload. Ned and one of the younger boys unhooked the full sled from the tractor and hooked an empty one back up so Rob could quickly get back to the field. Rob scanned the faces of the workers and knew most of them.

"We appreciate ya'll," he said, and he nodded at Ned before

heading back out with the old tractor chugging and blowing smoke from its small stack.

Rob had taken three loads to the barn and was hoping for one more before lunch when the tractor came to a halt. It sputtered and chugged and then stopped.

"Damn," Rob muttered, worried that this setback may throw his time frame off. The croppers glanced at him for a second and continued their work. They moved down the row but had to walk back to him to unload their bundles.

Rob jumped off the tractor and opened the lid over the engine, but he couldn't tell what might be wrong. They were far enough away from the barn that no one would see them. Rob thought if they were paying attention, they may notice that the chugging sound of the tractor had stopped. When no one came to them within a few minutes, Rob decided he would have to go find help.

"You men work as far out as you can," he told the croppers. "I'm going to head to the barn and see if anyone can take a look at this thing and get it going."

Rob sprinted to the barn. Even though he hated to ask for help, he knew he couldn't fix the tractor. When he reached the barn, he found Ned and explained what had happened. He hoped he'd have a solution.

"Well," Ned said thoughtfully. "What do you think you need to do about it?" he asked Rob.

The young man scratched his head. "I was hopin' someone here at the barn might know how to work on tractors," he said.

"Go ahead and ask," Ned prodded.

Rob cleared his throat. "Hey, men and ladies," he nodded towards the girls tying the plants onto the sticks. "Anyone here that can work on a tractor? It puttered out on me in the field, and I can't get it to turn over."

"Yes sir, I can take a look at it for ya," Bill stepped up. "I work on my daddy's tractor all the time."

Rob looked at the young man and tried not to show surprise. He appeared to be about 15 years old, but in this neck of the woods, kids showed their talents early. He nodded at the boy with appreciation.

"OK, young man. Let's go take a look."

They quickly walked back to where the stranded tractor sat. The croppers had gotten further away from the sled, making their job much harder as they had to walk back to the tractor each time. They kept working, though, despite the minor setback.

Bill had grabbed a wrench before heading out to the field. He tinkered around the engine, crawled underneath the front of the machine and worked fast.

When he scrambled out and dusted the dirt off his pants, he told Rob to fire her up.

The tractor cranked on the first try, and the engine hummed like new.

Bill grinned up at Rob, "just needed to make a few adjustments," he said. He nodded at Rob and took off at a jog towards the barn. As he watched the boy running down the row, Rob smiled and had a new appreciation for the ones who chose to love this life.

Rob didn't quite make his goal of finishing the day by 3:30, but he did have everyone paid out by 3:45. The field was cleared, the newly picked leaves were strung and hung in the barn, and everything was cleaned up. Rob was pretty proud of himself and the crew who helped.

"Well done, brother," Ned shook his hand as the last of the workers left. "It was a productive day."

"Yes, it was," Rob agreed. "It was a very good day, indeed."

When they walked up to the house, Robert had been rolled into the yard in his wheelchair. He watched solemnly as the two men approached, and Rob was unable to judge his thoughts from the expression on his face.

"Dad," Rob greeted him.

The older man nodded and looked towards Ned.

"Rob did a fine job today, sir," Ned said. "He took charge and got the job done in record time. He even had a minor setback with the tractor, but he got it going, and everyone stayed on track."

Robert's eyes met Rob's. "That true, son?" he said. "You were the foreman today?"

"Yes, sir," Rob answered, his eyes not wavering from his father's.

Robert stared at him for a few seconds, and Rob had no idea what he was thinking. His stomach was churning, and inside, he was shaking, but he would not show fear to his father. Was he mad because his son had wanted to take charge of the day?

At last, his dad spoke. "I'm proud of you, son," the older man's words surprised Rob. The two men locked eyes. "Thank you," Rob whispered.

When the shock wore off, Rob grinned. He realized that deep in his heart, these were the words he needed to hear. And that is why he wanted to be the man in charge of the day.

25

After another delicious dinner prepared by a few of the neighborhood ladies, Robert and Charlotte settled in their wheelchairs in front of the little black and white television in the living room. Lawrence Welk was coming on soon, and that was their favorite show. Rob positioned them side by side in the middle of the room and saw them take each other's hands. After more than 25 years of marriage, raising three children with one being difficult – him, of course – losing three at childbirth and one adult child, they still had a fierce love for each other.

Rob smiled at the site and slipped out the front door to sit on his favorite swing. He wanted to think and do a little writing in his journal. And he wanted to be alone. His parents would be put to bed after the show. Then he would drive over to Gram's, use the pay phone to call Eleanor, and maybe have a few minutes to catch up with Patti.

His thoughts were coming quickly, and he was writing some good stuff. He reflected on the day and the camaraderie of the neighbors who had signed on to work. He had forgotten how strong the work ethic was in this neck of the woods and was pleased to see it firsthand today. From what he saw, no one slacked off. Everyone worked together like clockwork and got their jobs done efficiently. And they even seemed to enjoy the work.

He compared the work ethic of today with what he lived in Atlanta. Folks there worked hard, but everyone seemed to be trying to climb the corporate ladder. Rather than work together, the climate was more cutthroat. You had to be on top of your game and be ready to jump at the latest story opportunity or hope to score a meeting with the big boss so he would know you by name and face. It was an entirely different world indeed.

"Hey, handsome," Rob felt the swing move as someone sat beside him, a little too close for comfort. He was jerked away from his thoughts. He had been so engrossed in his writing that he had not heard the car pull into the driveway or seen her step onto the porch.

He looked over into the smiling face of Karen. She sat down so that their shoulders were touching, and he could smell the sweet scent of her perfume. He noticed she was wearing a red sweater cut too low for his comfort, her lips were painted bright red, and she had a red scarf tied around her hair.

"Karen," he managed to stutter. "What brings you here this evening?"

"I wanted to check on you, silly," she smiled and put her hand on his knee. Rob wanted to remove it but didn't know how without hurting her feelings. But her proximity and now her bodily touch made him quite uncomfortable.

"I'm just fine," he said, hoping his voice didn't show the agitation he felt.

"Well, I heard you had a big day, and I just wanted to stop by and say congratulations. I thought you might want to get some fresh air, so we could take a ride in Ruby," she pointed to her red sports car. She had the top down, and he couldn't help but think how silly it was to name a car.

"Thank you for checking on me. I am doing well, but I'm going to pass on the ride. I want to finish up my project here," and he closed the notebook as he saw her eyes trying to scan what he had written.

"I heard you were a big writer up in Atlanta now," she said, feigning enthusiasm. "Tell me about it."

"There's not much to tell," he said. "I have a job waiting for me when I get back. That's about it."

He wasn't a man of few words, but he didn't want to share too much with this woman. He had a feeling it might be used against him at a later date, or the town may hear a new spin on it. There was no telling what the end result would be once it passed many lips.

"Well, I think it's just fascinatin' how you left here and followed your dreams. I know you are destined for big things, Rob," she reached up and stroked his hair. "Very big things."

Rob's discomfort level tripled. He didn't know a lot about women, but he didn't like where this was leading. Or where she was trying to take it.

"Come on and take a ride with me," she said with a pout in her voice. "For old times' sake."

Rob tried to think of an excuse so he could let her down gently. He knew if he got in that car, something would happen that he would completely regret. She was a beautiful girl, no doubt, but he was not in the least interested. She, on the other hand, seemed to be smitten with him for reasons he could not understand. He had to think fast.

"Gee, Karen, that sounds nice," he feigned a yawn and used that as an excuse to stand up and stretch, breaking her grip on him. "But I've been up since 4 am, and I am beat. I'm just waiting for Mom and Dad to go to bed so I can hit the hay myself. Their show will be over soon, and then it will be lights out."

She studied him for a minute, and he thought he saw her pull her sweater down a little lower as if that might make him change his mind. No doubt about it, she was a desirable woman. But he was raised a gentleman, and he had no intention of taking advantage of a woman, no matter how beautiful or how much she threw herself at him.

He held out his hand to help her up, and when she stood, she moved into him. With her cheek against his, she whispered into his ear, "I'll take a raincheck then. But I'll be back again soon." She kissed him on the cheek. "Sweet dreams." Then she turned and sauntered slowly towards her shiny red convertible.

Geroma and Margaret were on parent duty and were helping his parents settle in for the night. Rob peeked in to let them know he was going to run into town for a bit, and they waved him off.

It was just after 8 pm, and Patti would be closing down for the night soon. He also had to use the pay phone outside to call Eleanor. After their last conversation, he wasn't sure if she would even accept his collect call. Women, he thought. Why do they have to be so complicated?

He scanned the road as he drove, hoping he wouldn't see Karen. There were no customers in the diner, and Rob popped his head in the door.

"Hey, girl," he said as Patti was wiping down tables. "I need to use the pay phone outside, and then can I get a cherry coke and chat with you a bit?"

"That sounds great," she said. "But you don't need to use that hot, stuffy booth outside. You can use the phone in here. Is it a long-distance call?"

"It is, but I was going to call collect," he said. "And, no offense," he peered down at his shoes, "I need a little privacy."

"Well, I have a phone in the office in back," she smiled. "You can shut the door and have all the privacy you need. It'll be a lot cooler here. And," she added, "I have a business line, so it belongs to me only. No nosy neighbors listening in," she winked at him.

He blushed, wondering what gossip from his calls with

Eleanor had gotten around the town from Myrtle's prying ears.

"Thanks," he grinned, and Patti took him to the office.

After working outside in the heat all day, he didn't relish the idea of being cooped up in the stuffy phone booth outside. He would have to close the little folding door for privacy, and it would get steamy inside real fast.

He closed the door to the little office and sat down at the desk. He noticed how neat and tidy everything was. He wasn't sure if it was Gram's work or Patti's, but everything was orderly and well organized. The black shiny phone sat in the far corner, and when he picked it up, he was momentarily startled that no one else was on the line. Then he remembered that Patti had a private business line and breathed a sigh of relief. He didn't know how this conversation would go, and he didn't need extra ears listening in.

The operator came on the line, and Rob gave her Eleanor's number in Atlanta and asked for a collect call.

"Yes, sir, Mr. Mathis," a young voice said. Rob had no idea whose voice the operator's belonged to, but he figured by now he was the talk of the town. He held his breath when Eleanor answered, not sure if she would accept his call.

"Yes, operator, I'll accept."

As soon as the operator released the call, Eleanor's frantic voice came on the line.

"Baby, I am so sorry I ended our last call the way I did!"

"It's ok," Rob said, trying to send her comfort through the Southern Bell line. "We are both going through a lot right now, and I know I'm not there for you."

"I have so much to tell you! There are big opportunities for me right now and for you if you can hurry back." Rob grimaced at that comment. "But first, tell me about the funeral. Don't leave out any details."

Rob told her how pleased he was at the turnout and

described the service and the visitors who had been helping out tremendously.

"It sounds like your parents have plenty of help," Eleanor noted. "So, you can come back home soon. Right?" He heard the hope in her voice.

"Mom and Dad are both still in wheelchairs, and there is so much to do around the farm," he tried to explain, hoping not to cause another argument with her. "I just need a little more time to help them out."

Eleanor was quiet for a moment. She knew that no amount of arguing would convince him to change his mind. She would have to put Plan B into full force to get him back to Atlanta.

"I understand, darling," she said, trying to hide the frustration in her voice. "Take all the time you need."

Her words took Rob by surprise. That was not the response he expected, but he was grateful.

"Thank you for understanding."

"Of course," she said, almost too enthusiastically.

Rob sighed with relief. Maybe she's beginning to understand his situation, he thought.

"Let's talk again soon," Eleanor said with as much sweetness in her voice as she could muster. "Don't be a stranger."

"Goodnight, sweetheart," Rob said as they hung up.

As he put the phone back in its cradle, Rob had a new realization. Neither one had said, 'I love you.'

Patti had finished cleaning up when Rob came back into the main dining room. The front door was locked, the lights were dimmed, and there was a fresh cherry coke on the corner table. Rob smiled and slid into the booth while Patti took the seat opposite him. They made small talk, telling each other about their day. He didn't share his conversation with Eleanor, but he did tell her how uncomfortable Karen's advances on him were. Patti started laughing.

"What's so funny?"

Patti said through her laughter, "Word on the street is that you and Karen are becoming quite the couple!"

Rob was stunned. "And people believe that?"

"Well, you are a big city slicker now, and everyone knows Karen has been trying to find a way out of this one light town forever. What better way than to fall in love with one of her old high school flames who could whisk her away to the land of enchantment." Patti laughed again.

"You don't believe that, do you?" Rob focused on her eyes and wondered why that was important to him. But it was. He didn't care what the rest of the town thought. But Patti's opinion of him was important.

"I really didn't know what to believe, but I can tell by the expression on your face that it's not true." Patti's tone grew somber. "She's really coming on to you, huh?"

"I had to practically peel her off of me before I came here," he nodded. "That was an experience I can't say I've had before."

Patti giggled again. "She's made it clear to every girl between the ages of 18 and 30 that you are hands-off." She looked him straight in the face. "She's out to catch you as her ticket to bigger and better."

Great, Rob thought. Here was something else he'd have to deal with.

"Geez, Louise," Rob said. "This town has more drama than the entire state of Georgia."

"Ain't that the truth," Patti said, and they clinked their glasses together.

26

Eleanor's brain was reeling when she hung up the phone with Rob. She paced the floor of her tiny apartment, trying to come up with a plan to get him back to Atlanta. Her thoughts were running in all directions, and agitation had taken over reason. No matter what she said, Rob was in no hurry to come home.

Unfortunately, she needed him for the big assignment she was up for, and if he didn't come back to his job soon, she would lose this great opportunity. Sadly, in this man's world, women were still not respected for their own merits in the workplace. Her boss had made it very clear that he would give her this great assignment for a field reporter, but only if Rob was with her to oversee the writing and editing. If they couldn't start soon, he had no choice but to give the assignment to another couple.

The boss made it clear that Rob, not her, was his first choice, but he felt she would do a fine job with Rob's guidance. This infuriated her, but it was the break she needed to showcase her talent and skills. Then, maybe the next assignment would be given to her on her credentials only.

She plopped down on her bed, still with her dress and heels on, and tried to think. Most other girls would be sobbing by now, begging their man to come home. She was not a crier. Oh, no. She was strong-willed, determined, and knew how to get her way. If she could buy just a little more time from her boss, she'd have that man back in Atlanta and fix it so he would stay put.

27

Rob was surprised to hear the phone ring mid-morning. That was usually Myrtle's busy chatting time, so callers would get a busy signal when they tried to call in. He picked up on the second ring, and Myrtle's scratchy voice came through loud and clear.

"Who's this?" she demanded.

"Morning, Miss Myrtle," Rob mused. "My phone rang, so I'm just answering."

"Good morning, Rob. Ms. Myrtle," Freddie Black's voice came on the line.

"So, who's calling who here?" Myrtle demanded.

"Ms. Myrtle, I hope you're having a fine day," Freddy crooned to her. "I didn't mean to disturb you, but I called Rob. May I have a quick word with him, and then you can go back to your conversation."

Rob grinned.

"I wasn't on no conversation yet," Myrtle said, "but I picked up the phone to start one, and you was on here. Don't be long," she demanded.

Freddie chuckled. "I just need a quick minute."

When they heard Myrtle's breathing still on the line, Freddie said, "Ms. Myrtle, may I please have a little privacy for my conversation with Rob?"

The older lady hesitated for a moment and then slammed her receiver down so the men knew she had given up the line.

Rob laughed. "Sorry about that, Mr. Black. How can I help you?"

"First of all, call me Freddy. You're a grown man now. Not my student prodigy," the older man said kindly.

He continued. "I have an opportunity for you that I think you might like. How about coming down to my office early this afternoon?"

"Ya'll done yet?" Myrtle picked up the line and chimed in.

"Almost, dear," Freddie said. "Give us two more minutes."

The receiver slammed down again, this time a little harder.

"I think it's safe to say I'm wide open this afternoon," Rob said.

"Wonderful. Come by at 3. I look forward to seeing you," and Freddie hung up.

Rob stayed on the line, and in two seconds, Myrtle picked up.

"Who's on here?" she demanded.

"It's Rob, Ms. Myrtle. I just wanted to say I hope you have yourself a wonderful day." And he realized he meant it.

Myrtle paused for a second too long. She wasn't used to people being nice to her. "Ok," she finally said. "You, too, I guess."

Rob grinned and gently laid the receiver in its cradle.

Rob loved everything about the small-town newspaper office and was eager to see his old mentor again. He arrived early for his appointment and was greeted once again by the over-enthusiastic Mary Anne.

"Hey, Rob, I'm so happy to see you again." She threw her arms around his neck before he realized what was happening. He remembered seeing her at Connie's service, and she had briefly hugged him then. But this show of affection was just a little over the top.

"Ya know, I'm still waitin' on you to take me out for that cup of coffee," she smiled like a cat looking at a canary.

"Nice to see you, Mary Anne," he said once he was able to unfold her arms from his neck. "I've been busy with my parents and the farm."

"So, I've been hearing," and then, with pouted lips, said, "and spending time with Patti at the diner." It wasn't a question but more of an accusation. He was beginning to recall the other reason he left town without a word to most people.

"Well, a man's gotta eat, right?"

Mary Anne folded her arms and inspected him from head to toe. He could almost feel her undressing him with her eyes.

"You've gotten too skinny since you've been gone. It's time you put some meat on those bones."

He laughed. Eleanor kept him on a pretty strict diet to keep too much meat off his bones.

"I make a mean T-bone steak," she continued. "I'd love to cook you up one with a nice fat baked potato."

"Thanks," he said, avoiding eye contact with her. "I'll keep that in mind."

She pouted her lips again but then walked behind her desk and assumed her professional demeanor.

"Mr. Black had to run take some pictures, but he'll be back shortly if you'd like to have a seat."

Rob almost laughed out loud at the sudden personality change in the woman. Instead, he asked, "Do you think Mr. Black would mind if I looked around a bit?"

"Not at all. Help yourself," and she waved towards the door leading to the production area of the newspaper. "It's messy. We just went to press last night, and you remember how hectic that day is."

"I do," Rob smiled at the memory.

He loved press day. The staff would leave late and exhausted but excited that they had produced another fine weekly edition of local news and events. Very seldom was the news earth-shattering.

Freddie and his main reporter would cover local government meetings, which were often mundane and repetitive. A parking curb might need to be fixed, or one of the employees retired, and the budget might need to be amended. Sometimes, the school board meetings got a little heated when a parent felt their child was spanked unnecessarily by the teacher or principal. On occasion, there would be a fender bender or a drunken fight at the rodeo outside of town. But, for the most part, the news recounted happy occasions.

Wedding announcements were huge. The bride would usually have a full-page write-up complete with pictures of her in her regal gown. New babies were a special feature as well. In fact, there should be something in this week's edition about Betty's new infant.

And when he picked up one of the newest papers, he saw the front page lead story shared the outpouring of love at the loss of Connie Mathis. Two photos were included. One of Connie and his parents smiling at her high school graduation and another of the massive crowd gathered outside the small town church right after the service. Both were front and center and above the fold, which showed the importance of the story. Rob smiled at the tenderness with how Freddie had treated the article.

He walked around the layout area of the room. This is where the paper begins to take shape after the reporters gather the news and write their stories.

The typesetting machine sat in the corner, and pages of handwritten stories and notes were scattered across the top and spilled onto the floor. Here, the typesetter would decipher the handwriting of a hurried reporter and load the information into the machine. One line of text would roll across the screen as she typed, and if she missed a mistake, it would have to be caught and fixed after it was printed.

Once a story was typed, the canister holding the film was removed from the machine and taken into the nearby darkroom for processing. Since the story was typed on "one column" paper, the processed film could be quite lengthy. Once it was processed, hung up, and dried, it was then placed in the middle of a large round table into the properly marked basket. There were baskets set up for various pages of the paper - "front page," "editorial," "social," "school," "classified," and "other."

Photos were processed in the same darkroom, and they were matched with the correct story and basket. The "layout" team would then work on each individual page, which was placed on a spread of lightboards around the center table. The school and social pages were laid out early, but the front page and editorial were always the last. And an inside page had to be reserved for the spill overs from the front page. Laying out a newspaper was like putting a giant jigsaw puzzle together. The task was fun but could be challenging.

Rob's first job at the paper was to clean up the layout area the day after the paper went to press. Instinctively, Rob started gathering the handwritten notes and putting them in a neat stack on top of the typesetting machine. He walked slowly around the layout tables and picked up pieces of film that had been hurriedly cut off. Exacto knives and blue non-reproductive markup pens were scattered around. He put on missing caps and put them back into their cubby holes, ready for next time.

He snickered at the same wax method Freddie still used for the film. Putting a newspaper together was ever-changing. Stories got moved around on the pages, words had to wrap around the pictures, and headlines had to be added. You needed a removable substance to make your film easy to stick to and easy to peel off. Freddie had fashioned his own "waxer" out of an electric skillet and rolling pen. Quite ingenious, Rob thought. The skillet heated the wax, and once it became liquid form, a little motor turned the rolling pin. The wax would coat the pin as it spun around, and you guided your paper across the spinning rolling pen until it was coated. Most everyone learned the hard way not to let your fingers slip and touch the pin. Rob could still remember the painful burning sensation he'd felt more than once.

"You know, we have a new kid who'll be here any minute to clean up," Freddie's voice broke into Rob's thoughts. "You've moved past cleaning the layout area."

Rob laughed and turned to greet his old friend and mentor. The men shook hands, and Freddie showed Rob around the production area before they wandered into the press room. Not much had changed over the years.

"The old girl's still got it," Freddie laughed, pointing to the massive press in the center of the area. "I've thought about sending the paper out to Greenville for printing. They bought a new fancy model and are printing area publications to help pay for the thing. But she hasn't let me down yet," he smiled and patted a corner of the machine.

"She broke down once, and the paper was a few hours late hitting the streets, but we got her going and haven't had any problems since."

"I remember you always saying, 'If it ain't broke, don't fix it,'" Rob smiled at the memory.

"Good words to live by, my boy. Why don't we step into my office? I have a proposition for you."

As soon as they sat down, Mary Anne brought in two steaming mugs of coffee and sat them on the desk. She turned and winked at Rob as she sashayed out of the room.

Freddie sure didn't keep a tidy office, Rob mused. Newspapers were scattered around the floor; the desk was piled high with papers, empty Coke bottles, and a few half-filled ashtrays. A sign on the wall read, "A cluttered desk is the sign of a busy mind."

Freddie took a sip of his coffee and leaned forward on his elbows.

"Actually, I have a great assignment for you if you're interested," he said, looking directly at Rob.

"As much as I'd love to work for you again," Rob started, choosing his words carefully, "I'm here to help my parents. I'm not sure I have time to get back on the clock."

"You won't be working for me," Freddie said. "I've been asked to write a piece for a national magazine on tobacco farming in the south." Rob's interest perked up. "I can do it, but I thought to myself, who would be the best one to tell this story? How about a young journalist who has lived it his entire life? Interested?" Freddie paused to let Rob take in what he'd just said. A national magazine. This was even bigger than his upcoming job at the Atlanta newspaper.

"Why would you give this chance up?" Rob asked incredulously.

"I've written for this magazine several times," Freddie leaned back in his chair and folded his arms behind his head. He acted like writing for a national magazine was no big deal.

Rob was stunned. How did he not know that information about Freddie?

"I'm ready to slow down, and you know that life better than any journalist I know," he heard Freddie say.

"Hold up, here," Rob threw his hands up. "What have you written, and why haven't I seen it?"

"I'm not in this business for the recognition," Freddie explained. "I just enjoy what I do and wanted to make a small difference in the world. That's all. I've used a pen name for my endeavors outside of our little world here." He paused to let Rob absorb his words.

Rob surveyed the messy office and noticed several books on

the top shelf of his bookcase, along with several issues of a national magazine. He had read two of the books, part of a fictional series in the mystery genre. They had been some of Rob's favorite books and had been written by a Frederick Green. There was not a photo of the author, and the bio was short and vague.

"Holy shit!" Rob exclaimed as the recognition dawned on him. "You're Frederick Green!"

Freddie held his forefinger to his lips. "Nobody, and I mean nobody, knows about that."

"But why? Your books are amazing!"

"As I said, son. I don't do this for the fame. I like my quiet life here, and I love writing. This way, I get the best of both worlds. And it doesn't hurt to earn a small nest egg to boot." Freddie grinned.

"I'm speechless," Rob said and threw his hands up. "I had no idea. How long have you been doing this?"

"For the last 20 years or so." At the astonished look on Rob's face, he said, "Yep. Right under your snotty nose," and laughed.

Freddie leaned forward in his chair and looked at Rob. "But seriously, son, your life is what you make it. You can have it all no matter where you choose to plant your roots."

He let his words sink in a minute, watching Rob as he absorbed what he just heard.

"So let's talk about this story opportunity."

Rob's head was reeling, and he couldn't take his eyes off the books that he had read and loved. He still had his copies back at the apartment in Atlanta.

"Earth to Rob," Freddie grinned. Rob turned his eyes back to the older man.

"So, are you interested in doing the story? They are sending a photographer down tomorrow. I've already cleared it with the publisher to assign it to my junior apprentice. They trust my judgment."

"I have missed writing," Rob said. "And you're right. I know this world inside out."

"The pay is not bad, either," Freddie mused.

"Well, that's an added bonus!" Rob laughed. He got somber for a momen and then said, "Freddie, I can't tell you what this opportunity means to me. Thank you. I'd love to do it."

28

The photographer arrived at nine the next morning. Rob met him at Freddie's office, and they spent 30 minutes laying out a plan for the day. Fortunately, there was no rain in the forecast, but the temperature was predicted to break 100 degrees. While Rob and Freddie both had on shorts and cotton t-shirts, the photographer was not dressed for North Florida weather. Rather, he was professionally dressed in pressed black slacks, a long-sleeved white button-down shirt, shiny patent leather loafers, and a gray fedora.

Rob smiled, "you came down from the north, right?"

"Yes, sir. My office is in Chicago, and I flew in last night. It's rather warm in this part, isn't it?"

"My friend, warm is not the word you will use when this day is done," Rob gave him a friendly slap on the back.

Freddie shook their hands and wished them a good day. He had meetings to cover, he told them, and Rob led the photographer to his dad's old pick-up. In hindsight, he wished he had borrowed Betty's car since it did have air conditioning. But then again, this guy needed to have the full North Florida farming experience.

Today, the gathering was at Ned's farm, which would be a perfect location for photos. They would also visit neighboring barns and get pictures, so there would be plenty to choose from.

As they drove down the dusty dirt road with the windows down, Rob noticed beads of sweat already forming on the photographer's forehead. He was in for a long day, Rob mused to himself.

Even with the heat, the photographer was skilled at his job. He expertly maneuvered his big camera to take multiple shots from different angles. By lunch, he had changed the film in his camera at least five times.

They had walked the fields and took pictures of the men cropping the leaves. They had been so engrossed in their work that they hardly noticed the camera. Ned was on the tractor and nodded briefly when they walked up, but he ignored them after that and kept his concentration on his job. The kids at the barn wanted to pose and smile, but the photographer was able to capture them when they thought he wasn't looking for a natural look. And when the entire crew gathered for lunch, he got shots of the women setting the spread of food out and even shots of the men during their brief naps.

By mid-afternoon, the photographer's work was done.

"Son, I believe I have plenty of photos to work with your story," he proudly told Rob. He was covered in dust from head to foot, his damp hair was sticking to his forehead under the fedora, and his shirt didn't look so white anymore. But he was in good spirits.

"I'm anxious to read your story and match the perfect photos to your work. It will be a fine collaboration."

"Glad to hear. I look forward to seeing your work as well." Rob dropped him off at the little motel in town. The men shook hands and wished each other well.

29

"Tomorrow is the first day of the sale, and I plan to be there," Robert announced at dinner that evening. "I ain't letting those Yankee buyers take advantage of our crop because I'm not there.

Sale day was a huge event for the tobacco farmers and the culmination of their investment. The tobacco warehouse was located on the edge of town. On the designated sale day, buyers came in from northern states to examine and bid on the southern crop.

Ned had unloaded the barn and hauled their dried leaves to the tobacco warehouse. There, they were placed in heaping piles and neatly stacked rows with other farmers' crops. Once the auction started, the buyers would move quickly, judging the leaves and placing their bid based on the quality of the crop. The sellers all mulled close by to make sure their crop brought a fair price. Seldom did a farmer dispute the price his crop was offered.

"Dad, your leg is still in a cast," Rob protested. "You won't fit in the truck, so how do you propose we take you to town and to the sale? Ned and I can handle the buyers."

Robert remained stubborn and held his ground. He crossed his arms over his chest.

"Nope. I've not missed a sale in 25 years, and I'm not about to start now," he boomed. "You're a smart man. Figure out a way to get me there."

Robert stared directly into his son's eyes. "If you can't get me there, I'll do it myself."

Rob sighed. The old Robert was coming back. He used to challenge Rob when he was a boy, and now the challenge has been given again. He had planned to work on his story after his parents went to bed, but now he had a more pressing task.

"I'll get you there," Rob said, matching his father's stare. Already, an idea was forming in his head.

After his parents were settled in the living room for their nightly TV viewing, Rob got to work. He wanted to call Ned first, but as soon as he picked up the phone, he knew that plan was out.

"I'm talking here." The familiar scratchy voice was back.

"Hey, Ms. Myrtle," Rob cooed, "how are you doing this fine evening?"

"I'm hot, and my bursitis is killing me," she snapped back. "How's your mama and daddy?"

"They are improving every day. Thanks for asking. Sorry to interrupt your call. I'll let you get back to it," and Rob hung up. He spoke much cheerier than he felt.

Rob grabbed the keys to the old pickup and started out the door.

"Where are you headed?" Robert called after him.

"Going to work on your chariot for tomorrow," Rob called back. "Ya'll relax and enjoy your program."

Robert chuckled. He knew his son would rise to the challenge, but he had no idea what Rob would come up with.

Ned was relaxing on the front porch when Rob turned the old truck into the driveway. He smiled at his brother-in-law.

"I figured you'd be busy working on your big story," he said as Rob approached the steps.

"Believe me, I'd rather be doing that than what I have to do."

"Everything ok?" Ned was suddenly concerned that something may have happened at the house.

"Oh, yeah. Everybody's fine." Rob sat in one of the rocking chairs and paused for a moment.

"Dad insists he's going to the sale in the morning," he said flatly.

"Hmmm. Does he have a plan on how to get there?" Ned asked.

"Nope," Rob drew out the word and sucked in a breath. "But he said if I don't come up with a way to get him there, he'll go on his own." Finding that possibility quite amusing, Rob smirked at how Robert thought he would get himself to town. His cast stretched from his hip to his toes. He wouldn't fit in the cab of the truck. The hospital had provided an ambulance to take him to Connie's service, but he doubted they would provide that service again just to go to a tobacco sale.

"Don't you have a utility trailer to pull your tractor on?" Rob asked.

"I do," Ned answered, "but I loaned it to Ava Lee to use for the upcoming Sweet Corn parade. She's the queen this year."

Rob grinned when a thought hit him. "How much of the decorating do you think she's done?" he asked.

"Probably quite a bit," Ned answered. "The parade is this Saturday. Why are you asking?"

"That's perfect!" Rob chuckled. "Let's borrow it back for tomorrow. I'll fix any of the decorations that might get damaged."

What Rob was proposing dawned on Ned, and he laughed. "Are you serious?"

"I hope she has it decorated to the hilt. Hell, I'll help her finish it tonight so we can take Dad to the sale in style!"

"Well, let's go see her." Ned stood and spoke through the screen door to tell Betty he was taking her brother for a ride. Both men bounded down the steps in unison, grinning like little boys.

Ava Lee didn't live far away. She was enjoying the summer before her senior year in high school and was proud to represent her town as the newly crowned Sweet Corn Queen.

The festival and parade would be this Saturday, and she and her friends had been busy for days decorating her float. After borrowing the trailer from her neighbor, Ava Lee, and her friends painted a huge banner proclaiming "Sweet Corn Queen." They had attached it on posts 6 ft high so it could be seen by everyone who would line the streets for the parade. Every inch of the trailer frame was covered in yellow and green tissue paper shaped into corn stalks with a cardboard corncob perched atop each stalk. Artificial grass had been laid on the bottom of the trailer, and a huge throne was already in place. The throne was passed from queen to queen each year to be used in the parade.

No one remembers where or when the throne was built, but it was a massive wooden structure painted bright yellow, accented with shades of green. That throne had been the place of honor for the queen for as long as anyone remembered. The Sweet Corn Queen was the highest honor for the girl who was crowned each year at the Sweet Corn Pageant.

Rob smiled when he saw the float sitting in the front yard of Ava Lee's house.

"Perfect," he grinned.

"I don't know how you are going to talk Ava Lee into letting you take it," Ned cautioned. "Remember, our Sweet Corn Queens take their position very seriously. She's been working on this thing for days."

Rob winked at him. "I can handle Ava Lee," he said.

The young queen was adding some finishing touches to her

float when they walked up. It was covered from front to back in yellow and green, and Rob couldn't imagine what else she could add.

"Rob!" the young girl squealed when she saw him.

"Ava Lee! Look how you've grown up," Rob smiled at her.

She threw her arms around him and gave him a bear hug. "It's so good to see you."

"Same to you, Ava Lee. Congratulations on your crown. I don't know anyone who deserves it better," Rob gave her his best smile.

"Thanks. I'm so excited. How do you like my float?"

"It's beautiful," Rob said admiringly. "I think it's the best Sweet Corn Queen float ever."

The young girl beamed, and Ned coughed.

"Ava Lee," Rob started. "I need a huge favor."

"Anything for you, Rob," Ava Lee grinned.

"Be careful, Ava Lee," Ned warned with a laugh.

"My dad insists on going to the tobacco sale tomorrow," Rob explained. "But with his huge cast, there is no way we can get him inside of a vehicle." He paused for effect.

"I was thinking that we could load him and his wheelchair onto a trailer and drive him to the sale."

As the idea of what Rob was proposing dawned on her, tears formed in the corner of Ava Lee's eyes.

"You want my float?" she said in barely a whisper.

"Think about it. You would forever be known as the generous Sweet Corn Queen," he emphasized the word generous. "And I promise, if we do any damage to your decorations, I'll fix them for you. And," he hesitated, not wanting to offer what he was thinking but knowing it might clinch the deal, "I'll stay as long as you need me on Friday night to help you finish the decorations."

Ava Lee had always had a little girl's crush on Rob, and he

knew it. He hated to play on her feelings, but he didn't have much time to figure out how to take Robert to the sale in the morning. Plus, pulling up to the busy warehouse with his dad perched under the Sweet Corn Queen sign would be a hoot.

Ava Lee hesitated and stared down at her feet. Seconds went by before she looked at Rob. "I guess it will be okay for you to use it." Rob didn't miss the hesitation in her voice. "After all, it is your trailer, Ned," she added.

"You know I'm desperate, or I wouldn't ask," Rob said. "You are doing a great thing, Ava Lee, and I'll be sure everyone knows about your generosity."

She didn't seem entirely convinced.

"I promise," Rob put a hand on her shoulder. "Your float will be perfect for the parade."

"OK," Ava Lee smiled slowly. "But you have to help me fix it Friday night."

"Deal," Rob said and offered his hand for a handshake to clinch the deal.

"Brother, I don't know how you did it," Ned laughed as they left, pulling the float behind them. They parked the trailer under Ned's barn with a plan that Ned would pick them up early in the morning.

30

Rob awoke extra early. He'd begun to have second thoughts about towing his father into town atop the Sweet Queen Corn float. If his dad didn't like the idea, he would probably strike out down the country dirt road in his wheelchair. Rob knew that even though he would give it all the strength he had, he wouldn't make it far.

When Ned left last night, he had attached a chain to each side of the large throne and then secured the chain to the trailer sides. Once he was locked in the chains, the wheelchair wouldn't move, and he would ride alongside his dad on the float. For a fleeting moment, he thought about making a fake crown as a joke, but somehow, he didn't think Robert would find that too funny.

He strolled into the kitchen and made a full pot of coffee as he had a feeling Robert would be up early as well. As if on cue, there was a light tap on the front door, and the nurse's aide came in.

Robert had asked her to come early so he could be up and ready to be on the road by 8 am. After Rob let her in, he took his steaming mug out onto the front porch and sat in the swing to take in the sunrise. He took a sip of the hot liquid and sighed contentedly.

Morning time in the country was special. The birds were

waking up and singing their sweet tunes; it was still slightly cool, and the sunrise was spectacular. Rob didn't get these special effects in the city, and he hadn't realized how he had missed them. Shortly after, Ned drove up, pulling the queen's float behind him. Rob walked down to greet him, and together, they attached a small ramp they would use to wheel Robert into place.

"I have to admit, I'm a little nervous about this," Rob said with slight dread in his voice.

"I think it's perfectly safe," Ned answered. "I'll take it slow. We want your dad and the decorations on this thing to arrive safely."

"It's not safety I'm worried about," Rob grinned. "Dad may flip when he sees this thing."

Rob heard the nurse rolling his dad's wheelchair towards the door and held his breath. When they came onto the porch, Robert sat in stoned silence. He studied the float, gazed at Rob, then Ned, and back at the float. Rob swallowed hard, having no idea what his dad was thinking. Ned was grinning at the astonished look on the nurse's face,

And then, the older man let out a huge belly laugh that resonated in the neighbors' homes. Rob had not heard his dad laugh like that since he and his sisters used to play tricks on him when they were young. He always enjoyed their antics and played along with them. Rob didn't realize how he had missed that laugh, and hearing it now made his heart feel as warm as the north Florida sun.

"Now that!" he laughed more. "That is ingenious! I wondered how you were going to get me to the sale, son, and I have to say, this is a good one!" He laughed again until he almost had tears in his eyes. "Everyone will know when Robert Mathis arrives. Hell, where's my crown?"

Rob let out a long, low whistle and laughed with his dad. "I almost made you one, King Robert," he proclaimed in a fake royal voice, "but, by George, sir, I ran out of time." Now, he wished he'd followed through with his idea of a cardboard crown.

"Well, put me on my royal chariot, gentlemen," Robert said grandly. "I am ready to take my ride."

The nurse had wheeled Charlotte onto the porch, and she watched with pride as the men in her life worked together. Seeing her son and husband laugh together again after so many years of pain between them filled her heart with love and happiness. Losing her youngest daughter had been devastating, and she still silently cried herself to sleep every night. But she also believed that every death had a reason. Maybe Connie knew that leaving this world was her way to bring her brother and father back together again.

Rob sat next to his dad in a folding lawn chair he had put on the trailer while Ned slowly pulled the trailer towards town. Young children playing in their yards pointed at the Sweet Corn Queen's float and waved. The two men smiled and waved back, and by the time they reached the tobacco warehouse, they felt like they were the hit of their own parade.

The most crowded place in a small town is the tobacco warehouse on sale day. If a farmer had tobacco on the floor, he was there to see how his work paid off and how his crop compared to others. He also wanted to make sure he was given a fair price. If not, he had the option to pull his load from the sale.

That didn't happen often, as the farmers knew what the buyers were looking for, and they were skilled at putting out a top-notch crop. The buyers represented big tobacco companies and strived to offer as fair a price as possible on a quality crop. Most of the time, it was a win-win for all involved.

Ned maneuvered the truck and trailer as close to the warehouse door as possible so they could unload Robert. The two men on the queen's float got a few stares from people outside of the community, but most of the folks clapped and smiled and waved at the family. Some of the men ran over to help get Robert in his wheelchair from the trailer and congratulated him on making it to the sale.

Robert lifted his face to the morning sunshine and inhaled the sweet smell in the air. When the warehouse floor was full of the crop, the sweet and pungent smell drifted out of the warehouse doors. You could enjoy its honied aroma throughout the town. It was a smell that brought a nostalgic feeling to many every year as they recalled days gone by with generations of family and neighbors.

"Hey, city boy," the soft southern drawl behind Rob gave him a feeling of dread in the pit of his stomach. "I was hopin' you'd be here today."

"Karen," he said as he turned around to face her. "What are you doing here?" he asked with little enthusiasm.

"I came with my daddy, silly," she crooned as she put her hand on this arm. "I just love sale day. All the people and everyone is so excited."

"Nice to see you, Karen," Rob said as he delicately removed her hand from his arm. "I need to get my daddy out of this heat. Best of luck to your family today." He turned and spoke to his dad, "Ready to go in?"

Robert had seen the exchange. He could tell Rob was anxious to step away from the beautiful blonde who obviously had her sights set on his son. He was enjoying the cool morning air, but he took the hint.

"I appreciate that, son," he said. "The air is already heating up out here. Let's go find our place inside."

Ned had delivered his and Robert's crops early yesterday morning. He took Robert to his crop so he would be there when the buyers came by. They were on the fifth row near the front of the warehouse. It would be a couple of hours until the bidders reached them. Rob spotted Karen a few rows over with her father, and he noticed how she kept looking his way. He didn't feel like getting into more conversation with her, so he did his best to avoid her stares.

"I'm going to take a walk, Dad," he said to Robert and Ned. "Probably walk over to the diner and get a cherry Coke. Either of you want anything?"

"Sure, I'll take a Coke," Ned said and pulled a quarter out of his pocket.

"Put your money away," Rob waved him away. "I've got it."

"I'll take an RC Cola and a moon pie," Robert said.

"You got it," Rob grinned and sprinted away before Karen could catch his eye.

Gram's Diner was several blocks away, but Rob didn't mind the walk. Other than the walk from the funeral home to the newspaper last week, he had driven through town, usually in a bit of a hurry. He had not taken a fresh look at the buildings he remembered so well.

As he turned the corner onto Main Street, he noticed nothing much had changed. The feed store at the south end of the street was still owned by the Williams family. The store had been in their family for several generations and was still going as strong as ever. They offered cracked corn, hay, fertilizer, and most anything the local farmers needed.

There were several small dress shops, a lingerie store, and a family-owned grocery store in the center of the block. Downtown was bustling on Saturday mornings when families would load up their station wagons or their pick-ups and make a weekly trip into town. The kids would go into the general store and pick out penny candy. Dad would purchase his supplies from the feed and hardware stores, and Mom would shop at the grocery and dress shops. They often would meet up at Cramer's Pharmacy at the end of the block for ice cream and cherry cokes.

Rob could have stopped there to get their drinks, and his

walk would have been shorter. But he preferred to trek an extra two blocks with the hope of seeing Patti and buying the drinks from Gram.

"Well, well, if it ain't the sweet corn princess," Patti laughed when she saw Rob walk in the door. It was mid-morning, so there were few people in the diner.

"I guess news still travels fast around here," Rob laughed back.

"Ya'll were quite the talk this morning at breakfast," she said. "How in the world did you pull that off?"

"Dad needed a ride that would accommodate him and his wheelchair. I convinced young Queen Ava Lee to help her fellow man, and Dad thought it was a hoot. We had a great time waving to our fans as Ned pulled the float into town." Rob smiled at the memory of his dad's laughter.

Patti laughed with him. "What brings ya in here?"

"I need two cherry cokes and an RC cola," he told her. "I'm taking them back to the warehouse."

Patti cocked her head at him. "Your walk would have been much shorter if you'd just stopped at Cramer's to buy drinks," she said.

"True," Rob said thoughtfully, and then before he caught himself, "but you weren't there."

His words shocked him as soon as they left his lips. What in the hell was he doing? He was engaged! But here he was, acting like a schoolboy again and flirting with this girl he had known his entire life. Not to mention, he had butterflies flitting all through his stomach.

He thought he saw a slight blush creep up Patti's cheeks. Her hair was pulled back into a neat ponytail high on her head, and a couple of strands had worked their way loose and were hanging down on her forehead. He wanted to reach up and tuck those strands behind her ears. Even more, all of a sudden, he had a strong urge to kiss her.

They gazed at each other for what seemed like hours, but it was actually just a few seconds. A tear formed behind Patti's eyes, and she blinked and turned away. If he only knew that Rob had been the boy of her dreams. Her heart was broken into millions of tiny pieces when he left town without even a goodbye or a see ya later.

She took a deep breath to gain her composure before turning back to face him.

"Well, city slicker," she tried to keep her voice light. "Let me get you those drinks, and I'll drive you back to the warehouse."

"You don't have to do that," he put his hands up.

"If you walk the six blocks back to that warehouse, those drinks will be hot as a steaming cup of coffee. It's heatin' up out there fast."

He stared at her again and didn't know what to say. The idea of a few extra minutes with her was a pleasant thought.

She fixed his drinks, and he paid. She put them in a small box, along with the moon pie, so he could easily carry them.

"Peggy, I'll be right back," she called to the other waitress.

"Take your time. I've got this," she answered and smiled as Patti led Rob to the back door of the diner. She and the few customers had noticed the very hot sparks between them.

Patti still drove the old pick-up she had in high school. Again, Rob wondered why she had not done anything further with her life. She still worked in the same job she had in high school and drove the same 20-year-old truck. While he had moved on, she seemed to be stuck in time.

It only took a few minutes for her to maneuver the turns to the warehouse, but she had been right. The heat had really cranked up, and nothing would stay cool for long. She stopped right in front of the main door and smiled.

"Catch ya later, city boy," she grinned.

"Thanks for the ride. I'll come by and see you later." He

could hardly take his eyes off of her. But he forced himself to open the truck door and step out, carefully balancing the drinks.

She smiled, shoved the truck into gear, and pulled away.

As soon as he entered the warehouse, he saw Karen standing with Ned and Robert. She had seen him step out of Patti's truck and had a slight frown on her face.

"Sugar, I could have run and got those drinks for you," she cooed as he walked up and handed the men their cold beverages. "Besides, Cramer's has the best drinks in town," she said with a slight hint of sarcasm.

"I like Gram's drinks better," Rob said flatly.

"Hmmm," she said as if she knew exactly why he liked those better. She is going to have to up her game, she thought.

The auctioneers were getting closer, and Rob sensed Robert's nervousness. You could never predict what the buyers were going to think of your work. Sometimes, they would hesitate before a crop and whisper to each other. It was those times when farmers were short of panic mode, wondering if the buyers had seen a flaw with their crop.

The buyers were now looking at Robert's spread. He had ten sheets to sell today. To him, it looked damn good, but Ned and Rob had overseen all the work, so he hadn't controlled the quality. He glanced over again, and the buyers were writing on their clipboards.

Karen inched a little closer to Rob and her arm through his.

"I think your crop is beautiful," she said in her sweetest voice.

"Thanks," Rob said dryly. He took a step away from her and dropped her arm as gently as he could. He was nervous, too, and just needed to concentrate on the buyers.

"Crop of 10 sheets on the floor, numbers 103 through 112," the announcer called, and the bidding began. The auctioneer walked backward down the row, calling the numbers quickly, and in three minutes, the bidding on Robert's crop was over. His crop brought an average of 55 cents per pound.

"Hot damn," Robert shouted with excitement. "Boys, I have to hand it to you. Ya'll did an excellent job. This is the highest my crop has ever brought." He slapped both men on the back.

Ned was listening as they auctioned off his 12 sheets, which brought 52 cents per pound on average. He was pleased as well.

It took about an hour for their checks to be ready. Once the men were paid, they pushed Robert back to his place of honor on the Sweet Corn Queen float. As they pushed his wheelchair into place, Robert waved to the onlookers.

"Ya'll have a good day," he shouted to the small crowd. "Be sure and tell little Miss Ava Lee that she is a fine Sweet Corn Queen, and you appreciate her helping out her neighbors."

Ned slowly pulled away and pulled the trailer back towards their homes. Karen stood at the entrance and waved at Rob, but he never looked her way.

"Miss Ava Lee, we appreciate your generosity in letting us use your float today. It meant the world to my daddy," Rob told her when they were unhitching the trailer back at her house.

Ava laughed. "I heard ya'll were quite the sight in town today."

"Man, word still travels like lightning around here," Rob shook his head. "We didn't do too much damage to it, but I'm a man of my word. What do you need me to do to restore your throne back to its original glory?"

"It looks fine to me," the young girl said, examining the tissue paper leaves and corn stalks. "My friends will be over later to help put the finishing touches on it. Just be sure and wave at me in the parade tomorrow."

"You got it! Thanks again," and the men loaded up in Ned's pick-up and headed home.

31

Eleanor paced the floor, getting more agitated by the minute. Rob hadn't called in several days, and every time she tried to call his parents' number, the line was busy.

She didn't like the vibe she had gotten the last time they spoke, and she regretted losing her temper on the phone. If she couldn't find a way to convince Rob to come back to Atlanta soon, she could kiss her dream assignment goodbye. Her division chief had hired another female reporter who was showing almost as much ambition as Eleanor. She had to be on top of her game.

Even though she resented that the only way she would get this assignment was if Rob was here to "oversee her," she'd go along with the big boys for now. The assignment was to follow up with reports of a scandal in the Atlanta mayor's office. If she was the investigative journalist that she believed she was, this story would make her a household name in north Georgia.

She weighed her options. She and Leslie had not come up with a concrete plan, but they had thrown several ideas on the table. One, she would travel to that little hick town and surprise Rob and beg him to come home. That thought nauseated her. The idea of begging a man was well beneath her.

She could call and pretend to be severely ill, which might force him to rush back to her. That plan was risky, however, if he still insisted on putting his parents' needs first.

Then another idea hit her. And if Rob was half the man she thought he was, he would definitely put her needs first. She poured herself a highball and sat down at her little kitchen table. This would be the most difficult plan to carry out, so it would take creative planning to see this idea through.

32

Robert was still gloating about the high dollar his crop brought at the sale. His son had come through for him at a time when his family needed him most. When the boy had walked out of their home four years ago, Robert tried to put him out of his life. His only son had let him down.

Now, the father was beginning to understand that the boy had to become his own man in his own way. Even though he didn't agree with the way Rob had left, he was still flesh and blood. And while he would always have a void in his life now that his baby girl was gone, another void had been filled with his son's homecoming.

When Rob walked into the dining room where his parents had just finished lunch, Robert flashed his son a big smile.

"Thank you, son, for the work you did on our crop. You did a fine job," he beamed.

"Hey, I just finished what you started, Dad," Rob grinned back, completely surprised and pleased at his father's compliment. "A lot of hard work went into getting the crop ready for harvest. You should congratulate yourself as well."

Rob walked over and kissed his mother on the cheek as the ladies helping today stood discreetly in the kitchen. They, of course, overheard the conversation and were smiling at each other. The entire town remembered how Rob had left, and many had shared mixed emotions about the boy's departure. Now, the family seemed to be coming full circle. Having their only son back would do wonders for the Mathis family.

Rob wanted to work on his magazine article, so he decided to go to the paper's office and use one of their typewriters. Ideas had started forming, and he wanted to get them down on paper while they were fresh in his mind.

His deadline was next Wednesday, but his goal was to finish early. This was a big opportunity, and he wanted to show them he could not only meet a deadline but exceed the publisher's expectations. Once the article was done and submitted, he would think about the crossroads he found himself at.

A new road opened up this morning with Patti, and he needed to think things through. He thought he had been madly in love with Eleanor during the last year, but he had never felt the tenderness and tingling in his belly with her like he had this morning with Patti. This was an entirely new feeling and his head, and his heart, was spinning.

Freddie welcomed Rob to his office with open arms and even gave him a key to allow him to use the office at his convenience.

"Actually, son, I believe this is your key from when you worked here in high school," Freddie winked at him. "We've been saving it for you."

Rob thanked him, and Freddie pointed to the desk Rob had used when he was a teenager. It was piled with various newspapers, folders, and a few empty paper cups with sticky coffee remains in the bottom. Mary Ann hurried over and scooped up the papers. She smiled broadly at Rob.

"Sorry, hon," she said in her sweetest country drawl. "An unused desk is the catch-all for all the junk we collect around here." She cleaned off the desk and stacked clean paper by the typewriter for Rob's convenience.

He laughed at the amount of paper she brought. "I don't

think my magazine article is going to be that long."

"You never know what kind of inspiration you might be hit with," she winked at him. "Just making sure you have what you need. I put a fresh ribbon in the typewriter this morning, here's a clean trash can, and there are sharpened pencils in the drawer. Can I get you anything else?"

"I think I'm all set. Your efficiency is excellent." She beamed.

"Would you like some coffee?" she smiled.

"That would be great." And he put the first sheet of paper in the typewriter.

It felt refreshing to write again. The feel of the typewriter keys under his fingers was so familiar. He loved the click-clack sound as he struck each letter and the soft bell when he reached the end of each line. As he started to type, a feeling of peace washed over him, and he felt as if he'd come home.

Four hours later, Rob pulled the final sheet from the typewriter and laid it face down on top of the other pages. He hadn't expected to finish the article in one sitting, but once he started writing, the words flowed. He vaguely noticed Freddie and Mary Anne when they quietly went out and locked the door a couple of hours earlier. Mary Anne had turned off all the lights except the one over his desk, but it was still daylight outside, so he could see throughout the building.

Writing the story took him down memory lane in the tobacco fields and released feelings he had kept bottled up for years. As a young boy, he worked with his mother at the barn, carefully choosing the right leaves and handing them to her just right so she could string them quickly. He liked working with his mom, and Connie was always hanging around the barn with them.

As they got older, he started helping the other men in the barn while Connie became a hander. His teenage years were spent in the field cropping, and that was the part he was not so fond of. The other boys laughed and joked while they worked, and Rob laughed with them, but deep down, he wanted to get away and just think and write.

Cropping tobacco was hard work, but he kept up with the best of them. When the work day ended, especially if they finished early, they would take off to the nearby sand pond, which was always full of water in the summer. That was a nice treat to cool off and get refreshed at the end of a hard day. While one of the older boys drove the truck, the others would pile in the cab or in the back bed and enjoy the ride down the bumpy dirt road.

Rob remembered one time when his cousin Johnny was sitting on the side of the truck bed. Whoever was driving that day was going a little too fast, and when he hit a bump in the dirt road, Johnny tumbled right off the side of the truck. The driver didn't even notice he'd lost a passenger, and when the other boys stopped laughing, they called Johnny to make sure he was ok. He was, and after the boys beat on the back glass and got the driver's attention, he stopped so Johnny could catch up to the truck and climb back in. His ego had been a little bruised, but otherwise, there was no damage done.

Sale days were exciting, as that's when your hard work paid off, and a paycheck meant a trip into town for ice cream. Robert was extremely pleased with today's payday, but as Rob scanned the warehouse, some other farmers weren't so happy. You were at the buyer's discretion of what they thought your crop was worth and sometimes, the farmer just didn't agree. Rob remembers one time when a neighboring farmer got so irate at the buyers that he turned down their offer and took his crop back home with him. But for the most part, the farmers took the offer with the promise to themselves that the next sale would be better.

Rob stood up and stretched. Time had gotten away from him, and he didn't realize he'd been typing for almost four hours. His neck hurt, and his belly was rumbling. He briefly thought about swinging by the diner, but he needed to get his head straight first. He was afraid he might slip up and say too much, as he almost did earlier, and he wasn't sure that would be a good idea at this point. Instead, he locked the office door and turned the old pickup towards home.

33

The annual sweet corn festival was a monument event for the little community. Stores along Main Street decorated their windows in corn themes, Gram's served up her secret recipe of sweet corn pudding, and street vendors cooked corn in every way imaginable. A sweet smell filled the air with aromas of roasted corn on the cob, corn boiled in special sauces, fried corn fritters, and even fried corn on the cob.

Children had bright yellow balloons tied to their wrists with a soft ribbon. In years past, balloons had gotten away from the little ones when they carried them, and parents had to deal with the child's screaming meltdown because they had lost their balloons. Of course, they were always given a new one from the vendor.

The town mayor led the parade, wearing a specially made hat to resemble a fine ear of corn. The firemen, police officers, and city council members followed next. Then, the Sweet Corn Queen appeared in her float wearing a bright yellow gown with her court (the runners-up in the pageant), who all wore green to resemble corn stalks. Since Rob had dropped the float back at Ava Lee's house, she had added many more decorative touches. Balloons were strategically placed together to form the shape of an ear of corn, and green and yellow crepe paper wrapped around every inch that they could squeeze it into. Ava Lee, proudly wearing her crown, appeared to be sitting in the middle of a moving cornfield. She waved at the crowd, smiling broadly, and when she spotted Rob, she blew him a kiss. To be chosen as the Sweet Corn Queen was truly an honor and one that Ava Lee carried with diligence.

"Hey, city slicker," Patti sidled up next to him just after Ava Lee's float had passed.

He turned to face her. "I thought you never left the diner."

She smiled. "I locked the door. You can't be in town and miss the parade."

"And a fine parade it is." Rob watched as the high school marching band stopped right before them to display their talents and play a song they had worked on the entire previous year. Rob and Patti stood comfortably side by side while the band played, and when they moved on, Rob turned towards her.

Again, he had an urge to reach up and tuck a loose strand of hair behind her ear. They locked their eyes for a brief moment. He spoke first after clearing his throat.

"Since I have discovered that you can leave the four walls of your workplace," he grinned, "do you think we can meet somewhere later, maybe for coffee or something?"

Patti laughed. He was so cute when he was nervous, which he obviously was. And where else would they go in town for coffee, she mused.

"Tell ya what," she said, "everybody must go to the street dance. Why don't we meet in this spot around eight tonight, and you can whirl me around the street like you did when we were in high school."

At that moment, memories that he had kept locked away for four years flooded his mind. The street dance had been his favorite part of the festival, and he and Patti had danced the night away every year. He had stolen his first kiss from her in the ninth grade. The memory of that kiss made him want to kiss her again right there in front of the crowd.

"Hello, is anyone home?"

Patti's laughter brought him back to reality.

"I thought I'd lost you there for a minute," she said and touched his arm.

The touch sent a shock through his body. He realized at that moment he wanted to take her in his arms and never let her go. And that scared him, but he couldn't resist spending more time with her.

"This very spot. 8 pm." His voice was so low that Patti wasn't sure she heard him.

She squeezed his arm again, "See ya then, city slicker. Enjoy the rest of the festival." And he watched her sprint down the street towards her workplace.

The cub scout troop passed by, and Rob snapped back to reality. He smiled at the two younger boys in the front carrying their banner displaying 'Troup 129." They were followed by the Boy Scouts, who saluted as they went by. Next came the Brownies, smiling and waving, sporting their brown dresses and brown beanies on top of their heads. The Girl Scouts were right behind them, wearing their green dresses and sashes with merit badges showing their accomplishments. Everyone who was anyone was in the annual sweet corn parade.

Rob did a double take at the next parade float. It took him a minute to realize what he was seeing. Sitting in a rocking chair under a huge paper mâché oak tree was Myrtle. She was holding a sign that read 'save our tree!' Two women were walking on each side of the float and one of them shoved a piece of paper in Rob's hands. He read it and wasn't sure if he should laugh or jump on Myrtle's cause. He recognized the tree in the pictures. It was a centuries-old oak in the middle of a road just on the edge of town.

When the founding fathers put a road in, they split the road to go around the tree. Why they didn't cut it down at that time was a mystery to current residents. Many of the locals wanted the tree to be cut down now, as they said it was a nuisance and caused a dangerous setting for traffic. Myrtle and her friends from the local garden society had made it their mission to save the tree and vowed to do whatever it took to keep the tree intact. Their claim was that the history in the town was more important than new fancy roads. Their solution was to move the original road, which would cause even more havoc. That would put the road smack dab in the middle of someone's residence. He could see this was going to cause many heated discussions at future town council meetings. But he admired this side of Myrtle as she showed spunk in a cause she believed in.

The Songbirds of the First United Methodist Church followed next. This was a group of girls from ages 5 through 15. They were led by Louisa Snodgrass, who was a little older than Rob. Louisa had entered every talent show across three counties, but her singing 'talent' had never won her any trophies or runner-up ribbons. No one had the heart to tell the poor girl that she had absolutely zero singing talent, and some said she couldn't carry a tune in a bucket. But she never gave up trying. Even at church, she always asked for a solo part in the Christmas cantata. The choir director managed to persuade her that he couldn't find the right song to match her unique range of tone. Finally, someone came up with the idea of the Songbirds so that Louisa could put her passion to better use and perhaps teach the love of singing to the young. Their plan was working. Louisa put her time into planning the program and recruiting singers, so she decided she didn't have time to enter talent shows anymore. At their first official program, Louisa's off-key voice almost drowned out the sweet vocals of the little ones. Again, the choir director had to come up with a plan to silence Louisa. He suggested that perhaps her unique, very strong voice overshadowed her young charges and that maybe she should direct them only. Louisa thought that was a great idea, and from then on, she stayed silent while happily leading the young folks in song. Louisa smiled and waved at Rob when their float passed by as her young charges sang "This Little Light of Mine."

The parade began to wind down. There was a group of clowns handing out candy to the children as they walked by. The horses, owned and ridden by members of the local cattlemen's group, brought up the rear of the parade. Young men were following behind the horses, scooping up any droppings from the animals. They called themselves the 'pooper scoopers,' and Rob had been a scooper on several occasions. They were paid two dollars for their work, and that was great spending money when you were 12 years old.

Rob strolled down Main Street and looked at the vendors and their goods. The Baptist Girls Auxiliary, otherwise known as the 'GA's', was selling homemade cupcakes while the adult ladies ladled up golden fried corn fritters. He stopped and bought one of each, then made his way to the next booth. Various community organizations offered cotton candy, popcorn, crocheted potholders, and every craft you could imagine. He nibbled on his corn fritter as he walked and marveled how it was fried to perfection. Sweet kernels of cream corn were wrapped in a crispy batter, and it was delicious. When he finished the fritter, he stopped at the homemade ice cream booth, where he had a choice of vanilla, strawberry, or peach. Even as a child, he couldn't pass on homemade peach ice cream. He took out a quarter and happily paid for a cup.

"There's my favorite city boy," he recognized the familiar southern drawl just before she slipped her hand through the crook in his arm. He turned and Karen's face was too close for comfort.

"Vanilla is my favorite," she said. Taking the hint, Rob paid for a cup of ice cream for her.

"Nice to see you, Karen," Rob said with little sincerity.

She kept her arm through his as they stepped away from the booth. She was wearing her signature red dress with a red ribbon tied in her hair and bright red lipstick.

"You are coming to the dance tonight, right," she said, not as a question.

"I wouldn't miss it," Rob retorted. "The dance was always my favorite part of the festival."

"Oh yes, I remember," Karen said with a note of bitterness in her voice. "You and Patti always were the hot ticket at the dance." She peeked at him with a pout on her red lips. "I do hope you save a dance for me tonight," she said with a hint of suggestion in her voice.

"You mean there is still a spot for me on your dance card?" he asked, trying to avoid her question. "I would think your card would be full already with all the men here who would love to dance with you."

Karen giggled. "I'll always save a spot for you."

"Well then, I would be honored to have one dance with you," he said without a hint of sincerity in his voice. "Catch you later," and he unhooked her arm from his.

Noting the disappointed look on her face, he said, "I want to grab up a bag of those corn fritters and take to my parents since they still can't go out and about."

He almost sprinted to the Baptist ladies' booth before she had the chance to say another word. Rob would have loved to take them some of the homemade peach ice creams that the First United Methodist women were noted for. But in this heat, he would have walked in the door with nothing but a cup of peach milk.

His parents were napping when he got home, and the day nurse was reading a book in the living room. He glanced at his watch. It was only 2:00 so he had hours with nothing to do until the street dance. He had forgotten how lazy Saturday afternoons were on the farm. In Atlanta, he and Eleanor would walk through the downtown shops and stop at little cafes for coffee or a cherry coke.

With nothing around him but farmland, he was restless. He thought about calling Eleanor, but two reasons held him back. One, he didn't want his parents to overhear him as he had not mentioned her to them. And two, he was confused about her. He realized he didn't miss her, and he didn't understand why. He always enjoyed their time together, but had he confused the comfortable feeling of being with her for love?

He tried to remember when he had proposed. He had not gotten down on his knee or bought a ring in advance, or done anything special. He blushed at the memory of the one night they had made love. They had both been to an office party and had a little too much to drink. He had never been one to drink excessively, so it quickly went to his head. He remembered taking her back to her little apartment and the feeling of wonderment throughout the night. When he woke the next morning, his head was pounding, and she was sleeping beside him in her bed. She had rolled over next to him and smiled.

"Good morning, my future husband," she had whispered. Stunned for a moment, he assumed he must have asked her in his drunken stupor.

Not knowing what else to say, he answered, "Good morning, my future wife," and from then on, they became an engaged couple, even though he realized he was not ready for that next step in his life.

When he had a clear head, he apologized for taking advantage of her while he was inebriated and promised to not do that again until their wedding night. She insisted that she loved every minute of their night together. But she took advantage of his guilt to persuade him to spend most of his savings the next day to buy her the engagement ring she had picked out. From then on, they were in full-fledged wedding mode. She spent a lot of time with her mother and sisters planning the perfect wedding even though they had not yet set a date.

Now that he was back in the farmland he grew up in, he was questioning his decision to ever leave. He had loved college, and writing was still his passion, but there was something about the open air where you could see the stars at night instead of newly built high-rise buildings.

The pace was slower, and you never met a stranger. He knew Eleanor would never consent to moving to the "sticks," as she called it. Yet, he questioned whether he wanted to spend the rest of his life in the big city. Sure, there was always something to do, but did one need to be on the go at all times?

Shaking himself from his thoughts, he decided to ride over to the newspaper office and review the article he had written. Mary Anne would proofread it for him on Monday, and then it would be ready to send to the publisher.

When he entered the quiet office, the sweet smells of ink and paper made him smile. Freddie's family had owned this building for over 100 years, and it had the atmosphere that only a small-town newspaper could have.

He walked around the front room and noted that nothing much had changed. Three wooden desks were lined up in a row with old Smith Corona typewriters in the center of each. They were probably the same ones used by Freddie's father when he owned the paper.

Mary Anne had a newer portable typewriter on her desk. The teletype machine was behind Mary Anne's desk, ready for breaking news from other papers or law enforcement agencies around the country. Noting the half-full ashtrays scattered about, Rob realized he was probably the oddball in the journalism world by not smoking. He never had a taste for it.

In the back of the room, large bound books held a copy of every newspaper for the last hundred years. Rob enjoyed looking through them when he was younger, noting the change in writing styles throughout the years.

He sat down at the last desk in the row, "his desk," when he was younger, and rolled a blank piece of paper into the cylinder of the machine. After clearing his head for a few minutes, he began to put words to paper.

An hour later, he sat back, linked his fingers, and stretched his arms upward as far as he could. He turned his neck from side to side and heard it pop. He had gotten stiff as his body had moved very little once he started writing.

He had not planned for his story to take the turn that it did. Once he started typing, the ideas flowed, and the words kept coming. He didn't try to correct typos as he didn't want to interrupt the flow of his thoughts. If Freddie wanted to use the article, the typesetter would have to retype it anyway, and she would correct any grammar or misspelled words.

He read over his article, and for the most part, he liked what he had written. He thought for a few minutes and then scrawled a potential headline across the top of the first sheet – *Every Town in America Should Hold a Festival Like Ours.*

He had written in detail everything he had seen at the festival including the parade. But more importantly, he had noted how the festival brought families together, reunited friends, and offered the opportunity to make new friends. He described the vendors and the delightful smells of home-baked goods and fried treats, the sounds of laughter coming from every direction, and the colorful sights and sounds of the parade.

Freddie may not want to use his article, but it made him happy to write it. He only wished his parents were able to attend. It might have made their day a little brighter. Rob stacked the papers next to his magazine article and let himself out the door, taking care to ensure it was locked.

34

Rob dug his hands deep in his pockets and tapped his foot nervously as he waited at the designated spot for Patti. He had not been this nervous in high school when they danced the night away and snuck kisses behind the general store. Meeting Patti tonight felt right in so many ways, yet he couldn't help but feel a tug of guilt dating another girl when he was an engaged man. He tried to push thoughts of Eleanor away and convince himself that he was just enjoying the evening with an old friend.

Patti smiled and waved as soon as she turned the corner, and his breath caught in his throat. She always wore cute dresses to the dance, but he didn't remember her looking this beautiful. Since he'd been home, he had only seen her in her waitress uniform with her hair pulled up in a ponytail. Tonight, she was wearing a blue flowered sundress, and her hair hung like silk around her shoulders. She wore just a touch of pink lipstick on her perfect lips, and her blue eyes sparkled when she gazed at him.

"You look," Rob struggled for the right word, "just beautiful," he stuttered.

"Why thank you, city boy," Patti smiled at him. If she was nervous, she hid it well. "You look pretty spiffy yourself."

Rob blushed. He had not gone out of his way to get dressed

up for the dance. He had changed into a new pair of dungarees and had on a short-sleeved blue checkered shirt. He almost laughed out loud when he realized they were color-coordinated without realizing how the other would dress. People would start talking about them if they kept this up.

"I must warn you," Rob grinned at her. "Karen has already put me on her dance card."

Patti giggled. "I wouldn't expect any less from her."

"I may need you to rescue me. One dance only is all I promised her, and that was only to soothe her feelings."

"Don't you worry, city boy. I'll be your superhero and swoop in if she gets out of hand." She put her arm through his, and they began strolling towards the music.

The band had begun their first song, and it was the perfect number to kick off the festivities. The crowd was already moving to "Dancing in the Street," and the older generation were sitting on the sidelines in their lawn chairs and tapping their feet to the music. There were tables set up on each side of the street, and Sunday School classes were selling cups of ice-cold lemonade to keep the dancers refreshed.

The first three songs were fast numbers and the crowd clapped and cheered after each number. After the third song, Mayor Thompson took the microphone.

"I want to take this opportunity to welcome each and every one of ya'll gathered here tonight," his southern drawl boomed into the microphone. "Our annual street dance is the culmination of our Sweet Corn Festival, and we want you all to have a wonderful time and dance the night away."

The crowd clapped and cheered. When the noise died down, Mayor Thompson introduced the band and their singers.

"Now ya'll get ready to have an evenin' to remember," and the mayor handed the microphone back to the lead singer.

Rob grinned. He may have missed the last four dances, but the mayor's speech was still the same one he'd used every year.

"OK, ladies and gents," the lead singer announced. "This next song is for all you star-crossed lovers out there."

Just as he turned to take Patti's hand, Rob felt a tap on his shoulder. His stomach tightened when he turned and was face to face with Karen.

"How appropriate, Rob. I had you fourth on my dance card, and we get a slow romantic song," she purred as she ran her fingers up his arm.

He couldn't help but notice she was wearing a form-fitting royal blue dress that hit just below her knees. He noticed her tanned arms and how low-cut the dress was on her bodice. She had on her signature red lipstick and a matching ribbon tied in her hair. Of all the colors she could have chosen, she, too, had to dress in blue.

He glanced at Patti, who was grinning, but he thought he also saw something else in her eyes. A little regret, perhaps, that he was dancing the first slow dance with Karen?

"Excuse me," he whispered. "I promised her," his words trailed off, but he hoped she saw the regret in his eyes.

"I understand," she whispered back. "Go and get it over with."

Karen tried to lead the dance and pulled him into her too tightly. He tried to pull back, but she put her head on his shoulders and swayed to "Tears on My Pillow."

Rob began to think this was the longest song he had ever heard and peeked around over Karen's head. He saw Patti dancing in the arms of Justin Moore, who had been the high school football star, and a pang of jealousy hit him in the pit of his gut.

"I've missed you, Rob," Karen whispered in his ear. "You've become quite the handsome man, and I hear you have a successful career ahead of you in Atlanta." His jaw clenched at her voice in his ear.

She moved in as close as humanly possible, put her lips on

his ear, and said, "I can make you a very happy man. Just say the word, and I'll go with you back to Atlanta."

Rob stopped moving, and Karen mistook his action as an opportunity to move in closer. He glanced over and saw Patti's head still on Justin's shoulder. He also saw a tear form in the corner of her eye.

"What the hell, Karen?" he hissed under his breath.

She pulled back and looked at him, her eyes pleading. "Rob, don't you know I've loved you since high school? You broke my heart when you left without a word."

Rob took Karen's hand and pulled her to the side where they had some semblance of privacy. He ran a hand through his hair and tried to choose his next words with care.

"Look, Karen, if I ever led you on, I'm sorry," he said. "We dated a couple of times in high school, but we were never serious." He paused and saw the hurt in her eyes. But he couldn't tell if the hurt was from losing him or losing her ticket out of this small town. He was fairly sure it was the latter.

"My God, Karen, we only kissed one time when I took you home after our second date. How can you say you love me? You don't even know me."

"I do know you, Rob," and she began to cry. "I know you are a good man. You are smart and talented, and you love your family even though you had to leave here to find your place in the world," she sniffled, and he handed her his handkerchief. She wiped her nose and continued, "I think it's great that you came home when your family needed you, but you don't have to stay here forever. I'll go back to Atlanta with you, and we can start a new life together." She took his hands in hers and gazed up at him with tear-rimmed eyes. "I promise you won't regret it."

Rob stood stiffly for several seconds. The song ended and while the crowd cheered, Rob saw Patti several feet away watching him. She knew Rob wanted to escape Karen's grip, but she sensed that he needed to finish their conversation.

Rob shifted his feet and glanced down. "Karen, you can't go to Atlanta with me. I'm not even sure what I'm doing at this point." He looked directly into her eyes as she squeezed his hands.

"I don't love you, Karen," he said softly. "Not in the way you need a man to love you." He saw a tear roll down her cheek, but he wanted to finish this now.

"Karen, you are a beautiful woman, and any man would be lucky to have you. And I'm sure the perfect man is out there, just waiting for you to make him the luckiest man in the world. But it's not me. I love you as a friend. Nothing more." He leaned down and kissed her cheek.

What she did next caught him off guard. She slapped him across his cheek with all of her strength.

"Bastard," she spat at him. And she turned and stalked off.

Patti walked over and offered him a cup of lemonade.

"Looks like that went well," she smirked as she put her hand on his cheek. He instinctively reached up and covered her hand with his.

"Guess you can say I won't be added to her dance card again," he laughed. "I had to say it, though, so she could move on."

Rob cocked his head towards Patti. "You looked mighty comfortable in Justin's arms."

She thought for a moment before speaking. "Justin and I are friends," she said. "I've been a shoulder for him through his divorce, but there's nothing more."

"Besides," she grinned up at him. "I had an unexpected empty slot on my dance card, and somebody had to fill it."

"So, I'm assuming the rest of your card is filled with one name only?"

"You assume correctly," she smiled. He took her hand as

they joined the crowd to finish dancing the night away.

They didn't see Karen the rest of the night, and the band ended with another slow number, 'I Only Have Eyes for You.' By the end of the night, Rob realized he would only have eyes for Patti for the rest of his life.

He couldn't tell her yet, though. He needed to make things right with Eleanor first. He also had to figure out how he could make a good living in a small town. When the song ended, Rob leaned down and brushed Patti's lips lightly with his. He felt a tingling in his belly he had never had before.

She smiled as he took her hand and said, "Let me walk you home." She nodded, and they strolled down Main Street as others gathered their belongings to go home for the night. Patti led him in a direction away from her house.

"Where are we going?" He was confused.

"I don't live at my parents' home anymore, silly," she said. "When Gram died, she left her house to me."

Her words surprised him. He hadn't seen Gram around, but he didn't know she had passed away. The diner still carried her name and he assumed she still helped cook and bake.

Her house was just a block away from the diner, so they didn't have a long walk. Rob was impressed when he saw the little house. It was a bungalow style, painted crisp white with blue shutters and a front porch that ran along the front. The yard was small and was enclosed with a white picket fence. There were several flower beds alive with summer plants. They walked slowly to the front door, and both seemed at a loss for words.

"I really enjoyed tonight," Patti began first.

"Even watching me get slapped?" he answered playfully.

"It wasn't funny at the time," she grinned, "but now that the red is gone, it was pretty funny." She reached up and touched the spot where Karen had slapped him.

Her touch made Rob want to grab her and pull her close. He wanted to run his hands through her silky hair and feel his lips on hers. He wanted to hold her and never let her go.

Instead, he said softly, "May I kiss you goodnight?"

Patti focused on his eyes for just a moment. "I was hoping you would." She wanted to say more, but she didn't want to break the spell of the moment.

Rob leaned down and kissed her tenderly. They didn't touch bodies or even hands. He just kissed her gently on the lips, and the sparks flew bright and high between them. When the brief kiss ended, they stared at each other for just a moment. Both of them knew that when the time was right, there would be the promise of more.

35

To say he had a sleepless night would be an understatement. When Rob arrived home, both parents were in bed. His mom had left him a note that they would attend church the next morning, and she would love for him to join them.

The church had modified their bus to accommodate both wheelchairs, and the driver would pick them up in the morning. They also arranged to drive his parents to their next doctors' appointments. Grateful for that information, Rob hoped to get a good night's sleep so he could help his parents in the morning and honor his mother's request to attend church with them.

But sleep didn't come. He tossed and turned and finally gave up. He moved to the front porch swing, the thinking swing, as his mom called it when he was a boy. Maybe he could think his way through how he had managed to put himself in this position.

He was living a double life. He was an engaged man with a nice apartment in Atlanta and the promise of an up-and-coming career. He followed his dream of getting a college degree in the field that he loved and wanted to pour his passion into journalism. He thought he loved Eleanor. She had always been sweet and loving and encouraged his dreams. While he couldn't remember the actual time of engagement, he had grown to like the idea of marrying her and starting a life together. He admired her passion for her work. She would be a successful, if not famous, television journalist. She already held her own as a woman in a mostly male-dominated arena.

Now, he couldn't clear his thoughts from sweet Patti. They had sort of dated in high school, but he had been more focused on leaving this one-stoplight town. He always enjoyed being with her, but she didn't share the same passion he did for work.

She began waitressing at Gram's in high school, and now, as an adult woman, she was still a waitress. He thought she would have moved on to a more professional position or, like so many of the girls they had graduated with, would be married with a child or two.

He didn't understand her commitment to a restaurant when the owner was now deceased. Was she working for a corporation that had snapped up the little diner for pennies? Or perhaps some of Gram's relatives who didn't want to run it themselves?

And he kissed her! But what a natural kiss it had been. The look in her eyes told him she wanted more, but he had to get his life sorted out. Now he had two women on the hook, and one or both were going to be hurt when this was over.

His thoughts turned to Connie. Her life had been cut way too short, and he discovered she had an amazing talent that no one was aware of. Surely, her teachers had seen the talent in her. Why didn't someone encourage her to use her talents more? Why didn't he know she had such a talent? He rubbed his chin and let out a long sigh, suddenly feeling miserable about his whole life.

36

Patti couldn't sleep either. She tossed and turned before she eventually gave up, threw on her silk robe and slippers, and walked out onto her front porch. She sat down in her swing and admired her little front yard, where the plants were blooming even during the sweltering heat of summer.

She was falling for Rob again, no matter how hard she tried to fight it. After he left four years ago without a word, she vowed to never allow herself to fall in love again. The pain was agonizing, and she cried for months. Gram helped her put her life back together and was the shoulder she needed.

It took almost a year before she was finally able to make it through the days without thoughts of him consuming her. Then he walked back into her life unexpectedly. She had planned to keep her distance when she saw him the first night he was back. But it was hard. He was more handsome than ever, and the way his mouth turned up just so when he looked at her melted her heart once again.

She thought it was funny that Karen was pouring herself all over him and, in a way, hoped he would move on to her. That way, at least, her heart could remain closed. She couldn't help but cry a little when she was dancing with Justin because she knew her heartache was about to begin again.

And that kiss sealed her fate. All of her old feelings, along with new ones, came flooding back through her. She knew he couldn't stay in this little town forever when he had a promising career ahead of him. He would leave in a few weeks. And Gram was not here now to help her put the pieces of her heart back together   again.

37

The morning nurse prepared breakfast for Robert and Charlotte, and after they ate, she helped them prepare for church. Rob studied his face in the mirror, and he looked like he'd been run over by a truck. He took a quick shower, dressed in his Sunday best, and waited with his parents for the church bus to arrive.

"Did you have a nice time at the dance?" his mom asked. When she glanced at him, Rob felt his face flush, thinking that she sensed something was going on.

"Took me back to my high school days," he answered casually. "The band was great. Nice size crowd. It was nice." He took a sideways glance towards her and saw her smiling.

"Did you dance with any nice girls?"

"A couple."

"Anyone I know?" she prodded.

"Probably," he chuckled. "It is a small town, and I think you know almost everybody."

"Good God, Charlotte," Robert interjected, "why don't you just ask the boy if he was with Patti."

"I don't want to pry," Charlotte answered with a wink at her son.

"Yes, mom. It wouldn't be the Sweet Corn Festival if I didn't dance the night away with Patti Newton, now would it?" Rob grinned playfully, but inside, he wished they could end this conversation.

"Just like old times, huh?" Charlotte continued.

Robert groaned.

"It was a nice dance, Mom," Rob said as he leaned down and kissed her on the cheek. "We're not the same people anymore." As soon as the words came out of his mouth, Rob wondered who he was trying to convince – himself or his mother.

He was thankful to hear the rumble of the bus as it turned into the driveway.

As he breathed a sigh of relief that this conversation would finally end, he said, "Let's get you two loaded up and into the house of our Lord."

"Careful," Charlotte warned. "That sounded like it had a touch of blasphemy."

"Not at all, mother," Rob said as he smiled and carefully pushed her wheelchair down the ramp.

Reverend Stokes didn't allow a clock on the church wall, and he didn't wear a watch at the pulpit. He said he would preach as long as the good lord led him, and today, the lord gave the reverend a lot to say.

It's not that Rob minded the sermon; he was usually quite motivated by the reverend's words. But after very little sleep and the turmoil running through his head about his future, it was hard for him to sit still. He had glanced around the congregation and, thankfully, did not see Karen anywhere. He was disappointed when he didn't see Patti. Maybe she was a Methodist, he thought to himself. He was in the Baptist house of God.

As he tuned in to the sermon, Rob began to think that the preacher had read his thoughts. Know your heart, be true to yourself, and listen to your inner voice were the words that captured Rob's attention.

He glanced at the man in the pulpit, thinking sure he would be staring right through him. But the preacher had his bible in one hand and was looking towards the opposite side of the church. When he did look towards the area where Rob was sitting, he never focused directly on the younger man.

Thankful that he wasn't being singled out in a congregation of about 200, Rob put his head down and listened thoughtfully to the wisdom that was coming his way. Listen to your heart and be true to yourself.

The church ladies never disappointed when they prepared dinner on the ground. As a kid, Rob always wondered why it was called dinner on the ground since they set up their spread of meats, vegetables, and casseroles on rows of tables in the church fellowship hall.

One of his Sunday School teachers told him that in the very early days, picnics were held after church outside in the churchyard. Everyone would sit on blankets on the ground to eat and fellowship together. Rob thought that sounded quite unsanitary. As a child, he would imagine ants crawling all over the food laid out on the ground just for them.

The ladies had made a special place at the end of a table for both wheelchairs to fit so his parents would feel comfortable and their family could be together. Betty and Ned were getting their two little ones settled so Rob went through the line to fix his parents' plates. One of the ladies offered to take care of that for him, but he wanted to do it himself.

There were so many food choices, it was hard not to pile the plate too high to carry. Whatever he chose would be delicious. There were mounds of fried chicken, plates of carved ham, several bowls of fluffy mashed potatoes, fresh field peas with snaps, broccoli casseroles made in every way imaginable, squash casseroles, cream corn picked recently from the fields and scraped off the cob, green bean casseroles, stewed okra and tomatoes, macaroni and cheese, and so much more.

As he sat with his family while eating, Rob couldn't help but feel the void they all felt with Connie's absence. He saw the sadness in his mother's eyes, but he also saw the hope of a new life as she watched her grandchildren.

She insisted on holding the baby to allow Betty the freedom to eat, and little Dennis was content in his high chair. Rob laughed as the toddler scooped up a mound of mashed potatoes and shoved them in his mouth. White gobs spilled out the corner of his tiny mouth, and then he rubbed his hands through his hair. When the grown-ups laughed, he busted out in giggles and clapped his chubby hands together, spewing the remaining potatoes through the air.

Throughout the meal, people stopped at their table to welcome Rob home once again and cooed at the baby. As Rob studied his family and friends gathered together, a warm feeling enveloped his heart.

38

After little sleep Saturday night, Patti has a miserable Sunday as well. When she saw Rob walk into the diner just a few weeks ago, her heart had skipped a beat. She promised herself right then that she would not open her heart up to him again.

When he walked out of her life the first time with not even a goodbye, she had been heartbroken for months. Gram let her cry on her shoulder daily, and her parents did the best they could to help ease her pain.

Without even realizing it, she had now let herself fall deeper in love with him than ever. She had no idea about his life in Atlanta. He had shared almost nothing of that life with her except a brief mention of a girlfriend. She had seen his grief over losing his youngest sister. She had watched him tenderly care for his parents. And she had noticed how he had merged gracefully right back into the community he had left behind. But would he ... could he ... break her heart again?

She skipped church. Rob would be there, and she wasn't ready to face him. Truth was, she was not going to make herself easily accessible to him. If the kiss meant to him what it had to her, then he would come to her. She would not chase him. She chose the hours she would have spent in church to get caught up on paperwork and do a little baking for the week ahead. But she just couldn't focus.

That kiss had thrown her over the edge. He had kissed her with such tenderness that her stomach still fluttered when she let herself think about it. And all she did today was think about it! The paperwork looked foreign to her, and when she took the first apple pie out of the oven, something looked off. She tasted it and realized she had left the sugar out of the filling. She had made that pie hundreds of times and could make it in her sleep. But, one little kiss and the pie was junk.

"Damn it," she screamed since no one was around to hear her, and she threw the inedible concoction in the trash.

She fixed herself a cherry coke and sat in the corner booth in the dark. She couldn't turn lights on, or travelers passing by on the main highway would think she was open. She preferred to sit in the semi-darkness anyway.

She tried to pull her thoughts together and sort out her feelings. Maybe she should have gone to church. Sometimes, Reverend Stokes' messages spoke directly to her. Maybe she should talk to her mom. She had been her rock even though Gram was like a second mother to her. She cried on Gram's shoulder after Rob had left because she was too embarrassed to tell her mother how much she had really loved him.

Maybe she should find a psychiatrist to help her get over her mistake of letting Rob kiss her. Maybe, maybe, maybe. Instead, she put her head in her hands and cried.

She eventually locked up the diner and walked home. As she opened the gate of her little picket fence, her next-door neighbor called out to her.

"Myrtle has gone off the deep end," her neighbor laughed. "Rumor is, she's causing a ruckus at her beloved tree. We're going to ride over there and see what she's up to. Wanna come?"

"No thanks, I'm pretty tired, but you can fill me in later," she answered. She just wanted to stay in the safety of her home rather than see the show Myrtle was giving.

She went inside and tried to take a nap. No luck. She flipped through her favorite recipe books that Gram had given her, looking for some new menu options for the diner, but couldn't concentrate. She decided to get some air and drive Gram's old Rambler station wagon to the lake north of town. There, she could sit on the dock, dangle her feet in the water, and just let her thoughts wander.

39

The phone rang just as Rob got his parents inside the house and settled. The nurse told him she would help them lay down for a nap, so Rob ran to snatch up the receiver. Freddie's voice was on the other end, and he was surprised that Myrtle wasn't on the line as well.

"Rob, I need your help," the older man said hurriedly.

"Sure, what can I do?"

"That crazy Myrtle has chained herself to the big tree on the edge of town and won't budge," Rob couldn't tell if Freddie was in a panic or about to laugh. "I'm out of town at the moment and can't be there. Can you swing by the office and grab a camera and go cover this crazy lady's antics for me?"

"I'd be more than happy to," Rob laughed. He sure didn't see excitement like this in Atlanta, he thought.

"While you're there, grab yourself a press badge from the front desk," Freddie advised. "We want you to be official."

"My pleasure. When will you be back?"

"Not until tomorrow," Freddie said. "If you will see this through, I'd appreciate it. We'll settle up with all of your stories later in the week."

Rob hadn't thought about getting paid for the stories he was writing for the local paper. He was just happy to be allowed to use his journalism instincts.

"I'm not expecting pay, my friend. Just happy to help." And the two men hung up.

Rob made sure his parents were in excellent hands, even though he already knew they were. He jumped in his dad's old Ford and made his way to the newspaper office.

He mused at how Freddie had immediately brought him back into the folds of the small-town paper. He had his old key back, was about to use the paper's camera, and now had an official press badge. He'd forgotten how good it felt hanging that badge around his neck.

A small crowd had gathered, most of whom were there to cheer Myrtle on. Myrtle had wrapped a heavy chain around herself, padlocked it, and hid the key. She had wrapped it snug two times around her thickened waist so it would take excessive force to pull her out.

Of course, someone could sneak up behind her with heavy cutters and get her out, but they had not gotten that desperate yet. Two of the city police officers were talking to Myrtle while another was holding the crowd back. The city developer was standing at the front of the crowd. He was visibly agitated and clearly wanted this tree gone so his new housing development would move forward.

The tree that was the center of attention was estimated to be more than 100 years old, and over the past several years, developers had built houses too close to it. Now, with population growth, they needed a two-lane road, and the large grandaddy oak stood smack in the middle of the road. The city planner had declared the tree to be hazardous with all of the cars that were now on the road. He claimed that a driver's visibility was reduced, causing dangerous conditions.

"This tree will stay!" Myrtle proclaimed loudly, and her entourage began to shout with her. "Long live the oak, you people are a joke."

Rob suppressed a smile as he remembered fondly how feisty

his neighbor had always been. She was a prude on the telephone, but when Myrtle took up a cause she believed in, there would be hell to pay.

When the crowd saw his press badge, they stepped back to let him through. He was able to move in close enough to take several shots of Myrtle, the officers who were earnestly pleading with her, and the ladies holding up signs and chanting with their leader. He even managed to get several photos of the city developer with a huge scowl across his face.

The mayor arrived, shook Rob's hand, and walked up to Myrtle. She was not pleased to see him.

"You are not taking down this tree!" she proclaimed to him.

"Why, Myrtle," the mayor crooned. "You know it's not up to me. I have to do what the council recommends, and they take their recommendation from the city planner."

"You can find another way to build your road! Use that brain God put in your heads and build your town while preserving the beauty the good Lord gave us." The crowd cheered, and Rob had to admit he was impressed with her speech and her passion. The first time he'd seen her when he arrived home, he thought she appeared old and frail. Her determination today gave her a strong, youthful demeanor.

The mayor was speechless for a moment.

"Look here, you old coot," the city planner headed towards Myrtle. "There are plenty of other trees around here. You are just trying to stop progress for our town. Why are you so hell-bent on saving one tree?"

The mayor held up his hand and spoke up. "Let's don't start name-calling here." He glanced towards Myrtle and continued, "But Myrtle, he is right. We have many beautiful trees in our fair town. Why is this one so special?"

Tears formed in Myrtle's eyes, and Rob snapped the photos as fast as the camera would let him. He worked quickly to capture her obvious passion and emotion. "It just is," she said in a whisper that the crowd wasn't sure exactly what she had said. But the mayor understood, and his face softened.

He put a hand to his head and thought for a moment. Then he called the planner, one of the officers, and Rob over to the side where they could talk without being heard.

"Look, I don't know what it is about this tree, but Myrtle deserves to tell her story. This isn't the right place, however." He thought for a moment.

"It's getting late on a Sunday afternoon. Folks have training union and church starting soon. Let's call a special council meeting for Tuesday night and let Myrtle say her peace."

"I have special equipment arriving tomorrow to start taking this damn tree down," the planner objected. "A delay will throw us back for weeks."

"Well, it will just have to be delayed," the mayor snapped. "There's more here than meets the eye, and we need to get to the bottom of it."

"This is plum crazy," the planner snapped. "I'll head to the office and try to stop the construction company from bringing the equipment. Ya'll are as crazy as Myrtle," and he stomped off.

The mayor went over to tell Myrtle that she had won this battle, and the tree removal was being delayed. He told her she would have to make her appeal to the city council on Tuesday at 6 pm and he offered to unlock her chain.

She hesitated, not sure if she should believe him, but the officer assured her that he would see that the mayor made good on his promise.

She finally relented and reached into her bosom for the key. Seeing its former location, the mayor reluctantly took it from her. But then flashed Rob a big smile as he put the key in the lock.

When the film was developed, the photo showed the mayor grinning smugly from ear to ear and Myrtle with a sour look on her face just as the chain fell to the ground.

Two hours later, Rob was pleased with the words he had put to paper. He tried to capture Myrtle's passion for her belief in the tree, along with the city planner's frustration of not being able to move forward with his development project. Very objective. Just who, what, when, where, and why.

Even though Myrtle was a pain in the ass on the party line, he admired her for standing up for her beliefs. He had to agree that the tree was a beauty. The top of the tree could actually be seen from the center of the town, and the trunk stood tall and proud. The branches draped gracefully over the passing cars and showed no threat of endangerment. Rob hoped the city would come up with a solution for both parties.

He laid the pages on Maryanne's desk and went into the darkroom to unload the film from the camera. When he worked here during his school years, Freddie would sometimes let him develop film, and the smell of the chemical residue in the darkroom brought back fond memories. He had always enjoyed seeing the photographer's eye come to life as the black-and-white image slowly came into focus on paper. Once the image was crisp and sharp, he would move it from the developing solution into the 'fix' solution to stop the image from over-developing. From there, he gently placed it into the wash to remove all chemicals and then hung it on the line above the sink to dry.

He was tempted to develop his own film, but he didn't want to ruin his shots when he hadn't developed a film in years. Freddie had gotten a new exposure machine and Rob had no idea how to work the thing. He put his roll of film in the lightproof canister, turned on the lights, and then placed it in the basket next to the door.

As he locked the door to the newspaper office, Rob blew out a deep breath. He had been tied up with church with his parents, then the Myrtle story, so he hadn't had a chance to really think about what he needed to focus on most. That kiss.

After Rob left the office, he drove home to check on his parents. The nurse had them both at the table, getting ready for supper. They asked him to stay and eat, but he was too antsy. He wanted to talk to Patti. He sat with them for a few minutes and shared the whole Myrtle story with them.

"Lord, that woman!" Charlotte laughed. "I don't know what it is about that tree. She has big oaks in her own yard. Why don't she just chain herself to one of those?"

Rob was glad to see Charlotte laughing, and even his dad smirked at his wife's comment. As he sat at the table with them, he began to question his reason for ever leaving his family in the first place. Had life really been so bad here?

He was a teenager when he'd left, and now he was a man. He had a college degree, an apartment of his own, and a promising career in journalism. But seeing his parents together, after suffering such grief recently, he saw a bond between them he had never noticed before. No matter what they faced, for better or worse, he saw in the way they fit together that they were in it for a lifetime.

He didn't think they had ever left the state of Florida or Georgia, but that didn't matter to them. What mattered most was their love for each other, their family, and their community.

Would he ever have that bond with Eleanor? He didn't think he had it now. Was it something that grew as time passed? He rubbed his hand through his hair, and his head started to pound. Man, he had to think.

He decided to take a ride to try and clear his head. After thanking the nurse for taking care of them, he gave his mom a peck on the cheek and squeezed his dad lightly on the shoulder. With a promise to be back before they went to bed, he headed out the door.

Once he turned onto the highway, Rob had no idea where he

was going. He just needed time to clear his head and think. Even writing didn't appeal to him at the moment. The night air was stuffy, so he threw his hand out the window to feel the balmy breeze. He let it flap in the wind like he did as a kid when he wrote shotgun by his dad. He would pretend that if the wind caught his hand just right, it might float into the sky. Silly, childish nonsense, he thought.

As he suspected, there was little to no traffic in town. Some stragglers were just leaving their evening service at church, but most others were already getting settled in for the evening to prepare for another hard week ahead.

He knew the diner would be dark, and he was right. Maybe he was hoping to catch Patti working, but he was kind of relieved that she wasn't there. He made a left on the main highway through town, and two blocks up, he turned right onto the two-lane road that would lead to the lake.

He passed Myrtle's tree and grinned once again at her antics this afternoon. The "under construction" sign that was there earlier had been removed, and he was glad to see that Myrtle's tree had gotten a reprieve.

He would love to catch the sunset over the lake, but that was still a couple of hours away, and he promised his folks he'd be home before they went to bed. Still, 30 minutes or so sitting by the lake should give him some much-needed fresh air to clear out his brain.

It took him 10 minutes to reach his destination, and there were several cars parked in the sandy lot. He spotted Gram's old Rambler and wondered if Patti had the same idea as him. There was no turning back because he saw the slight movement of her head signaling that she had seen him first.

He shut the engine of the old truck off and sucked in a deep breath, and blew it out fast. He had no idea where this conversation was about to go. So much for clearing his head, he thought.

"Hey, you," he smiled once he got close enough to speak.

"Hey, back," she said, and she flashed him a soft smile.

"Mind?" he asked, gesturing to a spot beside her. "Looks like we both had the same idea," he smiled.

"I do believe it's a public lake," she said with a hint of fun in her voice. Both were nervous.

They sat in silence for a few minutes, both lost in thought and looking at the gently lapping waves on the lake. A family with several children was playing next to the dock, and the children's laughter filled the air. Light from the day was growing dim, but the sunset was still another hour away. The thought occurred to Rob that he would love to sit here and take Patti in his arms, holding her tight until the sun had slipped below the trees.

He cleared his voice.

"Should I go first?"

She peered straight into his eyes and nodded. "Please."

"Patti, I have to be brutally honest with you," he began, not really knowing how much he was going to say.

"Growing up here, I never felt like I fit in with my own family. I always thought I was a disappointment to my dad because I hated the farming life. Even as a kid, I loved to write silly stories, and when I would try to read them to my parents, my dad would just shut me down, saying I didn't need to spend my time on such nonsense."

"What about your mom?"

"She would smile and tell me what a good job I was doing, and when my dad wasn't around, she would read them and tell me they were nice. But she also told me family came first, and in our family, that meant taking care of our legacy, the farm."

He paused for a few minutes, trying to hold back tears that were choking the back of his throat.

"You were the highlight of my high school years." He gazed

into her face but couldn't read her thoughts.

"Well, you and Mrs. Cherry," he laughed.

"She saw my passion, and while I thought my writing would never be good enough to even think of having a career, she began to encourage me to continue. She took me to Freddie's office and talked him into hiring me on the spot. After my first real newspaper story, he said, 'Boy, you've got a gift, and we are going to teach you to use that gift for the benefit of mankind.'

Patti chuckled. "I remember reading some of your stories, and I always thought they were well written."

"Thanks. That means a lot coming from you." When he peered at her, he noticed a strand of her hair had fallen from the scarf, and he wanted to reach up and tuck it back in. But he held back. They needed to talk, and he had to make things right with the two women now in his life.

"In my junior year, Mrs. Cherry helped me apply to several colleges and to apply for scholarships. I received a full ride from Georgia State, and when I told my dad, he completely blew up. He pretty much disowned me. My mom and sisters would never have crossed him, so they went along with him, and I was basically excommunicated from my family. I felt so ashamed that I almost changed my mind and was willing to give up on my dream.

He paused when one of the children on the dock started crying. The parents were gathering up their things to leave, and one of the little ones was not ready to go. After his mother dried him off, he jumped back into the lake, causing a mad parent and a squealing child. Rob turned back to Patti.

"God, I was scared. I had never been 30 miles away from this county, let alone a big city in another state. I was just a country bumpkin thinking I could make it in the big league."

"Why didn't you talk to me?" Patti asked.

"I was scared, I was ashamed, and if you had told me not to go," he paused, "I would have stayed right here."

"I would have never told you not to go!" Patti answered. "I always wanted what was best for you and for you to have what you wanted."

She looked down at her skirt and picked off a leaf that had fallen from the oak tree.

"I cried for months," she said so softly that Rob wasn't sure he heard her correctly.

"The last thing I wanted to do was hurt you," she noted the anguish in his voice. "There is no excuse for what I did, and I felt horrible for not saying goodbye. I planned to write once I got to Atlanta, but things were so crazy at the dorm I got caught up in that life. Things move a lot faster in the big city than they do here. It didn't take long for my old life to fade away from memory."

"So, I faded from your memory?" The light was growing dimmer. Patti sniffled faintly.

"You never faded away, but the longer I waited to write you, the harder it became. I assumed you had moved on and found a good job and maybe even a new fella."

"Neither," she said, with no emotion in her tone.

"So, tell me something about you. Why in the world are you still waitressing tables?"

"Well," Patti said as she blew out a long sigh.

"After you left, Gram and I became very close. We'd always cared for each other, but she seemed to understand my heartache in a way that my parents didn't. They tried to help me, but they were getting frustrated at my incessant tears. Whenever I talked to Gram, she would listen for as long as I wanted to talk."

The pit in Rob's stomach grew larger as he realized how much he had let Patti down, what he wouldn't give now to take that heartache away from her.

"I enjoyed helping at the diner, too, so after we'd close up at night, we would share a dessert and just chat. After several months, I began to feel back to normal. And then,"

Rob saw a tear forming at the corner of her eye.

"Then Gram dropped a bombshell on me. She told me she had just been diagnosed with cancer, and it had already taken over her body."

"Oh my gosh," Rob was shocked.

"She had no family, and she told me I was like a daughter to her. She said nobody would care for the diner more than me. She and her husband had opened it 40 years ago, and it had become a staple in our little community. She wanted me to carry on the tradition, and she wanted me to have her home and everything else that was hers. She handed me deeds that night to the diner and her home, and she signed the title to the old Rambler to me. What little money she had left, she transferred to an account she opened in my name. All that she asked was that I help care for her when she was unable to do so."

Rob noticed that she was crying freely now. He took her in his arms and hugged her.

"I am so sorry you had to go through that. What a burden it must have been for you."

"It wasn't a burden at all!" Patti straightened and pulled away from him. "Gram was like a second mother to me. I told her, of course, I would take care of her, but she shouldn't leave everything she had to me. She could have at least given it to charity, but she insisted. She said if she'd ever had a child, she would have wanted her to be just like me, and the child would get it all. So, she proclaimed me her adopted child."

Both sat quietly for a moment.

"How was it taking care of her?" Rob asked.

"She was a trooper to the end. She only lived three months after that conversation. I took over the day-to-day responsibilities and learned as much as I could from her. She died peacefully in her sleep, but she'd been bedridden for two weeks prior. It was the hardest thing I'd ever had to go through."

"I can only imagine," Rob said. He noticed the sun was beginning to sink lower into the sky, and he was not going to make his promise to his parents.

"So, I suppose selling the diner is out of the question." It was a question, but he said it as a statement, and he held his breath, waiting for her answer. Maybe if she sold out, she would move with him to Atlanta.

"Absolutely not," she answered firmly. "Gram spent too much of her life building that business into what it is today. I'm not selling it just for financial gain. It not only belongs to me, but it belongs to the community as well. You should see the old coots who come in early every day. They would be lost if I sold out." They both laughed, and Rob felt the tension beginning to ease. And then she dropped the next question.

"What about you? How serious is it with Eleanor?"

Rob stiffened. He couldn't lie, but he didn't want to tell her they were engaged. He had decided for sure during this conversation that he would break off the engagement. Before he could form an answer, Patti blurted out.

"So, I can tell by your silence what the answer is. Robert Mathis, Jr., you have been leading me on while you have a steady girl back in Atlanta! You are not doing this to me again." She got to her feet.

"Patti, it's not like that." He stood beside her.

"I just need time to make it right with her so I can be free for you," he blurted out.

"Free for me?" Her voice got louder. "Free for me? What the hell, Rob? Are you married to the girl?

He dropped his head.

"We're not married," he swallowed hard and studied her, "but we are engaged."

The color drained from Patti's face. She stared at Rob for two seconds and then slapped him hard across the cheek.

"Go to hell," she spat at him, and then she turned and sprinted towards the old Rambler.

Rob dropped to the ground. He scanned the sky just as the sun dropped down behind the trees. The golden light of day faded into the night. He saw the sunset after all. But he watched it through his tears.

40

Driving to the newspaper office the next morning, Rob knew he had to come up with a plan. He had slept very little and tossed and turned most of the night. Thoughts of Patti ran through his brain, along with memories of the last four years with Eleanor. He had to decide which direction to turn.

He had no doubt now. He loved Patti. What he had felt for Eleanor, he wasn't sure. Or maybe he was just so shallow that he loved whichever girl he was with. No, he thought as he slapped the steering wheel. As much as he had been with Eleanor for the past four years, he had never had that feeling in the pit of his stomach like he had with Patti. She had been his first love, and she would be his last. Eleanor was pleasant and supportive of his career, and he realized now that he had felt fondly towards her. But now he knew what real love was. Her name was Patti.

"Great work, my boy," Freddie crowed as soon as Rob walked into the newspaper office.

"Our Myrtle is quite a character, but you caught her passion very well both in your story and these photos."

Freddie handed the photos over to Rob, and he had to smile at the shots he had captured. Photography wasn't his favorite thing, but in a small-town newspaper, you do a little of everything. In college, you had your reporters, and you had your photographers, and they worked together as a team.

"Thanks, Freddie. I appreciate your confidence in me," Rob shook the older man's hand.

"You've given me a reason to have confidence," Freddie said. "What say we head over to the diner for a cup of coffee and talk about how we'll cover the town meeting tomorrow night? It's going to be a doozie."

Rob cringed at the idea of going to the diner. He knew Patti would not be happy to see him.

"Why don't we just talk in your office?" Rob suggested. "We don't need extra ears listening in."

"Suit yourself," and he pulled out a dollar bill.

"Maryanne, would you be so kind to run over to Gram's and grab two cups of coffee for me and my friend here."

"Not at all," Maryanne sauntered up to the men and brushed Rob on the shoulder.

"Sugar?" She looked at Rob.

"Excuse me?" His look showed his confusion. "I mean," she drawled ever so sweetly, "do you take sugar in your coffee?

He tried to laugh to hide his embarrassment.

"Black is fine. Thanks," he stuttered.

The two men discussed Myrtle's plight with the oak tree at length. Freddie asked Rob to follow through with the story and cover the town council meeting on Tuesday evening.

"You've been on the forefront of the story, you might as well finish it," the older man said as he lit up a cigar.

Rob watched as the tip of the cigar lit brightly and smoke circled around Freddie's face. Rob took in the pungent smell. Many of his fellow journalists smoked tobacco, but he never acquired a taste for it. Even in college, his professors had lit up during class and encouraged the students to do so as well. Rob tried it once or twice but decided smoking was definitely not for him. Probably too many hot hours in the blazing sun getting the stuff ready to be made into what they now all smoked.

Rob filled him in on everything that had happened at the tree the day before, especially the things he didn't include in the article or capture in the photos. Freddie shared what little information he had gathered on the street about Myrtle's reason for wanting to save the tree. There were several versions of many stories, so he thought it best that they listen to the source directly.

And Freddie cautioned Rob to remain objective even if he found himself taking sympathy with Myrtle. If necessary, Freddie said he would write an editorial offering his opinion so he could say whatever he damn well pleased.

Maryanne was out of breath when she came back with the coffee.

"I'd advise ya'll to stay out of the diner today," she huffed. "Patti is in rare form and is being short with anybody and everybody. I don't know what's gotten into that girl."

Rob swallowed hard.

"I haven't seen her like this since right after you," and she looked at Rob and stopped short.

Rob glanced up at her as he took his coffee.

"Since I what, Maryanne?"

"Never mind. I shouldn't have said anything. Just stay away from that place today."

She sashayed out and closed the office door.

Freddie took the lid of his coffee cup and took a sip.

"I believe she was going to say since you left," he eyed Rob cautiously.

"That's what I was afraid of," Rob admitted and took a sip of the hot liquid. "I might as well fill you in."

Thirty minutes later, Freddie sat back in his chair, folded his hands, and touched his lips with both forefingers. They had finished their coffees, and Freddie's cigar was down to a stub.

Rob had shared that after he finished Myrtle's story, he would be catching a bus to Atlanta to wrap things up with Eleanor and his prospective job. He had to pack up his little apartment and figure out how to move his belongings back to Florida.

After a few minutes of silence, during which Rob was pretty sure he held his breath, Freddie leaned forward and took a set of keys out of his desk drawer.

"You can take my Chevy so you can load everything up in the car and make one trip. I'll run it over to Bill's Garage today and have him check it out to make sure you won't have any problems on the trip."

Rob was shocked and knew he couldn't accept such generosity.

"Freddie, that's mighty kind of you, but I can't take your car. That's a five-hour trip just one way."

"You can drive, can't you, son?"

"Yes sir, but"

"You have a license?"

"Yes, sir."

"This is my way of paying you for writing these two stories. Will that work?"

"Freddie, that's still more than generous. Think of the miles I'll put on the car and the wear on the tires."

"You let me worry about that," He smiled at Rob. "You only find your soulmate once in your life. Don't let her get away."

"You encouraged me to pursue a career in the city, remember, Freddie?"

"I do remember, and I see that you've grown into a fine young man in the last four years. You have a gift for words, that's for sure. The world is changing, Rob, and one day you'll have global opportunities. You've even written an article for a national magazine, all in this small community. You can find what you're looking for even in a small town. Think of this as your home base. The rest will come."

Rob swallowed hard as he tried to absorb what his mentor was saying.

Finally, he stood up. "Sir, I can't thank you enough. For everything."

Freddie came around the desk and put his hand on the younger man's shoulder.

"You are more than welcome. You'll figure it out."

As Rob turned to leave the office, Freddie stopped him.

"Just one more thing," Rob turned to face him. "I'd stay away from that diner today if I were you. I'd hate to see meatloaf go flying across the room."

Rob laughed and gave Freddie a salute as he opened the door.

As he passed Maryanne's desk, he noticed she was reading over his story about Myrtle and was making an occasional proof mark. She would hand it over to the typesetter later today.

"See ya, handsome," she smirked as the bell clanked over the office door.

41

Rob rode by the diner, knowing that he wouldn't stop. He couldn't do anymore at this point to upset Patti. The parking lot was full. He shook his head as the customers inside would get the brunt of her emotional state. The locals would forgive and laugh, understanding that we all have a bad day. They might chat down the street, as Maryanne did, about what kind of mood that girl was in. But at the end of the day, everyone loved her and respected her business, and they would go back the next day.

Her place also brought in a lot of travelers who didn't know Patti, and they might not be as forgiving if they got bad service. He hoped maybe she would move to the kitchen for the lunch rush and let her helper handle the front. Rob hit his steering wheel with his fist while waiting for the light to change. Damn, he wished he could redo their time at the lake last night.

He decided to stop in and see Betty. He hadn't seen her much since the baby was born, and when he turned into her yard, she was sitting on the front porch smoking a cigarette.

"Would you like one?" she smiled, offering him the pack of Winstons as he sat in the rocker across from her.

"No thanks," he said, smiling back. "I'm an odd journalist, as I think I'm the only one in my field who doesn't partake. Where are your babies?"

"I finally got them down for a nap, so I am enjoying some rare me time. Ned is at the sale today. What brings you by?"

Rob wasn't sure how much he wanted to share at this point but decided to open up completely to his sister. He shared his feelings for Patti, his relationship with Eleanor, and his decision to move back home even though he had no idea how he would make a living.

"I don't know if I'll be able to win Patti back either." He finally said aloud what he had been dreading. "I'm just as confused as I was four years ago when I left here."

Betty listened quietly, helping herself to another Winston while he talked. When he had spilled his heart, he glanced at her, and she was watching him.

"Rob, I know you left here on bad terms four years ago."

When he started to respond, she threw up her hand.

"Let me finish," she said through a ring of smoke that she was blowing out.

"I am so damn proud of you," her blunt words took Rob by surprise. "You were a kid being pulled in many directions, but you were such a talented kid who didn't fit in with his own family. None of us understood you. But you had to follow your heart. But when your family needed you, man, you came running as fast as you could. You might not be a farmer at heart, but you are a smart and talented man. Any girl will be lucky to have you. And if you love Patti with the vengeance you have shown for your passions, you will win her back."

Rob felt a tear sting at the corner of his eye.

"Betty, your words mean the world to me. I wish I'd had the guts to talk to you before I ran off like I did."

"We all have regrets about the way we handled you," she said back to him. "Believe it or not, even mom and dad do. They probably haven't thanked you for coming home, but I can tell by the way they both look at you they are extremely grateful. And, Rob, always remember, they are your parents, and they love you no matter what."

They both heard the baby cry at the same time. Betty crushed her cigarette in the ashtray next to her.

"Hang on a minute, and say hi to your youngest nephew," and she jumped out of the swing and softly closed the screen door behind her.

Rob listened as she cooed to the baby and talked baby talk.

"Your little dipey is so wet; let's get you all freshened up."

He leaned back and relaxed while she changed and cleaned up her infant. She was proud of her baby brother! Well, he was proud of his big sister for being such a good wife and mother.

She chose her passion, and her love for her husband and children showed in her manicured house and yard. She took care of all of them while helping on the farm and helping her parents as well. He realized how much values were different in the country compared to the big cities. And he realized he wanted to find his country roots again and share in those values.

"Here's your Uncle Rob," Betty cooed as she gently placed the baby in her brother's arms. Rob peered down at the sweetest little eyes, looking back at him with open trust and innocence. The immediate feeling of love and a fierce need to protect this innocent child surprised him. This was the first baby he had ever held, and the feeling almost overwhelmed him.

"Betty, he is beautiful." Rob studied his sister, feeling a new sense of pride for her. "And you are amazing for producing him."

"Well, I did have a little help. He looks a lot like his daddy."

"Maybe so. But you did the hard part," and they both laughed.

Rob rocked the baby while Betty enjoyed another cigarette. When she was finished, he stood up and handed the sweet bundle back to his mom.

"Guess I'd better go talk to Mom and Dad," he said quietly.

"Want my advice?"

Rob nodded affirmatively at his sister.

"Right now, less is better. I'm not sure they need to know about Eleanor at this point."

"Thanks," he met her gaze. "You just confirmed what I was already thinking."

He kissed his sister on the cheek and turned and trotted down the steps.

"I'll stop by before I head north," he waved as he got into the truck.

"You'd better," Betty waved back and smiled. As she watched him turn onto the road, she thought how very proud she was of the man he had become.

42

Rob's parents were down for their afternoon naps, and the nurse was sitting on the couch, knitting and watching television. Helen, one of the neighbors, was in the kitchen preparing for dinner.

He grabbed his notebook from his room and headed out to his favorite oak tree in the backyard. He slipped down onto the ground with his back against the trunk and closed his eyes. It was still warm and sultry, but the shade of the old oak kept him from being too uncomfortable.

He heard the rumble of a tractor in the distance and breathed in the sights and sounds deeply. He wanted to savor this moment and remember it when he had to break things off with Eleanor.

Not sure what he was going to write, Rob opened his book and nibbled on his pencil. That was a bad habit he'd had ever since he could remember, and he would chew on every pencil he used. That used to irritate his teachers, but when he needed to think in between words, there was something soothing about having a pencil against his teeth.

After he nibbled on the yellow stem for a few minutes, he knew what he had to write. He put his pencil to paper, and the words began to flow.

"My dearest Patti," he began.

"I'm sorry I hurt you, and I am begging for your forgiveness. While I can put words to paper, sometimes I can really mess them up when they come out of my mouth. I know I should have explained things differently, but please know I have never felt for Eleanor the way I feel for you. Yes, we are engaged, but to be honest, I don't even know how that happened. We were at a party, and I'd had a little too much to drink. When I woke up the next morning, she told me how happy she was that I had popped the question! The next thing I knew, we were buying a ring and making wedding plans. I thought I had everything I wanted in Atlanta. I had almost forgotten my life back home and was caught up in the success of college and having my own place with a promising career ahead of me."

He paused and considered his next words carefully.

"I said I almost forgot my life back home. But I never forgot you. Patti, you were on my mind and heart almost daily, but after the way I left, I assumed you had moved on. I pictured you as a married woman with a baby or two. And the thought of you with another man hurt deeply, so I buried my feelings for you. And I thought I had moved on until I saw you again.

Please give me a chance to show you how deeply I love you. I'm leaving for Atlanta on Wednesday to pack up my life there. I will break off the engagement, pack up my apartment, and be back on the road to North Florida and to you as soon as possible. I hope to be back early next week if all goes well.

I know you are hurting right now, so I'm not going to bother you in person before I go. But you better watch your back when I return because I will be looking for you. And know I will be a single man, and I will court you properly. All I'm asking for is a second chance. Okay, I guess it's a third chance. But, hey, third time's a charm, right?

Please rest easy while I am gone, and I am praying that you find it in your heart to forgive me.

Forever yours, Rob."

He tore the page from his book and folded it over three times. He would find an envelope and then ask Freddie to deliver it to Patti in the morning. He sat under the tree for several more minutes, listening to the sounds only heard in the country. Then he stood up, brushed himself off, and went inside to face his parents.

The ladies on the volunteer shift were helping his parents get ready for supper. Rob didn't realize how much time he had spent under his thinking tree, but his parents were eating earlier than usual these days.

He helped get them to the table and realized how hungry he was. He hadn't eaten all day, so after their plates were ready, he fixed one for himself. The ladies excused themselves and said they wanted to eat on the porch and enjoy the evening air. Rob knew they were being discreet so the family could have a quiet dinner together.

He appreciated their gesture as it was still hot as blazes outside, and the bugs were out in full force this time of day. Not wanting to upset anyone's appetite, Rob waited until their plates were almost empty before beginning his conversation.

He first apologized for the way he left his family, and after that one sentence, they all poured their heart out. Charlotte cried and told Rob how much she loved him and how proud she was of him. Even as gruff as Robert had been towards his son, he shed tears and told Rob how proud he was of what he had accomplished.

They shared stories of Connie, and Robert confessed how guilty he felt, because he always drove the car. Connie asked to drive that night, so he let her. But he couldn't shake the feeling that if he'd been driving, the accident could have been prevented. He broke down and asked his wife and son to forgive him.

"There is nothing to forgive, Dad," Rob said with tears in his eyes, and he kneeled beside his dad's wheelchair.

"No one could have known what was going to happen. From what I understand, that truck was traveling way too fast. We'll never understand why Connie was taken at such a young age, but you can't blame yourself. You've always been the strongest man I know. Even if you were driving, the outcome might have very well been the same. You have Mom, Betty, and two adorable grandbabies. Keep your chin up for them. Connie would have wanted that."

They talked and cried a little more. Then Rob told them his plans. He didn't go into details about Patti but just that they were working to rekindle their relationship. He didn't tell them about Eleanor since she was soon to be part of his past.

"Son, I don't expect you to come back here and work the farm," Robert said firmly. "I know that's not your true calling."

"Thanks, Dad. I'm happy to help when needed, but I have a feeling Freddie will take me on full-time, and he's already hooked me up with a national magazine publisher. I think I'll be able to make a decent living right here in my hometown."

"Be safe, and hurry back," Charlotte added. "We've gotten used to having you around here, and it's been quite nice." She smiled.

"I will, but you still have me through tomorrow. Freddie wants me to attend the town council meeting tomorrow night and finish the story of Myrtle and her beloved tree."

"That Myrtle is a character," Charlotte laughed and rolled her eyes.

Almost as on cue, the ladies came in from the front porch.

"Those skeeters are out in full force tonight," the nurse said, shuddering as she came inside. "I'm shutting the door. Those bloodsuckers will find a way to come through that screen so they can nibble on me some more."

43

City hall was packed. Rob wasn't sure if it was because people honestly cared one way or the other about the big oak tree or if they wanted to see the show that Myrtle was sure to give. Everyone knew how dramatic she was when she wanted to be.

As the representative of the press, Rob had a reserved front-row seat along with Freddie, who would take the photos. A reporter from the neighboring town was given a seat next to them. It seems as if Myrtle was gaining fame in the whole north Florida region, Rob mused.

"Who knows," Freddie leaned over and whispered to Rob, "this might end up in a national magazine or paper, and you'll be the head reporter." He winked at the younger man, but Rob couldn't see a silly story about an old woman and her love for a tree going national.

Mayor Thompson hit his gavel to signal the start of the meeting. The noise of the crowd died down at once, and Rob noted on his pad the starting time.

He scanned the room and saw many folks standing in the back due to a lack of chairs, and some were craning their necks around the doorway, hoping to see the action. Mr. Jenkins, the town manager, was sitting at a small table to the left of the council bench. The five council members were seated in a row with nameplates in front of them. Mrs. Smith, the town clerk and only female in the group, was seated to the right of the council. She had her pencil poised and ready to take notes.

The mayor explained to the crowd that there was to be no excessive noise and no name-calling. There were two town deputies in the room, along with the county sheriff. Anyone who got out of line would be removed immediately. Rob glanced over at Sheriff Pete, who was leaning against the wall by the door, arms folded across his chest. He didn't look like he expected any kind of trouble tonight.

First to be called to the podium was the town planner, Mr. Jenkins. He was dressed in a suit and tie and looked as though he was prepared to go to a legal battle. He had drawings of the road with the tree, which included the proposed surrounding neighborhood. He gave copies to each council member and to Rob and the other reporter.

"Thank you, Mr. Mayor, and the council for inviting me to speak tonight," he began.

"The town has hired me to plan for future growth, and I take my responsibility very seriously," he paused for effect as his eyes scanned the crowd. "Right now, we have a sweet little town with quaint shops, a little restaurant that we all enjoy visiting and socializing in, and every other amenity we need within a few block radius. We have our own newspaper," he nodded towards Freddie, "a funeral home, pharmacy, tobacco warehouse, and even a photography studio. We are set, right?"

He waited a moment for the crowd to respond and smiled when many in the room smiled and nodded their approval.

"However," he paused again to make sure he had everyone's attention. "It is 1962. What is our town going to look like in 20 years or even 10? Will we have everything we need? Will our children have everything they need? We must consider the growth of this town." Another pause for effect, and there were murmurs in the crowd again.

"My concern with this tree," he drawled slowly and loudly, "is for the safety of this community. If this town wants growth, and you know we need it for the future of our children and grandchildren, we have to make sacrifices." There were a few mumbles throughout the room, and Mr. Thompson banged his gavel twice, warning the crowd.

"The road that this tree sits on, and might I add, sits in the very center of, is a road that feeds to a main artery, i.e., a road coming into our town from the county. That main artery, which is a county road, connects to the main artery, a state road, which runs east and west through our entire county. The tree in question is only a block off that main artery. In a few years, this will be an area of heavy traffic."

Rob glanced at Myrtle, who was sitting at the end of the first row. She had her arms crossed over her chest, and her lips were pursed so tight they were almost blue. He saw her biting her bottom lip to keep from speaking out before her turn.

"There is a small area on each side of this large tree for traffic to come in or go out. We call that ingress and egress," he chuckled as if educating a class of children and then paused for dramatic effect and to give the council members time to absorb his words.

"We must consider the safety of our citizens," Mr. Jenkins began again. He swept his arm towards the crowd to make them feel it was each of them he was showing concern for.

"The tree blocks the view of oncoming traffic from either direction. This neighborhood will have children playing in their yards, and if the tree is left as is, it will cause them to have smaller yards with very little room to play." He paused again for dramatic effect.

"As you see from my drawings, we are keeping the two current homes on either side of the tree. They are historic and have been well maintained. They will add that touch of historic charm and character for future generations to enjoy. I think you will see how much more feasible it is to keep the homes and let the trees go. If the tree stays, we will have to consider tearing down those beautiful homes."

"Can we have a copy of that drawin'?" one of the farmers yelled from the back of the room.

"Mrs. Smith can make you a copy when the meeting is over," the mayor said.

Mr. Jenkins continued. "I ask you," he paused for effect and stared at each council member as he called his name, "Mayor Thompson, Mr. Johnson, Mr. Sale, Mr. Flowers, and Mr. Green to consider the future of our town. And for the safety of our citizens, allow me to do my job as the town planner. The job that you hired me to do. I think we can all agree that losing one tree is a small sacrifice for the future plans of our town."

He glanced at the council members once more and then turned to the audience.

"Thank you all for your concern and for allowing me to share our vision for the future growth of our wonderful little town."

"Thank you, Mr. Jenkins," the mayor said. "We'll open the floor now for questions."

There were some murmurs in the crowd, and then one gentleman stood and cleared his throat.

"This might be a dumb question," he started, "but have you thought of moving the street since it has to be built anyway?"

"No question is dumb," Mr. Jenkins answered, "and we have thought about that. But as you know, this little street also feeds into the high school, so we would have to come up with a whole new traffic pattern for the school and that could get costly."

"I understand, and thank you, sir," the gentleman sat down.

No one else asked a question, so Mr. Thompson thanked Mr. Jenkins and asked him to take his seat.

"Next, we'll ask Myrtle to come up and speak to us."

The crowd broke into applause as Myrtle moved to the front of the room. Mr. Thompson banged his gavel again.

"Now I ain't no town planner," she began once the room got quiet. "I guess I'm just a crotchety old woman." There was laughter from the crowd.

"But let me tell you something," Rob was writing and trying to catch every word. "If you studied the history of this town, you'd know that tree was planted by someone very special to many of us. My great grandfather, Jesse Brown, planted that tree right before he went to fight in the Civil War."

There were sprinklings of "that's right" and "oh my" muttered throughout the room.

"He told my great-grandmother Rose to water it every day until he returned. They had a brand new baby, my grandfather, and my great-granddaddy promised to return in just a few months. He said it would then be his turn to water the tree." She paused for a moment.

"Now, how many of you know who Jesse Brown was?"

About half of the hands in the audience were raised.

"As many of you know, he had three brothers, and many of you came from that stock. He was also the first school superintendent of the county, which is why his house was so close to the school."

Heads were nodding.

"Well, my great grandaddy Jesse never made it home from the war. And great Grandma Rose watered that tree every day of her life. She taught her son, Jesse, Jr., about the tree, and when Jesse, Jr., my grandaddy, married my grandma, he carved their initials in that tree. And my grandaddy was a businessman who owned a feed and grain store on the edge of town. He helped many of you and your parents and grandparents through the depression when money was scarce."

Myrtle studied each council member one by one, making sure she made direct eye contact with each of them.

"To some of you, that's just an old tree. And I guess it is," she said firmly. "But it holds a part of our town's history. And if you aren't related to the Browns like I am, you can rest assured that the Browns touched your family in some way."

Rob saw Mr. Jenkins sitting across the room with his arms folded across his chest and a scowl on his face. He wished Freddie could get a picture of him.

Myrtle walked back to her chair and picked up a stack of papers.

As she approached the council again, she said, "Now, I ain't no engineer with a big college degree or anything, but I have given this a lot of thought. I took some measurements around that tree, and I've drawn everything out on this piece of paper. I made copies for all of you." She passed them out to the same people that Mr. Jenkins had, but she didn't give him a copy. She gave one to Rob and the other reporter. When Rob glanced over it, he smiled. Turns out, old mean Myrtle was a pretty smart cookie.

"If you look at this drawing, I showed how you can make a one-way road to the left of the tree for traffic to come in off the main road. It will then take the cars through the little neighborhood and down to the school, where traffic already flows in one direction. Traffic will move to the left in front of the school, and then cars can exit either right or left. The street on the left can be one-way only back to the main road. Seems pretty simple to me."

The room erupted in applause. Mr. Jenkins was frowning.

The mayor banged the gavel several times to quiet the crowd.

"Myrtle, would you hand one of those papers to Mr. Jenkins, please?" the mayor asked.

"More than happy to," she replied as she smiled and handed her plan to the town planner.

"Mr. Jenkins, do you see any reason why Myrtle's plan

wouldn't work?" the mayor asked.

Rob watched the expression change on the town planner's face. He slowly realized that Myrtle's plan would work, but he had to save face in front of the town. Her plan would cost practically nothing to implement. He had been so focused on removing the tree to make a bigger road he had overlooked what she came up with.

"Well, Mayor," Mr. Jenkins started as he rose from his seat.

"I do believe we could make that work. It will take a little planning and some official measuring, some new signage, but," he pretended to be thinking the plan through, "but, yes, I believe Myrtle stumbled onto something."

"Stumbled my foot," Myrtle muttered.

The council made an official motion, with a second, and the vote was unanimous to have Mr. Jenkins draw up new plans that would keep the tree and reroute the traffic.

When the meeting adjourned, several people crowded around Myrtle to congratulate her on her victory. Freddie took a picture of Mrytle and Mayor Thompson shaking hands and another one with the entire council gathered around Myrtle. She had become the town hero.

Once the crowd dispersed, Rob told Freddie he was going to the newspaper office to write his story so he could get an early start on the road in the morning. He handed Freddie the letter he had written to Patti and asked him to give it to her after he left. Freddie slapped the younger man on the back and wished him a safe journey.

"Get back here as fast as you can," he winked at Rob.

44

The drive back to Atlanta was uneventful and much more comfortable than the bus ride going south had been. Rob arrived close to 3 pm, just missing rush hour traffic.

When he unlocked the door to his apartment, he almost felt as if he were in someone else's home. He had only been gone three weeks, but now the apartment that had been his place of haven felt foreign to him. He recognized his things, but they no longer held the sentiments they had just a few weeks ago. The life he had built in this vibrant city no longer appealed to him.

Rob looked around the rooms, remembering how he had left things after his frantic departure. Eleanor had obviously been there and tidied up after he left. The coffee cup he had left in the sink was clean and in the dish drainer. The dirty towels were gone from his bathroom, and the bed was made much neater than he ever made it. He had only taken a few clothes with him when he headed south, and he had left those in Florida. He had plenty more to pack up in his apartment.

He thought about calling Eleanor at work, but he didn't want to have her excited that he had come home when he would just be leaving in a day or so. He assumed it would be best if he just showed up at her apartment a little later.

Since he had a couple of hours to kill, he pulled his old suitcase from under the bed. This was the same one he had left home with four years ago, and it felt good to start packing again. Gathering his clothes was the easy part. Luckily, the apartment had been furnished when he rented it, so he didn't have to worry about the heavy stuff. The mismatched dishes and pots he had bought at Goodwill and yard sales he would pack tomorrow and donate them back to Goodwill. Feeling detached from everything made it easy to leave it behind.

He decided to take a walk downtown one last time. As he walked down the sidewalk toward the center of town, he admired the tall buildings with their sleek windows and modern architecture. But they didn't hold the draw to him they once did.

Maybe one day, he could bring Patti to visit along with other places he always wanted to travel to. It would be nice to visit such places with her but then always return home to their special little community.

He stopped at the sleek glass door to the office in which he had a job waiting. Now wasn't the time to tell them he wasn't taking the job even though he was extremely grateful. He owed it to Eleanor to hear the news first. Everybody else could wait until tomorrow.

He sat down on one of the benches outside of a department store and watched the people passing by. Everyone was in a hurry to reach their next destination. Not one of them stopped to admire the beauty of the architecture around them or the dimming light of day as the sun began its descent behind the tall buildings. Most were businessmen running to their next meeting or trying to get home to their wives, who would have dinner waiting on the table.

He could pick out the tourists as they were normally a young family, and they would stop and point up at the buildings. He smiled at one dad, looking at a map, trying to figure out where they were and where they needed to go next.

The hustle and bustle that he used to love was still going on.

Just a few weeks ago, he was part of that life, hurrying to get to the next interview or impress a would-be editor. Now, he enjoyed sitting on the sideline, watching the seeming chaos around him.

He thought back to the story he wrote last night. The decision on which perspective to write from was a difficult one. In reality, Myrtle was the hero. She had come up with a solution for the road that the educated and experienced town planner had missed. He had obviously been embarrassed that he had not seen the same solution. His focus had been solely on removing a tree that he felt was not necessary. Had he taken a step back from the situation and looked at the road from all angles, he might have come up with the same plan as Myrtle.

However, Myrtle's passion for saving the tree forced her to look for another alternative, and that is the way he wrote the story. Mr. Jenkins would be able to keep his dignity in the community with the way Rob had presented it. Myrtle would be a celebrity for what she did. And it was her belief and passion that forced her to look outside the box.

Rob gazed up at the tall buildings again and realized that he, too, had been in a box. He had talked himself into believing that the only way to have a successful career as a journalist was to be in a big city where the important news happened. He had not looked outside the box where stories could be found anywhere, even in small towns. Heck, even a reporter from the larger town nearby had come to cover their tree excitement. Rob chuckled at his own thoughts.

45

Freshly showered and casually dressed, Rob left his apartment at exactly 6 pm and headed two flights up to Eleanor's place. If she followed her normal routine, she would have come home around 5:30, changed into comfortable house clothes, fixed herself a glass of wine, and settled on the couch to watch Walter Cronkite on the news.

She had just started working for a large television network, and Walter was her idol. That would be her one day, she often said to Rob. He hated to interrupt her time with Walter, but if she had a meeting or event to go to later, he might not catch her today. And he wanted to get this over with as soon as possible.

"Rob! Oh my God, am I glad to see you!" Eleanor threw her arms around him after opening the door. She hadn't answered at first, so he had to knock a couple of times before she came to the door.

"Hi, Eleanor," he said with reserve in his voice and hugged her back. Normally, he would have used a term of endearment, such as baby or honey. She didn't seem to notice, however, as she took him by the hand and pulled him into the apartment. She put her arms around him again and held her face up for a kiss. Deep breath, he thought to himself and kissed her lightly on the lips. He sighed when they pulled apart. There had been no feeling in the kiss, at least for him.

"Rob, come in and sit down. Can I pour you a cocktail? You seem tired." Eleanor sensed the difference in him. Rob walked into the living room and glanced around. There were boxes stacked in the corner with labels showing small kitchen appliances, dishes, linens, and other items needed to set up house.

"Shit," he thought. She had either been buying for a new house or had been thrown a bridal shower by her friends. Either way, this was going to be harder than he thought. He also noticed the big diamond he had spent most of his savings on was sparkling bright on her finger.

"A drink would be nice," he said as he walked over to the pile of packages.

"Aren't you excited," she squealed. "The girls at work threw me a shower last week. We got some really nice gifts!" Walter was talking in the background, giving his viewers an update on the Cuban missile crisis. He thought how Myrtle's victory paled in comparison to the world's issues.

Eleanor came up behind him and put the drink in his hand. He took a sip and realized he had not tasted bourbon in over three weeks. It was good but stung a little as it went down his throat. His parents would never allow bourbon or any kind of alcohol in their home.

"So, tell me all about Florida," Eleanor was saying as she led him to the sofa. "You must be so glad to be out of that bug-infested swamp," she laughed. "And look at you, all nice and tan. Did you work in the crops every day?"

Rob noticed that she didn't mention his family. He couldn't remember if or when she had asked about his parents, Connie's death, or Betty's childbirth. The words 'bug-infested swamp' kept running through his head.

He already knew the rest of this conversation was not going to go well. How did he think he loved someone so shallow? She had been here having parties and showers and being self-absorbed while her chosen life partner was in his hometown dealing with a family tragedy. And she couldn't even ask him about it.

He realized at that moment that he had never been in love with her. He loved the idea of having a successful wife who would have pushed him to have a successful career in a world that was completely foreign to him. He had let those ideals overshadow his true self and the idea of true love.

He set his drink down on the coffee table and turned to face her.

"Eleanor, we need to talk," he said flatly. "Please turn the television off."

She glanced at her beloved Walter Cronkite talking on the small black-and-white screen. She had such a crush on him, and it was her evening ritual to sit and watch him with a glass of wine or a cocktail in hand. From the tone of Rob's voice, however, she could tell she would be missing Walter tonight.

Eleanor gracefully rose from the couch, walked over to the little television set, and switched it off. She had no idea what was on Rob's mind, but she felt in her heart that he was about to drop a bombshell. She quickly thought about how to implement plan B and drop her own bombshell. She turned to face him.

"I'm starving, darling. Aren't you hungry?" She smiled her sweetest smile and held out her hand.

"Let's walk down to that little café on the corner and grab a bite. We can talk there."

As much as Rob wanted to get this behind him, he realized that he had not eaten since breakfast. All of a sudden, he was famished, and his energy was fading fast. The idea also hit him that if he broke the news in a public setting, her reaction may be lessened. He had no idea that she had the same plan.

After they were seated and the waitress had their order, they leaned back in their chairs with cocktails in hand. Rob didn't usually drink cocktails back to back, but he needed to maintain his courage for the battle he was about to face. Seeing all the gifts in Eleanor's apartment made the engagement a reality. Family and friends were involved, so it was going to be even harder to break off.

They made small talk for a while. Eleanor told him about her recent interviews with city officials and how thrilled she was at having real air time on television.

"I can take you down to the station tomorrow and ask one of the boys to replay it for you," she smiled excitedly.

"I'm sure you did a beautiful job," he smiled back but did not match her excitement.

Then she dropped the first bombshell.

"I got my wedding dress!" she blurted out and clapped her hands. "It's so beautiful. You are just going to love it!"

Rob smiled, knowing the smile didn't make it to his eyes to show the pleasure that he knew she wanted.

"Darling, aren't you excited? Everything is coming together so well. I know we haven't set a date, but I was thinking we could go ahead and plan something soon. The alterations on the dress will be done next week, so I can pick it up. My sister is going to get all the flowers ready, and Mother has already ordered a cake. All we have to do is order you a tuxedo and reserve the church. We'll just keep it a small affair with family and close friends. Do you think your family would come?"

She gazed at him with the most innocent expression she could muster.

Luckily, before he answered, the waitress brought their food. Rob downed his drink and held up the glass for another one.

"My my, you are drinking a lot tonight. Did you turn into a raging alcoholic down in Florida?"

He studied her for a moment before speaking.

"Actually, I didn't drink any alcohol while in Florida. I was too busy making funeral arrangements for my sister and taking care of my parents once they were discharged from intensive care. And I was too busy working on the farm that my family has had for generations. So, no, my darling, I did not turn into a raging alcoholic in Florida." He couldn't stop the bitterness in his voice.

He watched as the color drained from her face, and she set her mouth in a tight line. He saw her nibbling her bottom lip to either keep from crying or from lashing out at him.

"You've changed, Rob," she hissed. "You are not the same man who left here three weeks ago."

Rob took a deep breath and swallowed hard.

"Let's eat before our food gets cold," he said with no inflection in his words. "Then we'll talk."

They ate in silence. She barely ate but pushed her food around on her plate with her mind whirling in many directions. He ate most of his food because he was starving, and he knew food would take the edge off the alcohol. He was already feeling braver than he should, and he wanted to be able to choose his words wisely and let her down gently.

He tried to remember how one intoxicated night turned into an engagement with a ring he could barely afford, a full-blown wedding with a dress, gifts, flowers, and a preacher. After she talked him into buying a ring, they did not discuss the details. They hadn't set a date; no venue had been picked out. They had not even made a formal announcement.

Now, he comes home and is told he's about to walk down the aisle. Jesus. He put his fork down and scanned the café. Luckily, it was fairly busy, so maybe she wouldn't make a scene.

"Penny for your thoughts," she flashed that sweet smile at him again and covered his hand with hers.

"I know this is all happening so fast, and I'm sorry I didn't keep you informed. It was hard to reach you down there in Florida. Your parents' phone was busy all the time, and you didn't call me very often."

"You're right, I didn't," he conceded. "As I already mentioned, I was pretty busy with my family. For what it's worth, my parents are both still in wheelchairs, needing around-the-clock care, and my older sister just gave birth to her second child. We've had a lot going on."

Eleanor lit up a cigarette, and he watched as she inhaled and then leaned back in her chair and blew smoke in his direction. She held the pack of cigarettes towards him, and he shook his head. He looked around and realized he was probably the only one in the restaurant not smoking, but he didn't care for the taste or the smell.

"Eleanor," he sighed, trying to choose his words carefully. "I dreaded going home more than you can imagine. I left my family on bad terms, and as you know, we didn't speak for four years. We probably would still not be speaking if it weren't for that horrible accident and the loss of my younger sister." She was taking in every word, and her silence gave him courage.

"But what I realized once I was back on my home soil is that family roots run very deep. No matter how mad you get with each other or how much you think you hate each other, your family is your root system. And those roots are hard, tough to break."

She just kept looking at him, slowly smoking her cigarette. Her eyes were narrowed ever so slightly.

"I think you understand that. You have a close-knit family."

"My family is now your family, darling. We talked about that," she said with a hint of coldness in her voice.

"Yes, we did talk about that. And I thought I had cut ties with my family. When I walked away from my parents and sisters and didn't hear from them again, I believed they had cut me out, too. But even my father welcomed me with open arms after all the hurtful things he had said to me. We lost the baby of our family, and that tragedy brought us back together in a way I never imagined."

She continued to stare at him.

"Your family is wonderful and loving, and I hope you never face a loss like we've had. But they are not my blood family. We don't have a past together."

"But we do have a future," she quickly interjected.

"Eleanor," he paused and took her hand this time. He looked directly into her eyes. He saw no sign of tears, but he saw an expression that caused a shudder deep in his belly.

"I don't think we are going to have a future," he said gently. He watched the color drain from her face for the second time this evening. She slowly withdrew her hand from his.

"I'm moving back to Florida," he said flatly.

She just stared at him for what seemed like an eternity, and when she finally spoke, her words made him nauseous to the core of his very being.

"You can't leave me, darling," she said coldly. She paused for dramatic effect and then dropped the bombshell. "We're going to have a baby."

He couldn't have had the breath knocked out of him any harder if she had punched him in the gut.

"What?" This time, the color drained from his face. "How?" He was confused.

"If you don't know how then you lived in those sticks way too long," she mocked him.

"I know how, but the only night that was a blackout for me was the night I got drunk and stayed in your apartment. The night I woke up, and we were engaged." He was the one with the cold stare now.

"Bingo," she said with sarcasm.

The waitress brought the check. She could feel the tension between them, so she laid the check next to Rob and walked away.

"I need time to think and to process all of this," Rob said wearily. He took out his wallet and pulled out enough money to cover the bill and tip.

"Eleanor, I need some fresh air. Let me do some thinking, and we'll talk again tomorrow," he stood up to leave.

She studied him for a moment with a mixed expression on her face.

"Don't take too long," she smirked at him. "The clock is ticking," she paused and then added, "Tik tok."

He turned and walked out of the café. Not sure where he wanted to be at the moment, he just started walking. The town he once loved and admired was now becoming a prison to him.

How in the world had he let himself fall into such a predicament? He had known Eleanor for four years, and when they first met, he admired her spunk and ambition. She was a beautiful young college student who knew all the right people to help him in his chosen field of study. They had worked on the school newspaper together, co-writing articles and interviewing professors and even the university president for one story. They were a solid team, so it was only natural when they became a couple and fell in love. At least, he thought it was love. But no kiss and no smile from her had ever touched him the way Patti's did.

Darkness was falling, but the streets were still alive with people. No doubt about it. Atlanta was an amazing city for those who wanted a busy life. But already, he missed the evening sounds of crickets chirping and frogs singing their tunes. The north Florida sunsets were magnificent. You had to drive far out of the city to catch one of those in Atlanta.

He found his way back to his apartment. While he had calmed down slightly, he was still agitated, and fury began to set in. He couldn't be upset at Eleanor. He was upset with himself for being so careless and, for now, having to break Patti's heart a second time. The suitcase he had packed was still on the bed.

He shoved it on the floor and sat down on the edge of the bed. He cried out in anguish and began to sob. At last, he slid off the bed onto the floor and sobbed until he could barely breathe.

46

"Darling, wake up so we can talk," Rob could barely open his eyes. They were swollen from all of the tears he had shed. He finally fell asleep on the floor at about 4 am and then dragged himself up on the bed, where he was restless for the rest of the night. He must have just fallen into a relaxed, deep sleep, and now he heard a voice bringing him back into the light of day.

"Rob, darling, I don't understand why you are so upset," he opened his eyes fully and looked into Eleanor's sparkling blue eyes. She was beautiful, there was no doubt about it.

"We're going to have a baby, a little bit of you and a little bit of me," she said softly through her smile. "Don't you want children?"

Rob blew out a sigh. Of course, he wanted children. But when the time was right. He had not even gotten his career off the ground, and now the mother of his child was a woman whom he realized he never really loved.

"Why don't you freshen up while I fix you a cup of coffee," Eleanor was still talking. "I don't have my first meeting until 9, so we've got a little time," she rubbed her hand lightly across his face.

"You're going to make a wonderful father," she smiled and sashayed off the bed.

He crawled out of bed, pulled on a t-shirt and yesterday's blue jeans, and headed for the bathroom. He splashed water over his face, trying to ease the puffiness in his eyes. When he stepped out, Eleanor handed him a steaming cup of coffee and smiled.

"Talk to me, Rob," she looked at him with anxiety in her voice. When he didn't respond, she continued talking.

"I know this isn't what we expected, but for the life of me, I can't understand why you're so upset. We've been together four years, and I've never seen you upset like this."

They sat at his little breakfast nook in the kitchen, and he sipped the hot liquid. It felt good going down and helped to lift the fog in his brain.

"Eleanor," he began. "I don't mean to make this hard on you. I'm just caught off guard. You've always told me how you wanted a career more than anything. We never even talked about children. When I left for Florida three weeks ago, we were just talking about a wedding. We hadn't even set a date. Now I come home, and you have a dress, shower gifts, and we have to get married in the next two weeks. This isn't at all how I pictured this all going down," he searched her eyes for a hint of what she was feeling, but they remained steel blue. He couldn't quite decipher her facial expression, but she didn't look like she was going to cry. In fact, she was tapping one foot and showing more agitation than sadness.

"Going down?" she snapped. "This is our life we are talking about."

"You're right. It is our life, and now we have another life to consider," he conceded, running a hand through his uncombed hair.

She smiled, knowing that he finally acknowledged their child to be.

"I was in shock last night," he continued. "Let me make some phone calls today and get my life in order so I can be the kind of husband and father-to-be that you deserve." he swallowed hard and almost choked on his words. "I've got to talk to the paper here and make sure I still have a job, and," he hesitated, "I've got some loose ends to tie up back in Florida."

"Well, I have a feeling one of those loose ends might be a girl," she watched for a change in his facial expression but saw none.

"I just have to talk to an old friend," he said and left it at that.

He took both of their empty mugs to his sink and rinsed them out before putting them in the dish drainer. When he turned around, she was smiling at him with her head tilted. He tried to smile back but only managed a lopsided grin.

"What?" he said.

"Rob Mathis, you're going to make one hell of a soul mate. We can have our careers and our babies. I just know it." She put her arms around his neck and reached in to kiss him. He kissed her back gently because that's what fiancés and fathers-to-be do. He just hoped to God that one day he felt something special in her kiss.

47

The first person Rob wanted to talk to was his mentor and friend. After he showered and straightened up his little apartment, he sat down at the phone nook and dialed the newspaper office. Mary Anne answered on the second ring. He didn't want to make small talk, especially with the long-distance charges, but if he blew her off, the secretary would know something was wrong.

"Morning, Mary Anne. You're sounding bright and cheery early in the day," he said.

"Good morning to you, Rob. I wish I could say the same thing, but you don't sound so cheery," she could always read his moods.

"Sorry. Atlanta mornings aren't as soothing as they are in north Florida. And, this is costing me money for every minute we speak," he tried to laugh to take the edge off. "Is Freddie in?"

"He sure is, doll. Just one quick thing. Patti was in a much happier mood yesterday. Just thought you'd want to know."

"Glad to hear," and he took a deep breath.

"Good morning, my boy," Freddie's voice boomed on the line when Mary Anne transferred the call. "Things going well in Atlanta?"

"Not at all, Freddie," Rob answered. "I need some advice. It seems my situation here has turned sticky."

"Hang on, and let me shut my office door."

Freddie was back on the line in just a moment. "What's going on?"

Rob filled him in on everything. The pregnancy, the quickly planned wedding, and his heartbreak over Patti.

"I can deal with the mess I've gotten myself into," he said flatly. "But the thought of breaking that girl's heart a second time is killing me," he tried to hold back his tears.

"I know she's trying to rush you into this," Freddie said with authority, "but, son, don't do anything too rash. Try to buy some time."

"Why?" Rob was confused. "She said if we don't marry soon, people will figure out that the baby was conceived before we were married. I don't want to bring a child into this world with a stigma on his head."

"You are a journalist," Freddie said. "Journalists investigate. Make sure you have uncovered every truth before you commit yourself."

"This is a sweet woman whom I've been with for four years. She was with me during some of my darkest times in college. I have no doubt she loves me, and I don't believe she would deceive me."

"I'm not saying that she is," Freddie answered. "But you owe it to yourself to be sure. You said you don't remember anything about the night you were intimate and got engaged. Start from there, my friend. I'm here for you any time you need me. Call collect if you want."

"Thanks, Freddie. You always put things into perspective for me. I'll get the car back to you in a few days."

"I'm not worried, my boy. Keep it as long as you need. I've got my old truck to rattle around town in. Promise me you won't rush into anything."

"I promise," Rob said, and they hung up.

While Eleanor was at work, Rob took Freddie's advice and tried to recreate that fateful night six weeks ago. Since it had happened in Eleanor's apartment, he used his key to let himself in. Her apartment was larger than his. While he had a studio with his bed tucked into a corner of the great room, she had a one-bedroom unit with separate rooms.

He walked into the bedroom and closed his eyes, trying to remember that night. They had been at a party in a co-worker's place in the same building. He remembered having one cocktail. He was never one to drink excessively, even back in the dorm when his classmates would have all-night parties. He always kept his wits about him. Yet, Eleanor had told him that he had gotten so intoxicated she had to practically carry him to her place.

He didn't remember anything after that first cocktail until he woke up with a splitting headache the next morning. How could he have made love for the first time in his life and not remember it? That was so unlike him. He walked around her familiar apartment, and no matter how hard he tried, no memories of that night came back to him. All he could remember was her smile the next morning when he woke up in her bed, buck naked. She told him what a wonderful night they'd had and how she said yes without hesitation when he'd asked her to marry him.

Rob left her apartment, and since he would soon be a husband and a father, he figured he'd better touch base with his new boss and make sure he still had a job. Even though he had not officially begun working for the newspaper, his boss had promised to hold his position open while he took care of his family. At the time, he had appreciated the gesture. Now, he felt it was one more tie binding him to this place.

48

When Rob and Eleanor moved to downtown Atlanta, they already had jobs lined up with the same communications company. He would be in the newspaper division, and she landed her dream job in the mass communications department. They chose their apartments so they could walk to work and just use a cab service if they needed to branch further away for interviews or nightlife. Otherwise, everything they needed was within a short walk. So, it didn't take Rob long to reach his destination.

The receptionist who greeted him was nothing like MaryAnne. She was older, and her shoulder-length brown hair turned up in a flip, a style he noticed on many girls these days. She wore a sleek, bright blue suit that showed off her trim figure and looked at him over the rim of her glasses.

"May I help you?" she said in a most businesslike manner.

"Yes, ma'am," he cleared his throat. She would be a tough cookie to get past if she didn't think you were worthy of entering the establishment.

"I'm Rob Mathis. I don't have an appointment, but I was hoping to see …"

"Rob, of course!" The receptionist got up and hurried around her desk to greet him.

"I'm Julia, and we haven't met, but I've heard everything

about you," she gushed at him. "I'm so sorry to hear about the tragedy that your family has endured. How are your parents?"

Wow, Rob thought. Gossip spread as quickly in Atlanta as it did in rural north Florida.

"Thank you for asking," Rob answered, bewildered that she seemed to know so much about him. "They are getting along well. It's been a big adjustment for them, but they are strong."

"Good to hear, sugar," she said, and she teetered on her heels back behind her desk.

"Mr. Webb is in a meeting, but I'll let him know you're here. He'll be delighted to see you. Welcome home!" she exclaimed as she strode to the back, where Rob assumed Mr. Webb's office was.

He sat down in the reception area to wait, hoping that Eleanor would not come this way. He wasn't ready to face her again just yet.

He surveyed the area and noticed that everything was sleek and shiny, with a lot of windows looking out over the city. This place didn't compare at all to Freddie's newspaper office, which had no windows and was dark and dingy inside. The openness made him uncomfortable, but he wasn't sure why. The building was several stories tall, and the ding of the elevator and the number of people coming and going was an overload to his senses. He felt like he was in a fog and just moving forward with the duties he needed to perform. This was not where he wanted to be.

"Follow me, hon. Mr. Webb is ready to see you, and he's thrilled that you're here!" Julia's southern drawl brought him back to reality, and he got up to follow her to wherever Mr. Webb's office was. His initial interview for the job was in a conference room on the other side of the building, so he had not seen this area before. He dutifully followed Julia down a long corridor, and she ushered him into a bright office with an oversized picture window. His new boss stood as soon as he entered.

"Rob, it's great to see you," he said as he stood and shook Rob's hand.

"Thank you, Mr. Webb, and I appreciate you holding the position open for me."

"Please, call me Jim. We're very informal around here," Jim's smile was welcoming. "Holding your position open was the right thing to do. Besides, we are excited to have you on board. You came with an outstanding portfolio from college, and your professors were very complimentary of your work. And Freddie couldn't say enough good about you."

That last sentence took Rob by surprise.

"You know Freddie from my hometown?"

"I don't know him personally, but he and my dad have been friends for years. They met at Florida State when they were in college and have stayed in touch ever since. My dad sat in on your interview. He was excited to hire one of Freddie's protégés."

Rob was surprised. Freddie had never mentioned that he had gone to college. He assumed his mentor had learned on the job working beside his father.

"Freddie is a fine man," was all Rob could think of to say.

The men sat down in the side chairs in front of Jim's desk.

"So, are you ready to start work?" Jim flashed him a smile.

"I am," Rob said and tried not to show anxiety over taking a job he no longer wanted. "I need to run back down to Florida this weekend," he added. "Freddie loaned me his car, so I want to get it back to him."

Jim looked a little confused as to why Rob would drive to Atlanta only to have to turn around in three days and drive back, but he didn't ask any questions.

"Alright. Today is Thursday. No need to start on a Friday, so how does Monday sound for a first day?"

"Sounds great," Rob agreed and managed to smile.

"Welcome aboard," Jim said as the men rose from their seats. He gave Rob a friendly slap on the shoulder.

"You've got a great future here. I just know it. You and that fiancé of yours are going to make a dynamic duo. You'll both go places, that's for sure."

"Thanks," Rob said. "I appreciate your faith in me. In both of us."

Jim escorted him to the door and pointed the way back to the receptionist.

"I'll see you on Monday, Julia," he said as he walked by her desk.

"I'm looking forward to it, sugar," she answered back.

The sun was shining high in the Atlanta sky, but Rob felt like he was drowning in a huge fog. He arrived yesterday to pack up and return to North Florida. In less than 24 hours, he found out he was going to be a father, he was getting married in less than two weeks, and he was starting a hot-shot job on Monday.

His world was spinning completely out of control, and he didn't know how to stop it. The one person he wanted to talk to was mad at him, and he had high hopes of shutting down this life and getting her to open up her world to him. Now, that seemed like a lost dream.

His stomach rumbled, and Rob realized he had not eaten since last night before Eleanor dropped the bombshell. After that news, he hadn't finished his dinner.

One of his favorite spots was a little deli close to his apartment building. Since the lunch crowd had already thinned out, he easily found a spot in the corner by the window where he could watch the outside world. He loved to watch the flow of people as they went about their daily routines.

He sighed and wished he could bring Patti here to see all of the sights. Maybe she would fall in love with the city like he had. His first trip to the big city seemed a lifetime ago. He was a scared kid getting off the bus, but it didn't take long for him to adapt.

He made friends easily when he moved into the dorm and sharing a room with guys he had never met came second nature to him. While he didn't join in their party scene, they accepted him and loved to tease their "country boy" friend.

He met Eleanor that first semester and the two became inseparable. With similar goals, they studied hard together and became best friends. In their junior year, he kissed her for the first time, and he thought he had found his true love. With a promising career ahead of him and this sweet girl by his side, Rob knew he could accomplish anything he wanted in life.

He thought about how, in four short years, he had erased from memory the life he left behind in Florida. He hated that life as a child, but he had never given it a chance as an adult. Now, he had to face so many regrets and figure out how to make things right, both in Atlanta and in Florida.

He needed a plan. Freddie cautioned him not to make any quick decisions, but Eleanor was pushing him to get married quickly. He didn't want people counting backward on their fingers when his child was born seven months after their wedding, and they were certainly getting close to that point.

But thoughts of Patti kept flooding his brain and his heart. He had to see her and tell her in person. And he wanted to make sure everything was in order for his parents. Once the baby was born, he would be sure to make regular trips for his or her grandparents to visit. One thing was for sure. He wouldn't keep them out of his life from this point forward.

He paid his bill and went back to his apartment with a plan in place. He would drive to Florida tomorrow morning, talk to Patti in person, and make sure his parents had what they needed. He would catch the bus back to Atlanta on Sunday.

Then he would be ready to start his new job on Monday. And he would be married the following weekend. He had committed to Eleanor, and one thing was for sure. He was a man of his word.

49

Eleanor used her key to let herself into Rob's apartment two minutes after five. He had expected her, so he wasn't surprised. He didn't expect the news she came to deliver, however.

"I have good news!" she exclaimed as she walked to him and put her arms around his neck.

"And what might that be?" He tried to show the affection he was not feeling.

"My parents are throwing us a grand party Saturday night. Sort of an engagement/pre-wedding party for our friends and family. I know it's last minute, but my mother has been on the phone all day inviting people. She asked for your parents' number so she could invite them."

Rob was taken back, and he pushed away from her.

"How can you plan a party without at least asking me? You know I have to go back to Florida this weekend." His anger was mounting, but he tried hard not to show how much.

"Darling, I'm sorry. Mother is so excited that you're back. You agreed to the wedding next weekend, so there's no other time. And she thought she was helping by having your parents come here."

"Have you forgotten they are both in wheelchairs?" Now, his anger was coming through. "How do you propose they even travel here if they wanted to?"

Eleanor didn't try to hide her tears. She sat down on the edge of his bed and put her head in her hands.

"I'm sorry," she cried. "There is so much going on in my life right now. You come home after three weeks and seem like a stranger to me. My body is doing crazy things, and I'm scared I'm going to lose you. Something is going on that you're not telling me." She gazed up at him with a fearful look on her face.

Rob took a deep breath and ran his hand through his hair. For him, honesty had always been the best policy, but lately, he seemed to be caught in a tangle of deceit.

"Honey, I'm sorry." He sat down next to her. "All of this is happening so fast for me. It's a lot for this guy's brain to process. My baby sister died a few weeks ago. I've had to reconnect with my parents, and my hometown for that matter. And yes, I did reconnect with my high school sweetheart."

She flinched at the thought of another girl with him.

"But, baby, I promise you. I am committed to you and our child. We have planned a life together, and even though it will be harder with a newborn, you are right. We will make it work. You are smart and brave, and you will be an amazing mother."

She studied him; her eyes were begging for the right answer to her next question.

"Do you still love me?" she asked in barely a whisper.

He hesitated just a second too long. She caught his hesitation, but she didn't let on.

"Of course I do," he said and put his arms around her. "I've just had a whirlwind three weeks, and I have to get my priorities back in order. We'll be fine." He smiled, but it didn't reach his eyes.

And for the first time, he placed his hand on her belly. Then he kissed her.

Change of plans, he thought to himself. He couldn't go to

Florida this weekend or next, if he was going to get married. He couldn't ask for time off now that he had committed to starting his job on Monday. How did life become so damn complicated?

Eleanor took the next day off work so they could shop for party clothes and make plans to combine apartments before the big day. Rob wanted to call Freddie again, but Eleanor was with him almost every second. She came down and fixed him coffee as soon as she knew he would be up. As they sipped the warm beverage, she laid out their plans for the day. While she talked, she lit up a cigarette, and Rob was dismayed that she was still smoking with a baby growing inside of her.

"Do you think it's ok to smoke while you're pregnant?" he asked with concern in his voice. "There has been talk that they may claim cigarettes are harmful to an unborn child."

"I haven't seen any warnings about it. It's just a little smoke. The baby will be fine," she answered flippantly as she blew smoke towards him.

He sighed but didn't say any more. He would address that another time.

While they waited for the stores to open, they munched on bagels and drank more coffee at the corner deli. Eleanor chatted excitedly about the wedding. Her parents had lined up the preacher, and they would hold the ceremony at their home. They hadn't been able to book a church this soon, but her parents had a grand home anyway. The ceremony would be next to the family pool, and there was plenty of room for the reception afterward. Her mother had managed to hire a band so the guests could dance the night away.

"Sounds like quite a big affair," Rob noted.

"We only get married once!" she shot back at him. "I want to have a wedding to remember."

"I think you are getting that," he replied with a hint of sarcasm.

They hailed a cab and headed to Lenox Square so Eleanor

could browse dresses at Rich's Department Store.

"My parents have a credit account here, so we can buy anything we need!" Eleanor was excited.

Rob didn't want to take money from her parents. But after buying the ring and his trip to Florida, he was running low on funds. This affair was much more than he had planned for, and he didn't have much left in his savings account.

He sat in the small waiting area while Eleanor tried on several dresses. Every time she put on a new one, she came out and twirled for him, asking his opinion. Of course, he said each one was beautiful on her, but he was growing weary after about an hour of dress modeling. She eventually settled on a shiny lavender satin gown that showed off her tiny waist. It was sleeveless with a V-neck and beige ribbon accents, including a satin bow at the waist. The beige lace fell gracefully along the pleated skirt that hit just below her knees.

Once that was added to her parents' account, she grabbed Rob's hand, and they rushed into the ladies' shoe department. Rob felt sorry for the patient shoe salesman as he slipped several pairs onto her tiny feet and waited while she pranced up and down the aisle, trying each one out. She squealed with excitement when the salesman opened a shoe box with a pair of beige satin pumps with a beige bow across the top. The toes were so pointed that Rob couldn't imagine how someone could stand in them for long. She chose those, and when Rob looked at the price tag, he almost choked. Eleanor didn't bat an eye when she signed the charge slip.

"Now we have to get you all fixed up," she said as she handed both of her packages to the store porter to hold until they finished shopping.

"You are going to be so beautiful, nobody will care what I'm wearing," he tried to laugh. He was already tired of shopping.

They made their way upstairs to the men's clothing department.

"I want something fast and practical," he told her as Eleanor went through the racks. She pulled out a three-piece brown tweed suit and found a beige button-down shirt. He tried everything on, and it fit well.

"Lovely, darling," she said, eyeing him satisfactorily. She picked out a matching tie and had him try on a pair of brown slip-on leather loafers that fit like a glove. After those items were signed for and given to the porter for safekeeping, Eleanor clapped her hands.

"Let's go buy your tuxedo!"

"Can't we rent that?" Rob was mortified to charge that to her parents. "I'll only wear it once."

"Nonsense. There will be lots of opportunities in our world to wear a tuxedo. It should be a staple in your wardrobe," Eleanor insisted.

Rob took a deep breath and closed his eyes. When he opened them, Eleanor was staring at him with concern on her face. He took her hand and led her to a bench just outside the store entrance.

"Eleanor, I will not go into a marriage totally dependent on your parents for financial support. The suit you just picked out is more than I'll make in a week, and I don't have the funds to cover it."

She started to speak, but he stopped her.

"I'll take that as a wedding gift from your parents. But I am not letting them pay for my attire at my wedding. We will rent a tuxedo, and once we are on our feet financially, I promise I'll buy one then. OK?

She knew from his tone that there was no need to argue. She nodded and led him to the rental section.

When all the clothing needs were settled, Eleanor wanted to browse for furniture.

"Why in the world do we need furniture?" he asked. "We

have two apartments full now. We'll have to scale down when we move into yours."

"I was thinking since we have a baby on the way," Eleanor whispered and chose her next words purposely, "maybe we should see about a larger apartment. You know, one with two bedrooms, so the baby will have a room of her own."

Rob rolled his eyes.

"Eleanor, you are shooting for too much too fast. We have almost eight months to plan, and the baby won't need a room of his own for a while anyway. Let's take this one step at a time."

He was beginning to get exhausted from her growing list of wants. He had never seen her spend money like she was doing today.

"I'm just so excited that everything is coming together. I'm ready to begin our new life together, and a new apartment will be a fresh start," she tried to convince him.

"Living in one apartment together will be a new experience and a fresh start," he reminded her. "We don't have the funds to move right now. When we save up our money, we talk about a bigger place. OK?"

She looked at him coyly and knew she was defeated.

"If you say so," she reached up and pecked him on the cheek. Then, she reluctantly turned away from the furniture.

50

Eleanor's sister picked her up early Saturday morning so the ladies could spend the day together before the party. They told Rob to take a cab and be at the house by 3:30 dressed and ready for the festivities, which started at 4. He was thankful for some time alone. He still didn't have his head wrapped around the drastic turn in his life plans. His world was spinning out of control, and he was helpless to stop it.

While he was sitting at his dinette sipping his morning coffee, he picked up the phone and dialed his parents' number. Hearing his mom's voice would bring some calm to his life. But, no surprise. The line was busy. He chuckled as he imagined Myrtle already on the phone chatting with her friends. The newspaper article about her plan with the tree and the road would have hit the streets yesterday. She would be calling people to make sure they had seen it. Heck, Myrtle had probably been on that phone non-stop since yesterday.

Next, he dialed Freddie's home number. He knew the publisher wouldn't be in the office today, and he was happy to hear his "hello" on the third ring.

"Good morning, Freddie," Rob was thankful to hear his friend's voice.

"Hello, my boy!" Freddie boomed into the receiver. "How are things going in the big city?"

"Moving along very quickly," he answered. "We shopped for furniture and a tuxedo yesterday," Rob continued with little enthusiasm in his voice.

"Now remember, don't move too fast," Freddie cautioned.

"I'm trying not to, but it is impossible to hold her back. "Rob sighed. "Her parents are holding a big soiree this afternoon to honor our engagement. The wedding is lined up for next Saturday. I feel like I'm on a freight train that won't slow down."

"I'm sure you do feel that way, son," there was concern in Freddie's voice. "And there is no way you can talk her into postponing this wedding?"

"Not at all," Rob said. "I'm not even sure I want to. She's already better than six weeks along, according to my calculation. People will be counting backwards on their fingers as it is when this child is born."

"Life can be tough sometimes, son," Freddie sighed. "You know best, and you do what you need to do."

"Thanks, Freddie," Rob hesitated. "I can live with what I've done. Eleanor is not at all a bad woman to have at my side. She's smart and beautiful. She's a little headstrong at times. I just hate what I've done to Patti. I left her once without a word. Then I came back into her life, and I know we had something special," his voice dropped. "And now, I'm walking out on her again."

"I gave her the letter," Freddie said. "I went in for coffee the next day, and she seemed much happier than she was the other day. Just be upfront with her. She knows you're an honorable man. You would never walk out on a child. She'll understand that, even if it hurts."

"I know you're right. And I'm sorry, but I can't get back down there for two more weeks to bring the car and talk to her in person."

"I told you. I'm not worried about that car. I do wish,

however, you could talk with Patti before you become a married man."

"You and me both." Rob sighed.

When the men hung up, Freddie tapped his fingers on his phone table. Something wasn't adding up to him. He decided to call his old college buddy Jim, Sr., and enlist a little help getting to the bottom of what in hell was going on in Atlanta.

Rob spent part of the day measuring the little bit of furniture he owned and deciding what he would take to Eleanor's place after the wedding. He wasn't going to try and move prior to. He already had too much going on next week with the new job. He had already started packing, so he would still donate most of his things to Goodwill. Eleanor had all of the shiny new gifts in her apartment, so they should be set.

He used his key to go into Eleanor's place and decided to look over the gifts she, or they, had received. There were all kinds of kitchen gadgets that he had no idea how to use. A shiny new coffee pot, bath towels engraved with their initials, a clock that was almost bigger than the wall space they had, sets of China, and various dishes and pans. She had been having wedding showers without his knowledge. Interesting.

51

Rob called for a cab to pick him up at 3 pm. He figured the traffic might be heavy, and Eleanor's parents lived outside the city. The new suit was stifling as he waited outside in the afternoon heat. Back in Florida, you only wore suits like that to a wedding or a funeral. This was just a party, for Christ's sake, he thought, and he was in tweed with leather shoes. Luckily, traffic was light, and he arrived at his destination a few minutes early. Eleanor came out to greet him, and he had to admit she was stunning in the dress she had painstakingly selected.

"Darling, thank you for being early," she squealed and threw her arms around him. He paid the driver, and she took his hand and led him up the steps of the grand home.

"Rob, it is so nice to see you again," Eleanor's mother exclaimed. She kissed him on the cheek. "We have all missed you. How is your family? We are so sorry about your sister."

The ladies led him through the expansive foyer, and he was glad to feel the coolness of their air conditioner.

"Thank you, Mrs. Butler," Rob said appreciatively. "They are doing as well as expected. My parents are strong people. They'll be fine."

"And I hear you got a new family member while you were there. A precious little baby!"

"Yes, ma'am. My sister had a healthy baby boy."

"There is nothing like a sweet, healthy baby," Mrs. Butler gushed. "I can't wait to be grandma," she winked at him.

Rob was thankful when Mr. Butler busted in and interrupted the conversation.

"Rachel, leave the boy be," he boomed and shook Rob's hand. "Come on out to the patio, and let me fix you a drink. You're going to need one to deal with this crowd."

"George, you hush," his wife said playfully.

The Butlers knew how to throw a party. There was every kind of drink imaginable, and comfortable chairs were set out around the pool. Rob thought it strange, once again, that he was wearing a three-piece suit and sitting by the pool.

Eleanor didn't leave his side, and he met so many people he would never remember all their names. At exactly 5 pm, everyone was invited to sit at tables and chairs on the side patio. The tables were dressed with white tablecloths, and name cards were placed on top of the fine white china. Eleanor led him to the table where they would sit with her parents, sister, and her husband. Each table had a matching centerpiece filled with summer flowers, and the silver flatware shined brightly in the dimming sun.

Servers dressed in black and white came from seemingly nowhere and exchanged the empty plates on the tables with full ones. Rob had to admit the food was delicious, and the wine served with the meal was tasty as well. About halfway through the meal, Mr. Butler stood up and clinked his glass with his butter knife.

"If I could please have everyone's attention," he said loudly as the crowd quieted down. "I'd like to make a toast. As you all know, we are here tonight to honor my youngest daughter, Eleanor, and her soon-to-be husband, Rob Mathis. These fine kids met in their first year of college and have been inseparable ever since. They have wonderful jobs with the largest newspaper and communications firm in the city, and they are going places together. Please join me in congratulating this wonderful young couple."

The guests raised their glasses, and 'congratulations' was spoken throughout the crowd. When Mr. Butler put his glass on the table, the guests did the same and broke out in applause. Eleanor grabbed Rob's hand and pulled him from his chair to stand while she spoke.

"I just want to thank you all for coming tonight and to thank my wonderful parents for giving us this very nice party." There were happy murmurs throughout the crowd. Then she put her arm through Rob's and continued.

"And I just want to thank this wonderful man for giving me the best college experience and for asking me to marry him. I just know we are going to have a long, happy marriage."

"Here, here!" several people shouted.

Rob smiled and waved at the crowd, but he was speechless. This public show of congratulations and adoration was more than he expected.

Knowing he needed to respond, he simply said, "And I thank you for agreeing to be my wife," and he leaned down and kissed her lightly on the lips.

The guests gushed oohs and aahs, and Rob smiled at his bride-to-be. She appeared so happy at the moment. He wished he felt the same giddy feeling that she felt.

After dessert was served, the guests began to dissipate, and only the closest friends of the Butlers stayed at length to chat. Rob began to relax somewhat. He found that he enjoyed chatting with some of Eleanor's old high school friends and with associates of Mr. Butler's law firm. Everyone was warm, friendly, and genuine. They were not unlike the folks in north Florida.

When the last guest left, Mr. Butler asked the family to gather in the living room. He passed cocktails around, but Rob noticed that he gave Eleanor a ginger ale. So, they do know about the baby, Rob realized.

"Now, Rob, I want you to keep an open mind about what I'm about to say," Mr. Butler began once everyone was seated with a drink in hand.

Rob's stomach flopped. He knew he was about to be admonished for getting Eleanor pregnant before the wedding, and he couldn't blame a father for doing so. Rob held his chin up as he looked at the elder gentleman and would graciously accept what he was about to say. Mr. Butler cleared his throat, and the words that came next were not at all what Rob expected.

"We are excited to welcome you into our family. Rob. You are a bright young man, and I can tell you are going to take excellent care of our daughter." He focused on Rob and added, "And our grandchild."

Rob swallowed before speaking.

"Thank you, sir, Mrs. Butler," he looked at Eleanor's mother, who was beaming proudly.

"I am so excited to be a grandmother soon," she gushed.

"You two are obviously in love," Mr. Butler continued, "and these things happen. We were young once as well," and he winked at his wife.

"Enough about that," he cleared his throat and continued his thoughts. "You are starting a life together, and you'll have added expenses that most young people don't have. You know, with the baby coming and all."

"Yes, sir, I have already thought about that," Rob interrupted.

Mr. Butler put his hand up. "I have no doubt. You seem like a very responsible young man. And we admire how you dropped everything when your family needed you and went home to take care of them."

"Thank you, sir," Rob muttered, wondering where this conversation was going.

"Mrs. Butler and I would like to help you two start out on the right foot." Eleanor beamed and put her hand in Rob's.

"What are you saying, daddy?" She sounded almost like a little girl expecting an expensive Christmas present. Rob's feeling of dread was growing by the minute.

"We are going to buy your first house," Mr. Butler announced with pride.

"Oh, daddy!" Eleanor squealed with delight at the same time Rob spoke in panic.

"Sir, that's very generous, but we can't accept this." Rob's stomach churned, and he felt like he might throw up. He was a man of pride and accepting charity, even from family, was not in his genes.

"What?" Eleanor and Mrs. Butler said at the same time.

"I come from a family that takes care of their own," Rob tried to explain. His face reddened as everyone stared at him with genuine disappointment and curiosity that he wouldn't accept such a generous gift.

"I promise I'll take care of Eleanor," he continued. "But, sir, please let me do it in my own way. We have an apartment close to our jobs. And once I build my savings back up, we'll find a bigger place. I give you my word."

Eleanor started pleading with Rob, but Mr. Butler held up his hand again to silence his daughter.

"I respect you for that sentiment, son. I do," he studied Rob for a moment and Rob held his eyes steady on the older man's face.

"Think about it like this. You are our family now, too. And, like you, we take care of our own." In those words, Rob knew he was about to lose this battle. Eleanor started to cry.

"Rob, we could give our baby a good start in a home of our

own. Not some dinky apartment," she said with tears falling gently on her cheeks.

Rob looked at his soon-to-be father-in-law and knew he was beaten. His mind whirled, and he came up with a lame plan to try and save face.

"I'll accept your generous offer on one condition, sir," Rob stood, trying to get a bit of an upper hand in a situation where he was outnumbered. "With all due respect, I want to pay you a fair rent."

Mr. Butler glanced at his wife and winked. Eleanor exclaimed, "Yes!" She jumped up and threw her arms around Rob's neck.

"I had a feeling you might say something like that," Mr. Butler grinned and held out his hand to Rob. "And I can live with that," he answered. The men shook hands, and Mr. Butler gave Rob a friendly slap on the shoulder.

"Now, here is an envelope with keys to three different houses." Rob gave the older man a questioning look, and Mr. Butler chuckled. "I have a client who is a real estate broker. He assured me these homes were solid, safe, and in a great neighborhood to raise children. "He'll meet you at the first one tomorrow at 1 pm. When you pick the one you like, give us a call. Mrs. Butler and I would like to come see your new home."

Eleanor jumped up and hugged her father and then her mother. "Thank you so much!" she cried.

Rob felt he had no choice but to graciously thank his future in-laws. He thanked Mr. Butler and turned to give his soon-to-be mother-in-law a hug. Eleanor slipped her arm around his waist and beamed up at him.

"I am the happiest girl in the world!" she said.

And I've just taken the final step away from the girl I truly love, he thought.

52

Rob had to admit, the house tour was pretty exciting. He was concerned that Mr. Butler had chosen homes as grand as his own, and he had no idea how he would be able to maintain the upkeep of such a grand estate. But the houses were perfect for a young couple starting just out.

They took their time going through each home, mentally placing furniture, and looking around the neighborhood. They were all in a newly built subdivision, just on different streets. They both agreed on a cute brick bungalow close to the children's park. Eleanor said she could see them pushing their baby in her stroller along the sidewalk late in the evening. The yard was small enough that Rob could take care of it, and the backyard was a perfect size for kids to play. Eleanor loved the modern appliances in the kitchen, and everything was shiny and new. As they stood in what would soon be their bedroom, Eleanor put her arms around his neck and said, "Welcome home, Mr. Mathis. Thank you for agreeing to our new home."

"Welcome home to you, the future Mrs. Mathis," and while he smiled on the outside, his heart sank on the inside.

53

Rob's first day on the job was chaotic at best. Working in a fast-paced newspaper in a large town was much different than he was used to. The atmosphere was more hectic than the school paper or Freddie's newspaper office.

He was given a small office in the inside corridor. Reporters with seniority and editors had offices with windows, but he was used to Freddie's dark offices, so having no windows didn't bother him. Several people came in and introduced themselves, and Jim's secretary told him he would be expected for lunch at the corner deli promptly at noon.

He took a self-guided tour around the editorial department and then wandered into the pre-press room. He marveled at the efficiency around him. A small crew was typesetting the stories given to them by the editors while another crew laid the type onto the pages spread around the room. They barely glanced up when he stopped to watch for a few minutes.

Next, he went into the stripping section, where the page-size negatives were being prepared for the press. Two ladies were marking out any lines left on the film with red markers while a young man came behind them and masked the various colors of the pages. It was an intricate process, but this group worked like a well-oiled machine.

He stood outside the press room as the door was marked

'Authorized Personnel Only.' He wasn't sure if he was authorized to enter, but he could see the massive machine inside getting ready to run tomorrow's edition later today. Rob mused to himself how Freddie's press resembled a tinker toy compared to this one.

He made it to the deli at 11:57, according to his watch, and Jim and another man were already seated in the back. They stood when Rob walked up, and the men shook hands.

"Rob, this is my dad, Jim, Sr."

"Nice to see you again, Mr. Webb," Rob smiled as the men took their seats.

"Please, call me Jim. When we're together, you can call him Junior," he pointed at his son and chuckled. Junior rolled his eyes.

"Well, as I told Junior, I do appreciate this opportunity. I'm excited to hit the ground running," Rob told the men.

Jim, Sr. studied Rob for a moment before he spoke. "My pal Freddie sure speaks highly of you. He said you made quite a stir recently with your story about that crazy lady saving the tree in your hometown."

Rob was surprised that the two men had spoken so recently. "So, you've just spoken to him?" Rob asked.

"Just the other day, as a matter of fact. He called me to see if I'd met you yet and to make sure I gave you a warm Atlanta welcome."

"Well, I think a lot of him, too. He was a great mentor during my high school years. Growing up in a farm family, I didn't quite fit the mold that they wanted me to. He was someone I could talk to who understood where I was coming from. He is like family to me."

"Let's hope we become like family as well. Atlanta is a great city to begin a promising career, and we're glad to have you and your lovely fiancé on board."

"Thank you, sir," Rob said as the waitress appeared and took their order.

The rest of the lunch was filled with friendly small talk. Rob felt he was going to like these men and was feeling a little more relaxed about the job.

When he got back to his desk, someone had placed a story lead on his desk. He was happy to get to work. He spent the rest of the afternoon making phone calls and working on his first story.

Eleanor was a chatterbox that evening, and he dutifully listened to her. She told him her plans for the wedding next weekend, moving into the new house as soon as her father got all of the paperwork signed and colors for the nursery. When she took a breath, he shared a little about his day and his lunch with Jim and Jim.

She looked at him with curiosity. "You had lunch with Jim Sr.?" He nodded. "I have yet to meet him. He's sort of a mystery figure around the office. They must have big plans for you."

Rob was thoughtful for a moment. "It was probably because Jim Sr is an old college friend of my publisher back home. I don't think there's any more to it."

After dinner at her apartment and a little cuddle time in front of the television, Rob kissed her goodnight and went back to his apartment. He refused to spend the night with her until their wedding night. He had already learned how just one night could change your whole life.

54

Late the next afternoon, Rob got his first call at his office. He was surprised when his phone rang. He had made several outgoing calls to set up interviews, but this was his first incoming call, and it excited him.

"Rob Mathis," he answered warmly.

"Rob, my boy, you sound so professional!" Freddie was on the other end of the line.

"Great to hear your voice as always, my friend," Rob chuckled. "How are you doing?"

"Never better. And I'm about to make your day a little better," Freddie laughed. "First of all, I just received a nice check with your name on it for the story you wrote about tobacco farming. The magazine was very pleased and paid you top dollar for that story. And you got credit on the cover."

"Freddie, that is great news! And the money couldn't come at a better time."

"Glad to hear. Jim was very impressed with you at lunch yesterday," Freddie cleared his throat. "I have probably meddled where I shouldn't have, so I will apologize in advance. You are like a son to me," Rob wasn't sure where Freddie was going with this. "So, I have played a little dirty with Jim's help. I want you to have a long talk with that fiancé of yours tonight about her immediate plans after the wedding. You've only got four days left to make absolutely sure that you are doing the right thing by marrying this girl."

"Freddie, I don't understand. Her family knows about the baby, and they are buying us a house. Well, I insisted on paying rent, and they are excited to be grandparents. Everything is lining up."

"So it seems, my young friend. I beg you, tonight, be the investigative reporter you know how to be. Just make sure everything is lining up like you think it is. I'm always here if you need me." Rob heard the serious tone of his friend's voice.

"Thanks, Freddie, and I trust you to meddle any time."

"We'll talk again tomorrow. Take care and be thorough," and Freddie hung up.

Rob hung up and mulled over Freddie's advice. Maybe his older friend was right. He had been so caught up in making plans for the next couple of weeks that he and Patti had not talked about what each expected from married life,

He decided if he were to interrogate Eleanor, it should be in a neutral setting. He was in the mood for Italian food, so he searched the phone book for a place nearby and then called for reservations at 6:30. It was getting close to 5 already, so he closed up his office and walked to the other side of the building to Eleanor's office. She was on the phone but waved for him to come in. She was smiling when she finished her call.

"Hello, my handsome husband-to-be. Are you picking me up today? If so, I like it."

"I am," he said, watching her closely. She seemed extra happy today. "I thought we'd go to a nice restaurant this evening and get to know each other a little better before we get hitched."

"Well, darling, I think I know you very well, but a quiet restaurant does sound nice." She picked up her purse and tucked her arm through his.

The restaurant atmosphere was just as Rob had hoped. The

lighting was dim, and they were seated at a quiet table in the back corner.

"How did you know I was craving pasta tonight?" she winked at him.

"Just a gut feeling, I guess." He held up his water glass, and she did the same. "To us," he said and clinked his glass with hers.

"To us!" she agreed and gave him her sweetest smile.

Rob waited until they had placed their order to begin his subtle interrogation. He trusted Freddie, so while he wasn't comfortable probing into her mind, he needed to find out what information Freddie knew, but he didn't.

"You know, darling," he began softly, "we've had so much to discuss that we haven't talked about you working after the baby is born."

"I thought we had," she said as she pulled a piece of bread off the plate and avoided his eyes. "I have read that it takes about six weeks to recover after giving birth. Then we'll hire a nanny, and I'll go back to my job. You agreed with me that we could have our careers and our family," she eyed him suspiciously. "You did agree, remember?"

"Yes, I did agree," he nodded. "And I want to make it work. But I've been reading, too, and pregnancy and childbirth is hard on a woman. There could be complications before the birth even. I just want to make sure we take the very best possible care of you."

"I appreciate that," she said as she shoved another piece of bread in her mouth. His investigative instinct told him this conversation was making her nervous, so he kept probing.

"OK," he tried to sound chipper. "Six weeks after the birth, not crazy about a nanny, but your income will pay for it. We can run home throughout the day and check on the baby." He was ticking items off on his fingers, "and what about prior to the birth? When do you want to take off to rest ahead of time?"

"Rob, why are you asking me all of these questions about the birth?" she was clearly getting agitated. "I need to focus on our wedding this weekend. I still have things to do, and you are quizzing me about something that won't happen for nine months!"

"Seven," he reminded her. She looked at him, and for just a moment, he thought he saw a flash of fear in her eyes.

The waiter brought their food, and they were silent for a few minutes. Rob dug into his pasta, but she barely touched hers.

"I thought you were craving pasta," he said with a note of tenderness in his voice. He hadn't meant to ruin her appetite.

"I was until you started interrogating me," she pouted.

"I'm sorry. I don't mean to upset you, but please understand. You and our baby are the two most important people in my world right now. I need to know that both of you will be safe and healthy. This baby is far more important to me than a 10-minute ceremony."

Her head snapped up. "So, you're saying this baby is more important to you than I am?"

He tried to put his hand over hers, but she pulled it away.

"Not at all, Eleanor," he sighed and sat back in his chair. "You are my priority, which is why I'm asking you this. I want to keep you healthy. That is my priority. Not getting all dressed up in front of your family and friends."

She finally took a bite of her food, and they sat in silence for a few minutes. When she put her fork down, she peered at him, and her eyes had grown cold.

"You fell in love with me because I was strong and independent. We are good together. People are saying we are the next power couple." He nodded. "You agreed to support me in whatever I chose to do. So, I need your support now. Not your questions."

He cocked his head, not sure where this turn of events was

going. He was all ears, however, and leaned forward slightly.

"I got a visit today from Jim, Sr," she told him firmly. "And I have been offered the opportunity of a lifetime." He realized this was what Freddie wanted him to find out. He listened intently, not wanting to stop her flow. That's what the best journalists do. Listen when the time is right.

"Our company is opening a satellite office in Paris, and they want me to travel over there and get it up and running. I'll be gone for six months."

Bingo, he thought. He kept his eyes on her and stayed calm. He needed to gently push her into telling him what he suspected. His appetite was fading fast.

"Wow, that is a great opportunity. But as your husband and the father of your child, I forbid you to be gone to Paris for six months," he calmly stated and sat back in his chair to study her reaction.

"You forbid me?" she almost spat at him.

"Sweetheart," he was laying it on thick. "Think about it. In six months, you will be eight months pregnant! What if you can't fly back to the States? What if something happens to you or the baby comes early, and I'm not there with you?" He paused and watched for her reaction. "This is crazy." He dropped his fork on his plate for emphasis.

The silence was heavy between them. Eleanor knew she was at a crossroads. Rob's words made perfect sense, but she couldn't lose this once-in-a-lifetime opportunity.

Looking down at her lap, Rob listened as his fiancé said, "I'm not pregnant." She said it so softly that he wasn't sure he understood her correctly.

"What did you say?" He was the one with the cold eyes now.

"I'm not pregnant," she said a little louder. Then she started to cry.

Rob felt as if the wind had been knocked out of him. In four days, he would have married this woman under false pretenses. She lied to him to lock him into a marriage he did not want. Thank God for Freddie's intervention, he thought.

He didn't know what to say, but he did realize that all of a sudden, his heart had gotten lighter, and he felt as if a load had been lifted from his shoulders. He would have stayed with her and loved their child more than life itself. But the truth had just come out, and now he felt like their entire relationship had been a lie.

"How could you fabricate something like this?" His voice was a little too loud, but he didn't care. "And why? You even lied to your parents!" he paused, and when she didn't answer, he continued, "And what was going to happen when no baby started appearing?"

She wiped at the tears on her face with her napkin and gazed down at her hands, "I was going to have a miscarriage next week after the wedding."

"Unbelievable," he sighed and threw his napkin on his plate. "Why in the hell would you do such a thing." It wasn't a question. He wanted an explanation.

"When you came back from Florida, you had changed, and I sensed I was about to lose you. There was a look in your eyes that I had never seen before," she was still crying, and she sniffled. "You hardly ever called me while you were away, and when I tried to call, all I got was a damn busy signal. You have been the love of my life for four years. We are so good together. We're the next dynamic duo, remember?" When she looked at him, her eyes were red, and mascara was running down her face. The look in his eyes scared her, though. They were cold as steel.

"Are your parents in on this lie, too?" he demanded. "Did they try to drag me in with the whole let me buy you a house thing?" His anger was starting to rise again.

"No!" she snapped at him. "They honestly believe I'm pregnant. Mom is already shopping for baby clothes."

They stared at each other for what seemed like hours, but in reality, it was less than a minute. The waiter had walked their way to check on them but realized that he shouldn't approach the table. He turned and walked away.

Eleanor broke the silence. "Rob, I truly love you. The thought of losing you breaks my heart."

He gathered his thoughts before he spoke. Part of him wanted to scream at her and shake her into understanding the magnitude of the lie she had told. But his rational side reminded him that he was now free to go back to Florida. He was free to rebuild his life with Patti. Let her bow out gracefully, he thought. He swallowed hard.

"I hope your dad hasn't signed papers on the house," he said softly. She shook her head, and he was thankful for that.

"Eleanor," he tried to choose his words carefully, "I don't think I have to tell you this, but our life together is over. I will never recover from a lie such as this, and I believe if you really loved me, you would not have made such a grave mistake."

She kept her eyes on her lap as tears flowed faster.

"Is the Paris trip real?" she nodded, still not looking at him.

"Okay. You need to pour all of your energy into going to Paris. That is a great opportunity for you and one you shouldn't pass up," he watched as she chewed on her bottom lip, so he knew she was listening to what he said.

"We had four wonderful years together in college, and we'll always have our memories. But we are different people now. You have more ambition now that you've gotten a taste of the real world. And to be honest, my heart is in my hometown. I'm not sure where that will put my career, but I have no doubt I'll figure it out," he paused, and she studied him once again.

"You were right about one thing," he said, keeping his voice even. "I came back here to end our relationship and tie up ends here so I could move back home."

He waited for her to respond, and when she said nothing, he

said, "Thank you for coming clean before we committed ourselves to a lifetime together. I'll be gone in two days."

She finally looked up again and nodded understanding. For once in her life, she had no words.

Rob stood up, pulled enough money out of his pocket to pay the bill, and left a generous tip. He leaned down and kissed her on the cheek.

"Go knock em' dead in Paris," he said, and then he turned and walked away.

55

Rob almost skipped down the sidewalk as he hailed a cab back to his apartment. He wasn't even upset with Eleanor for the stunt she had pulled. He realized he was more than thankful to be done with her. She would be fine as she was more career-focused than family-oriented. Once she got to Paris, she would dive into her work, and he would be a distant memory.

"Well, hello, Rob! I didn't expect to hear from you so soon," Freddie's voice boomed over the phone when Rob called him.

"I couldn't wait to tell you my wonderful news," Rob responded. "I don't know what you did or how you did it, but Eleanor came clean tonight with the whole lie she has been living."

"It sounds like you did some spot-on investigating," the older man chuckled.

"I'm pretty sure you were in the background doing some magic," Rob grinned, and Freddie was glad to hear the old Rob back in his voice. "Is the Paris job real?"

"It is. You may be disappointed to know that they were going to offer it to both of you after you were married. Can you see Paris in your future?"

"Absolutely not," Rob responded quickly.

"That's what I thought," Freddie said. "Come see me as soon as you get back, and we'll talk."

"See you in two days," Rob said, and they hung up.

Rob spent most of the evening sorting through his things and packing what he would take home. He decided to donate most of his household items to the Goodwill store, so he would take them over tomorrow.

He sat down at his little dinette, drank his last Atlanta cocktail, and penned a note to Eleanor's parents. He didn't know what to say but tried to express his appreciation for their kindness and support. He knew they would have questions and be disappointed with their daughter, so he kept his own feelings out of the note. He kindly asked that they forgive him for leaving and wished them a household full of grandchildren when the time was right.

56

When Rob turned onto US 41 South two days later, he rolled down his window and let out a whoop. A week ago, he had been told he was about to be a father and was being rushed into a marriage he didn't want. This last week seemed like a lifetime ago as he watched the Atlanta skyline grow smaller behind him with each passing mile.

He had tied up all of his loose ends yesterday and could leave Atlanta knowing he was on good terms. His landlord had released him from his lease as he already had people lined up wanting his small apartment. Check. Jim Jr was very understanding of his situation and wished him Godspeed, even though he only worked two days. Check. He mailed the letter to Eleanor's parents. Check. However, Eleanor would have some major explaining to do to her parents.

He couldn't stay mad at Eleanor even though he would never understand how she could drag everyone around her into such a shameless lie. But they had been sidekicks all through college, and he would always hold a special place in his heart for her. He had no doubt she would land in Paris and kick butt and no doubt that he would see her on national television one day.

The mountainous terrain and the hills grew flatter the further south he went. He didn't stop during the entire trip as he was hoping to arrive at the diner just after closing. Patti always stayed for a couple of hours after she locked the door to catch up on paperwork and plan the next day's menu.

He was torn between seeing his parents first, dropping by Freddie's, or going straight to Patti. Either way, whoever he didn't see first would get word that he was back in town once he was spotted. He grinned at the idea of returning to the small town where everybody knows and shares your business. But, also, everyone knows your name and drops what they are doing when you need a helping hand.

Traffic was fairly light, so he arrived back in Florida a little earlier than he planned. As luck would have it, he had time to go see his parents first. They should be up from their naps by now, he thought. He pulled Freddie's sedan into the driveway and glanced around once he had turned off the ignition. He was home. The place where you saw beautiful sunsets no matter where you were in the county, where the air was clean, and where his roots ran deep.

He knocked once before opening the door and stepping into the family living room. What he saw took him completely by surprise. The nurse was helping his dad take a few steps across the room.

"Well, look what the cat dragged in," Robert said with a smile when he saw his son.

"Yessir, I decided to come home and see what trouble my parents are getting into," Rob joked.

His dad took another step forward, and then the nurse helped him turn around and take a few steps back to his wheelchair.

"We were hoping to surprise you when you got home," Charlotte said. "We didn't expect you back so soon."

"I didn't know how long I would be, but things got wrapped up quicker than I expected," Rob said and bent down to give his mother a hug and a peck on the cheek. "I tried to call, but that dang phone is always busy."

"That's Myrtle for ya," Charlotte shook her head. "She thinks she's important now that she saved her tree. I hear she may run for town mayor."

"Well, I'm sure she can straighten some things out around here," Rob laughed and patted his dad on the shoulder once he was settled back in his chair. "You look good getting on your feet, Dad. I'm proud of you."

Rob turned and grabbed his suitcase that he had set down by the front door.

"Is that all you brought back from that big city?" Robert asked.

"I'm afraid so. I lived light, and I donated a lot of my household stuff to the Goodwill."

Rob chatted with his parents for a while, but he was getting anxious to see Patti. He had no idea how she would react to him, but he was eager to find out. He told his parents not to hold dinner for him and, if he wasn't back by their bedtime, to keep the light on for him.

"Go on, boy," Robert chuckled. "I bet she's anxious to see you, too." His dad gave him a wink.

"Thanks, Dad. I sure hope so." And Rob was out the door.

57

Rob realized that Patti had grown into a graceful and caring woman. When he first returned home, he thought she had no ambition. Now, he understood she was a trailblazer for women who wanted to own their own businesses. She loved her small town and wanted to serve the people in it. He sat in the parking lot for a few minutes, watching her through the window. However, before someone saw him and decided he was a stalker, he made his way to the door. It was locked, which didn't surprise him. He knocked timidly at first, but she didn't hear him, so he knocked a little louder.

The look on Patti's face when she turned and saw who was at the door is one he'll never forget. When she turned around, she appeared annoyed, thinking it was a customer trying to come in after hours. But when she realized it was Rob, her expression changed from sadness to surprise and then to utter joy. She broke out in a huge smile and sprinted to the door. As soon as she opened it, she was in his arms.

"I am so sorry I hurt you, Patti. I had to get my head straight and tie up things in Atlanta. Please forgive me?" He held her slightly away from him so he could see her face.

"There is nothing to forgive. I jumped to conclusions without giving you the chance to explain. Are you back for sure? No more Atlanta?" Her face was hopeful.

"No more Atlanta. I am free from everything and everybody there. I am home for good." He smiled, and this time, the smile reached his eyes. Her smile was full of joy.

And they kissed. With the door wide open, they stood on the threshold, held each other, and kissed. Rob had never felt like he did in this moment. He felt carefree and complete all at the same time. When they released each other, Patti pulled him inside and locked the door.

She brought them Cherry Cokes, and they sat in the corner booth and chatted. They talked about their high school days, and he shared stories about his college life. She told him more about Gram and some funny stories about customers. When they could talk no more, he took her hand and entwined his fingers around hers.

"It feels so right to be here with you," he said as he gazed directly into her sparkling eyes.

"I agree," she said.

"Together forever?" He smiled at her.

She smiled back. "Together forever."

58

Rob woke up happy, knowing he had his whole future ahead of him, even though he had no job. His dad would need help around the farm for sure, so he could always take on those duties. He wrestled with that thought, however, realizing that he left home to pursue a degree in the field he loved.

Maybe Freddie could use a hand, he thought. Maybe he could have the best of both worlds. He could help Freddie and his dad and make enough money to support a family. That thought made him smile. He and Patti agreed to be together forever, but they had not talked about marriage or family. That would come in its own good time.

He showered and dressed and grabbed a cup of Sanka. All of a sudden, he wanted to look at Connie's book of drawings again. His parents were still resting, so he padded into her bedroom and took the book. Then, he went to his favorite place on the porch and sat down on the swing.

He slowly studied each drawing and marveled at the talent his sister had. She had numbered each piece of artwork, and there were 48 in total. These belong in an art museum, Rob thought, or at least some place where others could appreciate them. He made a mental note to follow up on that idea once he got settled in.

After he put the book back in its place and washed out his

coffee mug, he decided to take Freddie's car back to him. He peeked in and his parents were still sleeping. The day nurse had arrived, so he was free to leave.

"Hey, Rob," Maryanne drawled when he walked into the office.

"Hey, yourself," Rob smiled back.

"I stopped at the diner for breakfast, and Patti was in an extra happy mood," she grinned at him.

"Glad to hear, and since I know you're dying to ask, yes, we had a long talk last evening."

"Well, I was hoping I still had a shot at ya, but congratulations. Everyone in high school saw how you two were meant to be together."

Rob was taken aback for a second. How in the world had everyone seen it but him?

"Welcome back, my boy," Freddie bellowed from his office. "Come on in and shut the door. Maryanne, grab us two coffees, will ya?"

"You got it, boss," she said and headed out the door.

Rob sat in the wooden chair facing Freddie's desk. He looked around the office and mused at the stark difference between Freddie's place and the Atlanta office. Freddie had newspapers spread all over his office and shelves lined with dingy bound copies of previous newspapers grouped and sorted by years.

The dark paneling added to the dreary look, and the one window looking out on the side street looked like it hadn't been cleaned in 20 years. But Freddie had done well with his family's business. He was respected in the community he served and was known for honest and fair reporting. Local citizens waited eagerly for each weekly edition to read the latest about their neighbors and friends.

There was a section devoted to births and weddings and

special events such as children's birthday parties and couples' anniversaries. The front page headlines seldom held news about tragic events, but occasionally, there was a car wreck, such as Connie's, and a dispute between elected officials. The local businesses supported the paper with their advertisements, and Freddie made sure to frequent them all to show his appreciation.

Maryanne knocked once and entered with two steaming cups of coffee from Gram's. She saluted Freddie and closed the door as she walked out.

"Freddie, you don't know how much I appreciate the use of your car and everything you did for me," Rob cleared his throat.

"Think nothing of it, my friend. As I said, you're like a son to me. With no kids of my own, you're all I've got." Both men sipped their coffee in silence.

"I take it you and Patti made up?" Freddie broke the silence.

"We did. All is good in our world."

"Glad to hear," the older man said.

Freddie sat back in his chair and put his fingertips to his lips, ready to choose his next words carefully.

"As you know, my grandfather started this paper," Rob nodded. "My father bought it from him, and I bought it from him." Freddie paused to let his words take effect.

"I, on the other hand, never married and never had children," Rob nodded again. "It bothers the hell out of me to think about selling this paper to someone who wouldn't share my passion and appreciation of what my family built." Rob wasn't sure where this conversation was headed.

"Isn't it a little early for you to think about selling?" Rob asked.

"You are too kind," Freddie responded, "but I am nearing that golden age of retirement. And you're not the only one sparking up a romance," he smiled slyly.

"I met a woman whom I've enjoyed spending time with over the last few months. She's a widow from South Georgia, and we've been seeing quite a bit of each other. At my age, you may think I'm crazy, but I'm ready to get married and enjoy life. We want to travel and see the world," he smiled.

"Freddie, that's amazing. Congratulations!" Rob was genuinely happy for his old friend.

"Thanks. So that leads to my dilemma," he paused. "Who can I sell the paper to that will love it like my family has?"

Rob was thoughtful. He had no answer for his friend.

Freddie looked Rob squarely in the eyes. "I want you to buy my paper, Rob."

Stunned, Rob sat quietly for a moment. He expected a job offer, not the entire paper. There was no way he could afford such a big expense. "I appreciate that, Freddie, I really do. But I don't have that kind of money. I mean, I'd love to have this paper, but I'm not financially ready to make such a purchase."

"Says who?" Freddie retorted. "Do you think I had a bunch of money when I was your age? I'm giving you the same deal my dad gave me. You pay me 10% of the net profits for ten years." He paused again. "And trust me, if you treat the people of this town right, they will support your efforts, and there is profit to be made. I'll work with you for six months to make sure you're on your feet. And then, my new bride and I will be off to lands unknown."

"Freddie, that is way too generous." Rob was stunned, but excitement was growing. This was the opportunity of a lifetime.

"It's what I want," Freddie said kindly. "I'll be happy knowing that the paper is in good hands for the next 40 years."

"If that's what you want, then how can I say no?" Rob laughed and jumped to his feet. He reached over the desk to shake Freddie's hand, but the older man came around the desk and gave him a quick hug.

"You're making an old man very happy," he said. "I'll have my attorney draw up the paperwork, and we'll make it official as soon as he's ready."

"I can't thank you enough," Rob said.

"It's you I should be thanking," Freddie grinned.

Rob reached into his pocket to fish out Freddie's car key. As he laid it on the big desk that would soon be his, Freddie said, "Keep it, my boy. That car belongs to the paper, so it's part of the sale. You might as well start using it now."

Rob choked up and studied the older man's expression. "Freddie, you are far too generous. I can't just take your car. You and your new bride can't travel in that old rattle trap pickup outside."

Freddie grinned. "My bride-to-be has a brand new shiny Oldsmobile that we'll be sporting around in. Don't you worry about me," the older man winked.

Without thinking, Rob grabbed Freddie in a bear hug. He couldn't speak for fear he would start bawling like a baby.

59

Rob's internal alarms started screaming when he pulled into his parents' yard. Sheriff Pete's cruiser was parked in the driveway, and when he stepped out of the car, he heard his father's booming voice. With fear and dread, Rob sprinted up the steps to the front porch.

"I don't want that bastard's money!" Robert was yelling.

"Dad, what in the world?" Rob asked as he slammed the screen door behind him.

"Pete came waltzing in here with a big check from that SOB that killed our daughter. It's dirty money, and I don't want it." Charlotte was sniffling in her wheelchair.

"Dad, calm down," Rob put his hand on his father's shoulder and looked at the sheriff. "What is this about?"

"The driver's insurance company admitted full responsibility for the accident," he explained calmly.

"I ain't taking it!" Robert bellowed.

Sheriff Pete continued, "They have offered a settlement for $200,000. They brought the check to me so I could present it to your parents."

Robert was shaking his head, getting angrier by the minute.

"Dad, you and Mom would live comfortably for the rest of your lives. Connie would be happy for you."

"Hell, no!" Robert boomed again. "Get that dirty money out of here."

The sheriff looked at Rob, hoping for guidance. Everyone was silent for a few minutes. Charlotte continued to sniffle, the nurse had slipped out the back door, and Robert sat with arms folded and a huge scowl on his face. Rob's mind was reeling. Then an idea came to him.

"Sheriff, do you mind waiting on the porch for a few minutes?" Rob asked calmly. "I have an idea I want to share with my parents."

"Not at all," the sheriff said and stepped onto the porch. Of course, he could hear the conversation, but at least it gave Rob and his parents a sense of privacy.

Rob got Connie's book of drawings from her room and brought it to his parents.

"Mom, Dad," Rob cleared his throat. "Did you know what a talented artist Connie was?" He held up her book with the big letters "private" scrawled across.

"I knew she doodled a lot, but she never shared what she was drawing," Charlotte said softly. "I saw that book, but I didn't want to invade her privacy. I haven't had the heart to look at it since," and her voice dropped.

"Well, I did look at it, and her work is amazing," Rob said.

"All kids draw!" Robert boomed. "Everyone thinks their child is the most talented. That don't mean anything."

Rob opened the book to the drawing of Betty in her wedding gown.

"Look at this," Rob walked to his parents and showed them the beautiful details. Charlotte sucked in her breath. Even Robert was speechless. Rob slowly turned the pages one by one.

"This isn't just any kid's drawings. This is the work of an extremely talented artist." Rob let his words sink in.

Both parents were trying their best to hold back tears. Rob

understood this would cause a new wave of grief for them. They had never seen the talent their youngest child had possessed. Even more, they had never had the chance to acknowledge it to her.

"I have an idea," Rob said and waited for his parents to respond.

After several minutes, Charlotte looked at her son. "What's your idea?" Robert was speechless.

"What if we create a legacy for Connie that will last forever? We can use this money to share her work with the outside world and teach others to love art and acknowledge their talents?"

"How will that money do that?" Robert asked, a little softer this time.

"We can open a school in her name. Create a foundation. Show her work and hire teachers to teach the love of art to young people," Rob's excitement was growing, and his ideas started flowing. "You know that old mansion in the center of town? It's for sale. Can't you see a big sign in front that reads 'Connie Mathis School of Art'? Her name would live on forever!"

"Rob, that is a beautiful idea," Charlotte whispered.

Robert wasn't sold as easily. The art world was foreign to him. Just as Rob's writing talents were unknown, he had to wrap his head around the art world. He took a deep breath and scratched his head. "I'll think about it," he said sternly.

"Well, that's a start," Rob grinned. "I'll tell the sheriff to lock up the check safely until we come up with a plan."

Charlotte grinned. Robert grunted.

60

Rob sat under his favorite oak tree in the backyard later that afternoon. He lifted his face to the sky, and the warmth of the sun invigorated him. Life could surely change when you least expect it, he mused. Even the best laid-out plans could take a twist with no notice. Six weeks ago, his life was headed in the direction he thought he always wanted. He had a promising career and a girl by his side.

In the blink of an eye, it all changed. His baby sister was taken from this world, his parents' lives were turned upside down, and a new life brought love and joy with the birth of Betty's second child. The woman he thought he wanted to spend his life with turned out to be someone he barely knew, and the truth came out just in the nick of time.

The girl he had a crush on during high school had become his forever sweetheart. She had blossomed into a smart young woman with a business of her own in a world where women were frowned on in the workforce. Now, they had a happy and promising future together.

And he was about to become the publisher of his community newspaper. There, he would be able to combine his love of the written word with his love of the community. He could showcase all that this wonderful place had to offer.

And the family farm he resented so much as a young boy

became the haven he wanted to come home to. He had tried to break away from his family and his past. But he finally found what was most important to him. His family and his community provided the roots and strength he needed to live the life he was truly meant to live.

About the Author

J.B. has lived in rural northern Florida most of her life. After growing up in a big city, the switch to small-town life was a bit of a culture shock, but she quickly adjusted. After she married a hometown boy, they settled down in a rural farming area. They now have two amazing sons, the best daughters-in-law, and the two most beautiful granddaughters on the planet. Besides running two businesses in her downtown area, she enjoys writing, crafting, and spending time with her family and fur babies.

Made in United States
Orlando, FL
04 December 2024

54762971R00163